D1272640

Dear Reader,

"The past isn't dead. It isn't even past." The old saying may be truer than we know. Of course, an antiques dealer like Sadie Speers knows a lot about how the past can enrich the present—the way living with things from another time reminds us of truths that we would otherwise forget: where we come from; what we've left behind or perhaps even lost; and what we have to be grateful for now, both in our present circumstances, and in the past that brought us to them.

In this book, however, Sadie isn't searching for the truth about an object's past but rather that of a person. She's searching not just for the history an object reveals, but the hidden history that each of us carries within ourselves: our grandfather's eyes, our mother's voice, the cowlick that we share with our brother. And the secret history of our own lives: the things that happen to us when we're too young to even remember, and the things that we remember clearly but perhaps can never understand unless a friend or relative helps us by filling in details we couldn't have known at the time.

I like to think that what Sadie does for her friend in the book is an echo of what God wants to do for all of us. He patiently helps us see the truth about ourselves that will help us to lead full lives, even when those truths might sting at first. But even more important, He's there for us as the truth is revealed, sticking close to us like a friend, to help us bear any surprise or disappointment. And, in the end, the fact that we have a friend like Him may be the biggest truth we can ever learn about ourselves.

Vera Dodge
writing as Carole Jefferson

Mysteries of Silver Peak

A Mountain of Mystery
Nobody's Safe
Silver Surprise
Wildfire
A Lode of Secrets
Time Will Tell
A Code of Honor
Empty Saddle
Reunion Dance

Reunion Dance

CAROLE JEFFERSON

Guideposts
New York

Mysteries of Silver Peak is a trademark of Guideposts.

Published by Guideposts Books & Inspirational Media
110 William Street
New York, New York 10038
Guideposts.org

Acknowledgments

Every attempt has been made to credit the sources of copyrighted material used in this book. If any such acknowledgment has been inadvertently omitted or miscredited, receipt of such information would be appreciated.

Cover and interior design by Müllerhaus
Cover art by Greg Copeland represented by Deborah Wolfe, Ltd.
Typeset by Aptara, Inc.

Printed and bound in the United States of America
10 9 8 7 6 5 4 3 2 1

Prologue

In the depths of midnight, a car turned onto the quiet street. As it turned, its lights cut out, but it still proceeded almost silently down the block, a dark hulk moving along dark curbs where no street lamps had yet been put up.

Most of the houses on the street were dark at this hour, even bigger and more mysterious than the drifting darkened car. But the bottom floor of one house was lit up as if a big party was going on inside, although no guests could be seen in the empty rooms.

It was at this house that the car finally came to a stop.

Two figures got out. They melded into a single shadow, then slipped up the front walk to the house. The door swung open, letting out a long swath of light that revealed the bright green grass of the lawn for a split second before the two figures stepped inside, the door swung shut, and the light was snuffed out.

For several long minutes, the street lay still, in perfect silence.

Then the door opened again, and the two figures came back down the main walk. One of them helped the other into the passenger side, then circled the car to take the wheel.

As the car pulled away from the curb again, lights still off, the muffled sound of a baby's cry broke the silence.

1

"I'm so glad you're here," Charlene Jones said with a grateful smile. "I don't know how we could do all of this without you."

"Well," Sadie said with a smile, "I know I'm not the only one in Silver Peak who's grateful for what you and Jason are doing here."

Charlene, a middle-aged black woman with a streak of white in her short, curly hair, grinned. "I hope they'll be even more delighted when we're all done," she said.

She and Sadie stood in the front room of the Parker House, one of Silver Peak's most beloved private homes, beside the remarkable fireplace grate, covered with filigree and fleur-de-lis, which had once protected the family's roaring fires when the house was still warmed primarily by wood heat.

The Parker House's gingerbread trim, whitewashed brick facade, and crisp green roof made it one of the most recognizable buildings in Silver Peak. And the fact that it stood quite close to the downtown business district meant that both Silver Peak residents and visitors passed it frequently on their way to do business in the town's shops. A drawing of the Parker House had even been featured for a few years as part of the logo on Silver Peak tourism brochures.

So when Josie Parker, the last of the Parker family who had originally built the house and owned it for several generations, had passed away earlier in the year, the house had been put on the market for the first time in a century. The town had reacted with a mixture of curiosity and trepidation. Would some out-of-town businessman sweep in and try to make a bed-and-breakfast out of it, chopping up the spacious old rooms and painting the facade in garish colors? Would a buyer even emerge at all for the big old house? It was beautiful, of course, but so large and old-fashioned that it wasn't really practical for many of Silver Peak's newer families. Would any individual family be up to the task of keeping up the house in the present day, not to mention preserving all the historical importance and beauty of the old place?

"This house means a lot to everyone in Silver Peak," Sadie said.

"I know there was even some talk about trying to turn it into a museum before we made our offer," Charlene said.

Sadie nodded. "I'm not sure that was ever much more than talk," she said. "Out here, people sometimes get the idea that everything ought to be a museum."

"But I hope what we want to do here is going to be even better," Charlene said. "When we turn an old place into a museum, it's always seemed to me like trying to freeze it in time. That place might have meant something in the past. And I know the past is important, don't get me wrong."

Sadie raised her eyebrows and nodded. Charlene was well acquainted with all the love and energy Sadie spent preserving the treasures of years past at Sadie's antique shop, the Antique Mine.

"But when we freeze something in the past, it's never really part of the present again," Charlene went on. "Everyone can go into a museum and look at a thing, but almost nobody ever picks it up again. Nobody ever drinks out of a cup that's put in a museum. Nobody ever sits in a chair. Thousands of people might get to walk by a painting in a museum every day. But nobody ever gets to live with it, see new things in it every day, understand how the way they see it changes depending on their mood, or what's happening to them, or happening in the world. Or find out how living with something—from a simple dish to a great painting—really changes them."

"I never thought of it that way," Sadie said.

"Of course, putting something in a museum means a lot more people get to go see it. But Jason and I have always dreamed about bringing one of these beautiful old places back to its former glory—as a living home. We bring it to life, and then live our life amidst it."

"The best of both worlds," Sadie said.

"That's our hope," Charlene said, nodding. Then she gave Sadie a meaningful look. "And it feels like a real gift that we found this place just as Jason and I were retiring. With my schedule as a lawyer and his schedule as a doctor, we haven't had much time in the past years. But I don't think either of us would take very well to doing nothing in retirement. This gives us a good project to keep busy with."

"Without all the pressure of work life," Sadie said.

"Exactly," Charlene agreed. "But I do have to admit that I feel some pressure to do this thing right. The fact that everyone in Silver Peak loves this place so much comes with a lot of responsibility. I know everyone in town will have their own opinion about what we're doing."

"Well," Sadie said, "they say whenever you have a hundred people in a place, you have two hundred opinions."

"I hear that," Charlene said, laughing.

"But I don't think the fact that you're moving here from Denver means that you don't have just as much a right as anyone to put your mark on this place," Sadie said. "After all, it wasn't someone in Silver Peak who bought the house. You did. And you know what? However much we may think we know and love a place, it's always good to get a new perspective. Sometimes people who haven't been in a place all their lives can see things the people who have been there all that time have forgotten to notice. I think we need your perspective. I think it'll help us do an even better restoration."

"I hope so too," Charlene said. "But we're also just so grateful to have you as our historical consultant. Because we think the perspective of the people who have known and loved this place for all those years is invaluable too. And yours especially. You don't just know this place. You've got such a strong grounding in history.

"So...," Charlene said, her eyes lighting up. "I've already given you the grand tour of the downstairs rooms. Do you want to see where we've been keeping all the historical documents?"

"What are we waiting for?" Sadie asked.

With a quick glance over her shoulder, Charlene led the way out of the front room to the main hall, where a flight of winding stairs led to the second floor. At the second floor landing, she paused before one of several doors that led away from it.

"They offered to clean all of this out for us before the sale was completed," Charlene said. "They thought all of the old papers

Josie had kept all these years were just junk. But we told them we wouldn't go through with the sale *without* the papers. I think they're going to be our road map. They won't just tell us how the house used to look. They'll tell us what life was like back a hundred years ago when this place was built."

"And that's always the more interesting question, isn't it?" Sadie said.

Charlene nodded and swung the door open.

Sadie held back a slight gasp as they stepped into a little room. "It's so cozy," she said. The room was less than half the size of any other room in the house, only about six by eight or ten feet.

"It's tiny, isn't it?" Charlene agreed. "From what we understand, it was originally a quarters for the maid. The family had a girl here to help with all the cooking and cleaning."

"That'd be helpful, to keep up a place this big," Sadie said.

"I tried to talk Jason into the idea of a live-in maid, but he was unconvinced," Charlene said.

"Even when you told him it'd be historically accurate?" Sadie said.

Charlene laughed. "I haven't tried that approach yet," she said.

Sadie couldn't contain her curiosity any longer. She stepped into the room. "I don't remember Josie ever having a live-in maid, though," she said.

Charlene shook her head. "I believe your memory's correct on that," she said. "From what we understand, Josie was using this as kind of an office."

Sadie nodded. That made sense. Crisp white curtains hung in the tall windows, which were so old that they turned the view of the backyard wavy because of the interesting imperfections in the antique glass. But that was the only domestic detail in the room. The rest of it did look like an office, although an old-fashioned one. Piles of papers and cardboard accounting boxes were stacked on the surface and reflected in the mirror of a simple antique vanity—the kind one might provide for a maid, Sadie guessed. More boxes stood in stacks in the left corner, piled almost as high as a handsome wooden filing cabinet that stood beside a simple desk. The desk and the vanity were settled somewhat awkwardly, side by side, with the desk overlooking the yard below and the vanity huddled in the far corner. The desk, though simple like the vanity, was more modern. It looked to Sadie as if it had been added quite a bit later than the rest of the furniture—probably around the time that Josie turned the room from maid's quarters into her personal office.

"That's quite a piece," Sadie said, pointing out the file cabinet. "There's a rage for original office furniture these days. If you felt like parting with that, it might fund a good chunk of your restoration."

"That's exactly the kind of advice we're looking for," Charlene said. "But we're not parting with a scrap of this yet. Not until we know more about what's in all of this."

"Well, I'm not sure which one of us is more excited about this project, you or me," Sadie said with a grin. "It's a dream job for me. I've been raring to get in here. My best friend kept teasing me that she thought I might start a renovation myself before the place was even sold."

Sadie looked around at the papers and boxes piled on the furniture. On the opposite wall, near the door, sat a rocking chair beside a small table that held a pretty blue glass lamp.

"Well, will you look at this amazing piece," Sadie said.

"Is it?" Charlene said. "It looked that way to me, but I'm not an expert on these things—yet. My guess was that it looked a little too fancy to have been bought in the early days of Silver Peak. I thought perhaps someone had brought it here all the way from Denver."

"My guess is that it's even older than that," Sadie said. "It looks to me like threaded glass. That's from the Victorian era, even before this house was built. So it may actually be a treasure that some member of her family brought all the way from the East Coast when they first arrived in these parts."

"Wonderful," Charlene breathed.

Sadie glanced past the glass at a set of several boxes that had been stacked at the foot of the chair. Unlike the other boxes, these seemed new, the ink on the cardboard still fresh and vivid, and each box marked with labels that were almost certainly printed by a computer.

She pointed at the boxes. "What are these?"

"You know," Charlene said, "I'm not sure those are going to be any good to you at all. But when we made keeping the papers a condition of the sale of the house, the executor of the estate brought these to us as well. They're Josie's personal financial papers. I'm not sure how much they'll tell us about the restoration project. But you can't say we left any stone unturned."

"No," Sadie said with a smile. "I guess not. Have you had a chance to look at any of it?"

Charlene shook her head. "To tell you the truth," she said, "I've been itching to. But we didn't want to disturb anything that might give you a historical clue. We're not sure what we're looking for.

We didn't want to get things out of order, or start throwing things out just because we didn't know enough to understand what they were trying to tell us. So this has pretty much been kept just as Josie left it, for you."

At this, Sadie's eyes lit up so much that Charlene couldn't help but grin. "I can see we've chosen the right partner in this project," she said. "I'm thrilled."

"Me too," Sadie said. "This is *so* up my alley."

Charlene smiled and reached into her pocket. She pulled out a key on a chain and handed it to Sadie. "Jason and I will be in and out from Denver, but we won't be local here for at least another few months. And we don't want you to have to wait until we're in town to make a new discovery. We'd like you to be able to come and go as you please."

Sadie took the key with a smile. "I will take very good care of the place for you," she said.

Charlene smiled. "I know that," she said. "And it might even help keep our contractors on track to have you around from time to time. It'll be good for them to know another person on the restoration team might drop by without warning."

"That never hurts," Sadie agreed.

"All right, then," Charlene said. "I'd love to sit down and crack the first one of these boxes open with you, but I promised I'd meet Jason to talk with the landscaper. So I'm going to leave you to it."

Sadie pocketed the key. "I'll dive right in," she said.

Charlene wrapped her in a quick hug. "Thanks again," she said. "I can't wait to see how this place looks when we're all finished with it."

"Better than any of us can imagine," Sadie said.

"Your mouth to God's ear," Charlene said, waving as she went out the door.

As Charlene's steps trailed down the front stairs, Sadie surveyed the small room, her heart full with the thrill of a new project. *Lord,* she prayed. *Thank You so much for this opportunity. Thank You for the Jones family and all the love they already have for this house. Thank You for all this mess, and for all the treasures and clues to the past it may hold. And please lead me through it to whatever You want us to know.*

When she was finished, she sank down in Josie's old chair. She glanced around for a moment, and then reached for the box that was closest to her. It was labeled *1961 and previous.* That was decades after the house had first been constructed, but it was as good a place to start as any.

Sadie pulled off the lid, laid it to the side, and picked up the first thing she found: an old-fashioned accounting ledger, handsomely cased in turquoise leather. She flipped it open and scanned the first set of numbers. Then she broke into a smile.

Josie Parker had spent her entire professional life working at the Silver Peak Lumber Company as the accountant. So it made sense that, instead of keeping a primitive personal checkbook, she would arrange her own finances in the professional accounting style she used at work. All of her personal expenditures were neatly noted, for things as simple as a ten-cent bag of roasted peanuts at the local fair. It was a wonderful way to understand the history of her life.

Sadie checked the date at the top of the page: January 1949, just a few years after the war had ended. Then she turned to the next page. There she stopped in surprise. Neatly noted in the deposits column was a surprisingly large deposit, almost five hundred dollars. At that time, Sadie quickly calculated, that would have been nearly a third of a teacher's salary for an entire year. And Josie might have been making even less. Where had that big sum come from?

As she scanned down the page, her eyes widened in surprise again. Several weeks later, the account was debited for five hundred dollars. But even though Josie had kept strict accounts of her ten-cent bag of peanuts, there was no notation to explain where the enormous sum of five hundred dollars had gone.

Sadie flipped through the next several pages, scanning for any other large deposits. It was probably just a small inheritance or gift of some kind, she told herself. And Josie hadn't noted it because it was such a large number that it would be impossible for her to forget.

But on several of the following pages, she found similarly large-size deposits and debits, spaced out over years.

The Parker family, as Sadie understood it, hadn't had much money. While she was still living, Josie had joked with Sadie frequently that she was in danger of going to the poorhouse keeping up the house that her relatives had bequeathed to her. "People around here think I'm rich because of this big house," she liked to say. "They don't understand that it's what's making me poor!"

So what were these large sums of money that had moved in and out of Josie's account?

Sadie flipped back to the first page of the ledger just as her phone rang.

At first she glanced at it with slight annoyance at the interruption. But then she saw the caller ID and gasped.

A moment later, she picked up the call. "Ann," she said. "I'm so sorry."

"I'm just glad you're okay," Ann said. "I've been sitting here worrying that something must have happened to you for you to miss our lunch date."

"I'm so sorry," Sadie said again. "I lost track of time."

Ann laughed. Even though Sadie hadn't seen her in years, she still sounded just the way she had when the two of them had attended high school together in Silver Peak. "Well, it sounds like you haven't changed a bit," Ann said.

"I'll be right there," Sadie promised, and laid the ledger aside to hurry downstairs.

2

It had been so long since she'd last seen Ann. Sadie looked around as she stepped through the door of the Depot, one of the favorite restaurants of Silver Peak's locals. She wondered if she'd recognize her old friend.

But even before the door swung shut behind her, Sadie realized there had never been a reason to worry. The instant she saw the attractive older woman with the smoothly layered blonde haircut sitting in a booth near the door, she recognized the face of her friend, familiar even over the decades. And the smile Ann broke into at the sight of Sadie wasn't just familiar. It was exactly the same as it had always been, warm, welcoming, and slightly mischievous.

She rose to her feet as Sadie entered, and the two women shared a long hug.

"You don't look a day over seventeen," Ann told Sadie as the two of them took their seats.

"I'm not going to call you a liar," Sadie said with a grin. "Not when it's been this long since I've seen you, at least."

Ann grinned back. "I took the liberty of ordering Spaghetti Western for both of us before you arrived. They haven't changed the recipe, have they?"

"I think the people of Silver Peak would tolerate a change in the town charter before they'd tolerate a change in the recipe of the Depot's Spaghetti Western," Sadie said. "And thanks for going ahead and ordering. I'm so sorry I was late."

Ann shook her head. "To tell the truth, I was a little late myself. There's just been so much going on with the planning for this reunion."

Sadie nodded vaguely. Her closest friend, Roz, had been talking Sadie's ear off for weeks already about the reunion, and for some reason, Sadie just couldn't seem to get that excited about it. She'd thought at first that maybe that was because she already lived in Silver Peak, and got to see so many of the people she had shared those early years with already. But Roz lived in Silver Peak too, and she seemed to be able to work up plenty of emotion about the reunion.

"I've been hearing about that a bit from Roz," Sadie said. "I guess the two of you are cocaptains for the planning?"

Ann's brow creased slightly, but she kept her tone bright, with evident effort. "We are," she said.

"Roz is wonderful at these kinds of events," Sadie said. "She's always got such a great vision for things."

Ann's brow creased even more deeply. "Yes," she said, but with a tone that made it clear that she didn't completely agree, "Roz has definitely got a strong vision."

"So can I get a sneak preview of what it'll be like?" Sadie asked, nodding her thanks as a waiter set a glass of water down at her place. "Where is it going to be held?"

"That's one of the details we haven't worked out yet," Ann told her.

"That sounds like kind of a big detail," Sadie observed.

"You could say that," Ann said. "Actually, we do have a place reserved already. I found a beautiful ranch outside town with a gorgeous event space, and ponies for the children to ride, and four-star catering. It's very sophisticated, but still with a country feel. They've even got a dance floor that they'll lay out for us in one of the old stock pens. They string those big, old-fashioned incandescent lights around the perimeter, and there's dancing under the stars. I thought it was perfect, and they book up quickly, so as soon as I found it, I made the reservation. The deposit was hefty. But I figured it shouldn't be a problem, if we got the numbers we thought we'd see for this reunion."

"It sounds lovely," Sadie said.

"That's what I thought. And I thought Roz agreed with me. But when I got here, I discovered that she'd taken out a permit to have the reunion right here in town, in the square."

"A lot of events do happen in the square," Sadie said, trying to stay evenhanded in what she was quickly realizing was a serious conflict between her two friends.

"Exactly!" Ann said with an air of triumph. "That's what I said. All the events in town happen in that square. Pep rallies. Bake sales. Political events. I want this reunion to be something special. Something different."

"I know Roz wants it to be special too," Sadie said.

"Yes," Ann said, with a strong hint of disgruntlement, "she's made that clear."

"So what are you looking forward to most about the reunion?" Sadie asked, trying to get the conversation on a more positive track.

Ann looked surprised at the question. "You know, I've been so caught up in the details that I haven't thought much about that," she said. "It's a good question."

She smiled as their waiter returned to place heaping plates of Spaghetti Western in front of each of them, along with side salads.

"It's not exactly health food, is it?" she said.

"It makes me happy," Sadie said, digging in. "And my doctor says that's good for my health."

Ann nodded, taking a bite herself. She savored it, then gave a satisfied nod. "Just as I remembered."

"What did I tell you?" Sadie said.

For a few minutes, the two of them enjoyed their Spaghetti Western in companionable silence.

But then Ann broke it. "I'm not sure what I'm looking forward to," she said. "Seeing you again was definitely high on my list."

"Oh," Sadie said, smiling, "likewise."

"I've really enjoyed seeing where people I've connected with by social media have ended up," Ann said. "I'd like to talk to Gertie Bowers about her dog training business, for instance. As I remember it, the Bowerses had the worst-trained dog in town when we were in school. I feel like he chased just about everyone in our class home at least once. And he was so big. What was he, a cross between a Great Dane and a German shepherd?"

"My dad used to say he was part pony," Sadie said. "That was the only thing that could account for his size."

Ann laughed. "Do you remember the time he treed Artie Dillinger?" she asked. "Somehow the Bowerses' dog got out of the yard and found a bunch of us down in the square. The rest of us scattered, so there was nowhere for Artie to go but up. The police chief had to come and take that dog home. And even he couldn't help laughing a little bit when he saw Artie up in that tree."

Sadie laughed along with her. "But he wasn't a bad dog," Sadie insisted. "The worst he would have ever done was to lick us to death."

"Yes, but he was so big! I think most of the kids had a heart attack just from the size of him, before they realized there wasn't a mean bone in his body. I just don't understand how someone from the family that raised that dog became a professional dog trainer."

"Maybe that's *why* Gertie became a professional dog trainer," Sadie suggested.

Ann laughed. "That thought did cross my mind," she said. "And what about you? Anyone you're interested in seeing in particular?"

Sadie looked around the restaurant thoughtfully for a moment. Then she shook her head. "I can't think of anyone," she said. "But I'm excited to go," she hurried to assure Ann. "It'll be great to see everyone all at once."

"There's no one in particular you want to see?" Ann asked.

She seemed to be getting at something, but Sadie wasn't sure what it was.

"Is there someone I *should* be looking forward to seeing?" she asked, knowing her face must be communicating the bewilderment she felt.

"I can't believe you don't know whom I'm talking about," Ann said, her eyes dancing with even more mischief than usual.

"What in the world are you so amused by?" Sadie asked.

"Well, I know most high school romances are only puppy love. But honestly, I always thought that you had something special even back in high school. I think we all did, really. Everyone who knew you two. And I know you and T.R. were very happy. But now that you're both single again, when I saw on the list that you were both attending the reunion, I couldn't help but think..."

In a flash, Sadie realized whom Ann was talking about: Sadie's high school sweetheart, Edwin. She was fishing to see if Sadie was hoping to rekindle that old romance at the high school reunion.

Sadie broke out in a ringing peal of laughter.

"Is it that ridiculous of an idea?" Ann asked, somewhat taken aback. "I mean, I know things change over the years. And I'm sure some things change too much for us to ever go back. But Edwin always impressed me as one of the good ones. And those don't come along every day."

Sadie's laughter finally subsided. She shook her head.

Ann shrugged. "Well," she said, "I guess I was wrong."

Sadie raised her hands in protest. "No, no," she said. "I'm laughing because you're so right."

Ann's eyes flared in triumph. "See?" she said. "I knew that old flame couldn't have totally died out." She leaned forward across the table, her voice conspiratorial. "So?" she said. "What do you think it's going to be like to see him again? Have you decided what you're wearing?"

Sadie grinned again, at the thought that two women their age should still be aflutter about what to wear when they were planning to see an old flame. But it was part of the beauty of life that they did still get aflutter about that, she thought. It was part of how they knew their hearts were still alive.

By now, though, Ann was so excited that Sadie couldn't bear to keep her in the dark any longer.

"The thing is," Sadie said, "I've actually seen Edwin recently."

"You *have*?" Ann breathed. "*When?* What was it like?"

"It was lovely," Sadie said. "He came and picked me up just as I was closing the shop, and we walked down here to get a scoop of ice cream for dinner. Then we came back up to Los Pollitos and had some enchiladas for dessert."

Ann's eyes widened. "Sadie," she said. "That sounds for all the world like a date. Do you think he's interested in you?"

"Well, I certainly hope he is," Sadie said.

"You do?" Ann said, her voice squealing almost as high as it had when they were both teenagers. "You two are going to wind up together! I just knew it!"

"The thing is," Sadie said, "we already are together."

She hadn't thought it was possible for Ann's eyes to grow any wider, but amazingly, they did. "You're *what*? How have you not told me this already? How did I not know this? How did this happen? Tell me everything."

"We've been seeing each other for a while," Sadie said simply. "And I'm very happy about that."

Ann's face broke into a grin. "I think that makes me happier than I would be if I reunited with my own high school sweetheart," she said.

"Jimmy Rhinebacker?" Sadie asked. "Didn't he run off and join the rodeo?"

Ann shrugged. "I don't know. He was one of the ones we couldn't get a certain address for when we were trying to send out the invitations. I left a message at an e-mail address someone had for him, but we never heard anything back. I don't think he's coming. And if he's spent all this time in the rodeo, he's probably walking with two canes now, if he's walking at all."

"Still," Sadie said. "I've always thought cowboys were kind of romantic."

"Not as romantic as the town mayor," Ann said, her voice teasing.

Sadie took the last bite of her Spaghetti Western and leaned back in her seat. "It's so good to see you," she said.

Ann smiled. "You too," she said.

"And I'm so glad you're helping head up this reunion," Sadie said. "I know it's a lot of work on your part that the rest of us are just going to get to enjoy. To tell the truth, I'm a little surprised to see you in town so soon. I mean, I was sure you wouldn't miss one of our big reunions. But spending a week in town is a lot for a girl who couldn't wait to get out of here. Especially now that you don't have family in town anymore."

For the first time since Sadie had sat down, Ann didn't meet her eyes. "Well, once you buy the ticket from California, it just makes sense to have a bit of a stay, I guess," she said.

That didn't ring true to Sadie. Ann's parents had passed away years ago, but even though her younger brother, Jasper, lived on the family ranch outside town, Ann was hardly a regular visitor to Silver Peak. And she was hardly hurting for money. From connecting with her over the Internet, Sadie knew Ann had done very well professionally, building her own personal shopping business with some of the biggest names in Los Angeles—as well as some customers who were so powerful that they managed to keep their names out of the press almost completely.

"So I guess you're enjoying catching up with Jasper, then?" Sadie asked with a smile.

Now Ann stared down the remains of her Spaghetti Western, as if she couldn't bear to meet the gaze of anyone in the place.

"Ann," Sadie said gently. "Is something wrong?"

"I was trying to decide whether or not to tell you this," Ann said, her voice low. Then she looked up and met Sadie's eyes, her own full of questions, and something else—maybe even pain? "But it's becoming clear I can't do it all on my own. And you might be just the person to help me."

"Do what?" Sadie asked.

Ann took a deep breath. "I'm not just in town for the reunion," she said.

By now, Sadie had all but figured that out for herself. But she kept silent. It was clear Ann was carrying a heavy weight, and she needed to tell her own story at her own pace.

"My niece is quite sick," Ann began. "They've been trying to manage her condition for years. But now she needs a kidney transplant."

Sadie's mind whirred, but she didn't immediately see what this had to do with Silver Peak. Jasper's daughter was in Denver, miles away. And although Silver Peak had a wonderful hospital for a town its size, it was hardly the place you'd pick to have a major, complicated procedure like a kidney transplant.

"So, of course, everyone in the family got tested to see if we were a match," Ann said.

Sadie nodded. She could understand why Ann might be especially emotional about something like that. It could be a huge disappointment to find out you couldn't help someone you loved, no matter what sacrifice you were willing to make. And on the other hand, some family members might feel pressured to make a sacrifice they weren't ready for if they proved to be a match for another family member in a life-or-death situation.

Ann looked up at Sadie, a plaintive look in her eyes, as if she didn't know how to go on.

"And were you?" Sadie asked gently.

Ann shook her head. Suddenly, tears stood in her eyes. "Sadie," she said, "the tests told me I wasn't even a member of my family."

"I don't understand," Sadie said. She had tons of memories of Ann with her family: her father picking her up from school in his beat-up ranch truck, her mother teaching all the girls how to make themselves look bigger in case they ran into a mountain lion on one of the trails outside town during Girl Scouts. Of course Ann was a member of her family. What could she be talking about?

"Genetically," Ann said. "I'm not a match with anyone in my family. Not Mom's siblings, or Dad's. Or even Jasper." At this, her voice broke. "They said we don't have any recent common ancestors," she almost whispered.

"You were adopted?" Sadie said, reasoning through it for herself.

Ann nodded. "I must have been," she said. "That's the only explanation. But Mom and Dad never said a word about it to me. And Jasper was born just five years before I was. He doesn't remember anything."

"Nothing?" Sadie said. "Nothing at all?"

Ann shrugged in despair. "That's all he'll say, that he doesn't remember anything. But he doesn't want to talk about it at all. As far as he's concerned, he says, I'm his sister, and Mom and Dad are our parents, and he doesn't see why I'd want to know anything besides that. But Sadie," she said, "I have to know."

"I can understand that," Sadie said.

Across the table, Ann fingered the chain of a necklace at her throat. As she did, a distinctive charm peeked out from the collar of her shirt, a delicate chain holding a thick ornament. It looked strangely familiar to Sadie, but she didn't have the time to think about it now. She could ask about it some other time, when Ann wasn't struggling with such a serious question.

"I came back to town so early to see if I could get some answers," Ann said. "You've been here in town so long. You know so much more than I do about how things work around here. And you've always been so good at getting to the bottom of things. I can't do it on my own. I'm too emotional. And I don't even know where to start. I know it's a lot to ask, but I don't know where else to turn. Sadie, will you please help me?"

Sadie stared back across the table at her friend. Then she took Ann's hand, squeezed it tightly, and nodded. "Of course I'll help you."

3

"GRANDMA!" THEO CRIED IN EXCITEMENT.

In the front window of the shop, Sadie carefully finished fastening the corner of a soft antique quilt to the long bar that would keep it evenly weighted, preserving the years-old fabric as it was displayed to the passersby on Silver Peak's street. Then she made a little half turn on the stepladder she stood on, and squinted toward the back of the counter, where Theo's voice had come from.

Despite Theo's exclamation, the shop looked just as it always did: a comfortable jumble of relics. It changed all the time as Sadie brought in new pieces and others went out the door in the hands of happy customers. But somehow, it also managed to feel the same, perhaps because the common factor in all the pieces was always a special something that appealed to Sadie herself. It wasn't just a shop. In some ways, it was almost an extension of Sadie's own home. And although it changed all the time, and she sometimes stocked items that she wouldn't keep at home because she knew her customers would like them, her store always did reflect the things she was interested in and attracted to—so something about it was always familiar, even though it stayed fresh enough to bring in a steady stream of new and returning customers.

"That looks nice," Julie, the young mother who worked for Sadie at the shop, said, stepping back and appraising with a sharp eye the job they'd done hanging the quilt.

"Theo?" Sadie called, still scanning the back of the shop for a glimpse of her grandson. "Is everything okay?"

Instead of Theo, her daughter, Alice, stepped out from behind the counter, brushing back her auburn hair with a smile. "I think you're going to be pleased with this, Mom," she said.

An instant later, Theo popped up like a jack-in-the-box from behind the counter, where he had apparently been kneeling or crouching. In his hand was a gleaming silver bowl.

"That's gorgeous," Sadie said. "I don't remember our having a silver plate in that size."

"That's because it was buried in the sort pile," Theo said.

A fuzzy memory came back to Sadie, that sometime in the past few months, she might have picked up a bowl of about that size and shape in one of the haunts and sales she frequented to stock the Antique Mine. Snapping up great finds was the easy part. It was going through the sort pile Theo had mentioned, pulling out the finds, fixing them up for sale, and pricing them, that took time. So the pile was always bigger than she meant it to be. Thankfully, it turned out that Theo thought of the sort pile as a kind of permanent treasure hunt. He had asked for permission to come into the store, poke around in his grandmother's new finds, and choose one to fix up for sale himself. "It looks familiar," she said. "But it certainly didn't look like that when I bought it."

"It took me three rounds of polishing," Theo said.

Sadie crossed the store to take a look at it. The bowl might as well have come straight from the silversmith's. Theo's work had been so thorough that there wasn't a hint of tarnish anywhere on it. "You did a beautiful job, honey," she said. "Thank you. I had no idea I'd bought anything so pretty."

"Well, I suspect you had some idea," Theo said. "If you didn't have a good eye, there wouldn't be so many great things here at the Antique Mine."

Alice ruffled Theo's hair. He ducked, and Sadie smiled.

"But look at this, Grandma," Theo said eagerly. He held the bowl up so that she could see a faint but beautiful monogram engraved in the lip of the bowl. A large *R* was surrounded on either side by an ornate *J* and *L*.

"My goodness," Sadie said, peering closer. "I can't say I even saw that when I bought it, through the tarnish."

"I don't think you could," Theo said. "I didn't see it myself until I did my second cleaning. And I couldn't really make it out until I did my third."

"That's some very nice engraving," Sadie said appraisingly.

"But do you notice the initials?" Theo said, his voice full of excitement.

Sadie strung the initials together in order: *J*, *L*, *R*. But it didn't ring any bells for her.

"Theo just did the unit on Colorado history last month," Alice said.

"Oh?" Sadie said, her eyebrows lifting. A smile tugged at her mouth at the fact that her grandson now apparently knew something about Colorado history that had slipped her own mind.

"John Long Routt!" Theo exclaimed.

"Colorado's first governor," Sadie said.

"And its seventh!" Theo added. "Not to mention mayor of Denver."

"Apparently, he was popular with the ladies," Alice added.

"Was he handsome?" Sadie asked.

"No," Theo said. "He believed they had the right to vote."

Sadie took the bowl from Theo, gazing down into the delicate letters. "Well, that's very interesting," she said. "Of course, there's no guarantee that this was one of Governor Routt's own bowls, just because it has his initials."

"Yes," Theo said, "but if it were any other set of initials, it'd be guaranteed it *wasn't* his."

Sadie laughed. "You're right," she said. "It'll be fun to track this down."

"What do you think we should do first?" Theo said. "Where do we start?"

The bell over the front door rang.

Sadie looked up to see a tall, handsome man in a sky-blue knit shirt and a pair of trim khakis step into the shop. His face was one of the most familiar in the world to her, but her heart still skipped a beat or two when she saw him.

"Hello," she said, deciding to make a joke so that she wouldn't act like a nervous schoolgirl. "Welcome to the Antique Mine. Have you been here before?"

Edwin, who was always quick on the uptake, picked up on her joke right away. "Once or twice," he said, coming over to the counter.

Alice gave him a warm smile. "It's Edwin."

"Hi, Mr. Marshall," Theo said.

"What have you got there?" Edwin asked.

"It's an antique bowl Grandma found somewhere. I just cleaned it up and we think it belonged to John Long Routt."

Edwin's brow furrowed. "Now, how do I know that name?" he asked.

"He was the first governor of Colorado," Theo told him.

"And the seventh," Sadie added, a twinkle in her eye. "And, apparently, a sympathizer with the suffragettes."

"Those troublemakers?" Edwin asked.

Sadie gave him a mock warning glance and adopted a jokingly chilly tone. "I'm sorry," she said. "Were you looking for anything in particular?"

"Actually," Edwin said, ignoring her tone as he leaned on the counter, "I was looking for you."

"And what were you thinking I might be able to help you with?" Sadie asked.

"Well," Edwin said, "from what I hear, there's a dance up at the high school this weekend."

"A dance at the high school?" Sadie asked.

Edwin nodded gravely. "I was thinking you might go with me."

Sadie glanced around. Alice and Theo had both faded to other corners of the shop, to let Sadie and Edwin talk in relative privacy.

"What makes you think I'm the kind of girl who goes to dances?" Sadie asked.

"You're too pretty not to dance," Edwin said.

To her chagrin, Sadie blushed. "You do have a point," she said. "But I mean, so much can happen to a girl in a week. What if somebody else asks me?"

"Then you can tell them you're going with me," Edwin said. His tone was still joking, but his voice had gotten louder, too, so that Sadie got the feeling that he didn't even like the idea of her joking about going with someone else very much at all.

Before Sadie could come up with a rejoinder to this, the bell over the shop door dinged again. Edwin glanced at the door with a slightly guarded look, as if another one of Sadie's imaginary suitors might actually be on the doorstep of her shop.

But Sadie broke into a bright smile when she realized who it was: Roz, her best friend, dressed in one of her predictably zany getups. Roz's taste ran to the unique, and sometimes, in some people's opinion, to the bizarre. Sadie just thought that Roz was always a bright spot in any room, and today that was definitely true. She had paired a deep purple tunic with what seemed like a king's ransom in turquoise jewelry, including bracelets that ran high above her wrist on both arms, a thick choker, and a leather belt studded with gorgeous chunks of the deep blue stone.

But her expression was anything but bright.

"Is everything all right?" Sadie asked, her eyes widening in concern.

At the sound of the alarm in Sadie's voice, Edwin reached across the counter to give her hand a squeeze. Sadie squeezed back gratefully. No matter how the two of them might enjoy a playful round of sparring, she knew Edwin would always be there for her if she needed him.

Roz barreled over to the counter, shaking her head.

"It's outrageous," she said. "Just outrageous. And at our age. You'd think we'd be old enough to know better."

"About...what?" Sadie asked. Roz was a woman of strong opinions, but she was usually able to hold them without getting bent out of shape if someone else disagreed with her. It was one of the qualities Sadie enjoyed most about her, because it meant that Roz was a great person to work through new ideas and real questions with. She didn't have to force you to believe what she did. She was willing to explore ideas with you. So what in the world could have gotten her so upset?

"Is everything all right?" Sadie asked.

"That remains to be seen," Roz said darkly, dropping her large, clunky bohemian bag on the counter when she reached it.

"Do you want to give me a hint?" Sadie pressed.

"I don't think Ann Cartwright has even set foot in this town in the last twenty years," Roz said. She spread her hands in a broad gesture that seemed to take in not just the whole contents of the Antique Mine, but the entire town beyond it, and perhaps the great state of Colorado—and maybe even the whole universe. "But now she thinks she owns the place."

Edwin gave Sadie's hand another squeeze and began to back away, as if he'd just discovered a live wire lying between him and Sadie, somewhere in the vicinity of the counter. "Maybe I'll just...," he said, with a glance at the door.

Sadie gave him a quick but grateful nod, and he headed for the exit.

It was unclear if Roz had even noticed that he was there in the first place. All her attention was still focused on her outrage—apparently over something Ann had said or done.

"What's going on?" Sadie asked as the door closed behind Edwin.

Julie, who had been in the back, putting the finishing touches on quilts for the window display, poked her head out and gave Sadie a questioning look, to see if Sadie needed help with a new customer. Sadie gave her head a quick shake to let Julie know she had it covered.

Roz gave the deep sigh of a valiant warrior, facing defeat, but unwilling to surrender. "It's this reunion," she said. "She's trying to ruin it."

Sadie thought back quickly on the conversation she had just had with Ann. Roz and Ann had different ideas. But Ann was hardly out to ruin the reunion.

"Are you sure that's what she's trying to do?" Sadie asked.

Roz straightened up. "It might not be what she thinks she's *trying* to do," she said. "But it's what she's *going* to do. Unless I stop her."

At this, her chin came up, and Sadie thought she got a quick flash of any of the grandfathers or great-grandfathers in Roz's history who had ever served in a military capacity.

"What is she trying to do?" Sadie asked.

"First of all," Roz said, "she doesn't even want to have it in town."

Sadie nodded, to show she was listening.

"She wants to have it out at the Lonnigan Ranch. As if any of us ever spent any time out there when we were in high school. There weren't even any Lonnigans in school when we were going through school."

"Maybe she thinks it'll be a special treat," Sadie said, thinking back on her recent conversation. "A change of pace."

"A change of pace is hardly what high school reunions are supposed to be about," Roz said. "They're about tradition. And memory. People are returning to town to visit a place they've remembered all their lives. Not someplace none of us have ever been to before."

"I can see your point," Sadie said, trying to keep out of it as much as she could.

"She keeps talking about how beautiful it will be, with all the stars out over the Lonnigan ranch," Roz said. "As if there aren't stars anywhere else in the world but over the Lonnigan ranch. As if they're a special feature God installed only for them."

"So what were some of your ideas for the reunion?" Sadie asked, trying to get Roz on the path of something positive, instead of concentrating on the problems with Ann's proposed plans.

"I just wanted to have a simple get-together down in the town square," Roz said, with a curt nod of her head, like a general laying out the strategy for the next day's battle. "You know, simple. Open air. Kind of like me." She grinned.

Sadie grinned back at her. "That sounds nice," Sadie said hopefully.

"It does, doesn't it?" Roz said. "And I'd already put in a request for the space with the city, and gotten it approved. I even got them to waive the fee, so nobody who's already spending all that money to get here from out of town has to pay any extra."

"Great," Sadie agreed.

"Well," Roz said, "except that *Ann Cartwright* had already gone ahead and put a deposit down on the Lonnigan Ranch, without getting any approval from me. Because she thinks it's so much more sophisticated than the bohemian shindig I want to throw in town. I don't see how a party in a barn is more sophisticated than my idea, which was just getting together a bunch of us, right here in town, and enjoying the open air and the stars and some good food and good company. And she might not think that seventy-five dollars a head is much, but that's a lot of money for some people. Especially if you're coming as a couple. And then I, for one, would like to meet people's kids, or grandkids, if they're around. Are we going to charge them seventy-five dollars a pop too?"

"I see what you mean," Sadie said. "And I think Ann's done pretty well. So she might not realize how tight things may be for some other people. What were you planning on having, if you go ahead and throw the reunion in the city square?"

Roz looked surprised. "What do you mean?" she asked.

"Well," Sadie said, "all those people. They'll want to eat something."

"That hardly matters, does it?" Roz asked. "I mean, they aren't returning to Silver Peak for the haute cuisine. They're coming home to see each other. Once we arrange for that, who cares what we eat?"

"Still," Sadie pointed out, "they'll need to eat something."

Roz shrugged. "We're all adults. I'm sure everyone can figure out something."

Sadie wondered how she would feel if she was one of the out-of-towners who would be traveling thousands of miles to attend the reunion. "It might be nice to have something planned," she said. "Just so that people feel welcome. Especially if they haven't been in a town for a while."

Roz waved her hand impatiently. "Well, I know one thing," she said. "There aren't many meals in Silver Peak that would set you back seventy-five dollars per person. On Saturday night specials, Sophia's is two for twenty... so that's... what is that?"

Sadie thought wryly that, as much as Roz and Ann might dislike working together, she was glad they were. Much as she loved both of them, she didn't want to go to the hypothetical reunions either of them would plan alone. But together, they might just balance each other out enough to come up with something that would work for everyone.

"That's five pizzas per person," Roz said, triumphantly. "With a couple of dollars left over for bread sticks."

"Are you really going to serve pizza at our class reunion?" Sadie asked.

Roz gave her an arch look. "Don't test me," she said.

"Have you two come to any decisions together?" Sadie asked.

Roz shook her head grimly. "Not yet," she said. "I'm on my way over to meet her now. I just needed to see my oldest friend for some moral support."

"Well," Sadie said, "keep in mind that Ann's one of our oldest friends too. I'm sure you can work something out. Remember how much fun we had sophomore year, the first time her dad let her take the car out by herself?"

Roz's eyes brightened. "His brand-new Mustang!" she said. "With the white seats and the convertible top!"

Sadie nodded. "It was right after a rainstorm."

"And there was that incredibly tempting puddle from the jammed drain over on Monroe Street," Roz went on.

"And Kent Luscombe was unlucky enough to be walking home just as we went by," Sadie continued for her.

"But when she tried to splash him, most of that puddle wound up *inside* the convertible," Roz remembered. "On us!"

"I'll never forget trying to get that thing dry before she took it home to her dad."

"Do you think he ever noticed?" Roz asked.

"I imagine we'd have heard about it, if he had," Sadie said, with a smile.

"That was a fun day," Roz admitted.

"Maybe you're right," Sadie said. "It doesn't matter so much exactly what we do at the reunion, as long as we all get together. It'll just be fun to all spend some time and remember stories like that one."

Roz didn't look exactly convinced. But she didn't look nearly as girded for battle as she had when she first came into the store. "We'll see about that," she said. "I'm not sure how fun it's going to be, if Ann gets her way."

Then she checked her watch. "I'd better go," she said. "I'm supposed to meet Ann in a few minutes."

"Let me know how it goes," Sadie called as Roz headed for the door.

Roz waved, and the door thudded shut behind her.

Julie came back from the front of the store and circled around the counter. She laid down a small pile of books on the Native American tribes, the last remains of the previous display of native art and artifacts they'd just removed in order to install the quilt.

"I think we're all set up there," she said.

"Thank you so much," Sadie said, looking over the window dressing with a practiced eye. "It all looks great."

"I love doing the displays here," Julie said. "I know we're a store, but it's almost like we're a museum too. We don't just sell our customers something. It's about history."

Sadie smiled. She had thought the same thing herself. "I think it's better than some museums," she said. "Because you can actually pick the things up and touch them. You get a real feel for what life must have been like in other times."

"I know I do," Julie said. She quickly shelved the books among some others nearby, then turned back.

"How are you doing?" Sadie asked. "Will you be in good shape if I go out for a bit?"

Julie nodded. "Of course," she said. "I mean, it won't be nearly as fun as it would be to have you around, but..."

"I'm sure you can handle it," Sadie said with a laugh, pulling her purse onto her shoulder. She was itching to get over to the Parker House. Since Charlene had given her the keys and access to the files to do her research, she hadn't been able to get over there once.

A few minutes later, she stepped through the door of the Parker House. From a new set of tarps, pails, and tools in the front entrance, she could tell that a new set of workers had been and gone since she last met with Charlene.

Before she went upstairs to the room that Josie had used as an office, Sadie stood for a long minute in the hall, listening and watching, reaching back into her own knowledge of history to try to get a feel for what it might have been like so many years ago, when the house was new and filled with family. Then she took a step into the cozy front room with its intricate fireplace grate.

Instantly, she started. In a flash, she knew what had been tugging at her memory when she thought she had recognized the interesting charm that Ann had been wearing around her neck when the two of them met for lunch. It matched the fleur-de-lis design of the Parker House fireplace grate. In fact, as far as Sadie could tell, it was identical.

Sadie stepped over to the grate. The resemblance between the intricate metalwork and the ornament Ann had been wearing was so similar that Sadie had the strong feeling that Ann's necklace must actually have been part of the grate at one time. But a first glance seemed to contradict this. All the visible parts of the grate were whole and perfect.

Sadie stepped closer. She ran her fingers over the entire face of the grate, looking for any imperfections. There were none.

Then she checked the left wing that angled back to the stone face of the fireplace. All the whorls and swirls of its metal were also complete.

But when she looked at the right side of the fireplace grate, she immediately saw a missing piece in the design. About halfway down, one of the fleur-de-lis that made up the pattern was broken off and missing.

And if Sadie remembered correctly, it was exactly the size and shape of the one she had just seen Ann wearing.

But could that even be possible?

4

Sadie saw Ann pull up to the curb outside the Parker House from the window of Josie's old office, where Sadie had been going through an old box of birthday cards and holiday greetings that Josie had carefully collected through the years. They were full of great examples of the popular greeting styles of previous years, with more austere designs during the war years, blossoming into bright colors and glitter in the postwar era. And they were a testament to Josie's popularity in town—it seemed like just about everyone in Silver Peak must have sent her seasonal congratulations of some kind to fill the banker's box Sadie was sifting through. But other than that, the box at least hadn't shed much light on the early history of the house—or the possible connection between Ann's necklace and the missing piece of the fireplace grate.

Outside, on the curb, Ann stepped out of the car and looked uncertainly up at the house. The expression on her face was more than the look of a woman checking for the correct address, wanting to make sure she'd arrived at the right place. There was a look of longing, a hint of worry, but also one of hope. Sadie knew Ann would find her way to the door on her own, but she hated the idea of leaving her out there with her thoughts, alone. She got up and hurried downstairs, where she stepped out onto the porch of the Parker House with a cheery wave.

"Ann!" she said. "You made it!"

The worry and wonder she had seen on Ann's face from her view in the upstairs window quickly disappeared, replaced by the smile Sadie had known for so many years. Ann came quickly up the walk and enveloped Sadie in a warm hug.

"I know I just saw you," she said, "but it's so good to see you again."

Sadie smiled back at her. "You too, Ann."

"I guess it's just been such a long time since I've been around really old friends," Ann said. "I mean, I have good people out in California. But there's just something about people who have known you all your life."

"I think I understand," Sadie told her. "My daughter, Alice, talks about feeling something similar when she moved back here from Denver. She really loved living in Denver. Of course, there are things you can get there that you can't get in a town the size of Silver Peak. And I imagine that's true for where you are in California too."

Ann smiled. "But there are also things you can get in Silver Peak that you can't get in California. Like a scoop of ice cream from the Depot."

"Alice does love their ice cream," Sadie said. "But she says she was surprised when she came back to Silver Peak by what a relief it was to be around people who had known her all her life. She had good people in Denver. And she'd been happy there. Both of her kids were born there. She liked her job. But she said it was wonderful to come back here, too, to be with people who didn't know her just for her job, or as her kids' mom, or as her ex-husband's wife. People who had known her even before she remembered knowing anybody. When she was just a tiny girl."

"And people who loved her back then," Ann said, almost wistfully, "before she was even sure who she was."

"You've got some people like that in this town yourself," Sadie said.

Ann gave a grateful nod. "I think I'm getting a taste of how it felt to Alice when she came back to town," she said. "But I've still got some important questions. I always thought I belonged in Silver Peak. I always thought this was where I'd come from. But now I'm not even sure about that anymore."

Sadie nodded.

"You said you might have found something for me?" Ann said.

"We'll need to take a closer look to see," Sadie told her. "But I think it's worth a look."

"I'm ready," Ann said.

Sadie put a hand on her shoulder and began to steer her toward the door. "Come on inside," she said. "We'll take a look and see what you think."

She led Ann into the house.

"I always loved this place," Ann said as they stepped through the door and into the main entrance, "but I've never been inside."

Sadie thought about the possible fit between Ann's necklace and the broken part of the fireplace grate, and wondered if that was really true. But she didn't say anything to contradict Ann. Not yet. Even though she knew Ann had gotten along well with her parents, the revelation that Ann wasn't biologically related to them had obviously hit Ann hard. So Sadie didn't want to introduce any more questions into Ann's life right now than she absolutely had to. And she hoped that the questions she was about to bring up about the necklace and the fireplace wouldn't just add to the many questions Ann felt she didn't have answers to right now. Sadie hoped that the questions she was asking might actually help lead to some of the answers Ann needed.

"It's beautiful," Ann said, looking around.

"It'll look even better when we're done with the renovations," Sadie said.

From the back of the house, she could hear the sound of workers busily replacing the plumbing in the kitchen. The Joneses wanted the renovation to bring the place back to its former grandeur—but one thing Charlene was committed to was a state-of-the-art kitchen under the historical facade. Sadie still needed to answer some questions about what the original kitchen had looked like, but they already knew enough to know that the most recent set of pipes, which had been installed thirty years ago, weren't going to be up to snuff. So the contractor was putting in the bones of a new system while Sadie put the finishing touches on the details of the historical renovation.

"We?" Ann asked.

"I'm consulting on the renovation," Sadie told her. "For a couple who have just moved here from Denver. The historical research I'm doing here is actually for the renovation. But I just happened to come across something that seemed like it might be connected with you."

"What made you think that?" Ann asked.

Sadie gestured for Ann to follow her into the front room. When they stepped in, Sadie watched as Ann glanced around, taking in the high ceiling, the remarkable windows that reached from a rounded peak all the way down to the floor, and, of course, the fireplace grate.

As Ann looked around, Sadie checked to see if Ann was wearing the ornament. Sure enough, the same delicate chain was still around Ann's neck, dropping down inside the crisp white shirt she was wearing. It must be a favorite piece of jewelry, Sadie reasoned, for Ann to wear it two days in a row. Most of the distinctive ornament was hidden from view, but Sadie could make out a glimpse of the verdigris.

Sadie was curious if Ann would recognize the similarity between the ornament she wore around her neck and the verdigris of the fireplace grate. But after a quick survey of the room, Ann turned to her with a look very much like the one Sadie had seen on her face as Ann first looked up at the Parker House when she arrived: uncertain, apprehensive, but still eager.

Sadie's heart tugged at the unease her old friend was feeling. As Ann watched her, Sadie walked over to the fire grate and pointed to it. "Do you recognize this?" she asked.

Ann's brow knit. "I don't know," she said after a minute, as if she wasn't sure what the right answer ought to be. "Should I? I've never been here before. Was it brought in from someplace else? From somewhere else in town?"

Sadie shook her head. "No," she said. "Actually, that's one of the few pieces of the Parker House history we're sure of, so far. This fire grate was part of the original design of the place. Mrs. Parker fell in love with it on her honeymoon in France, and Mr. Parker had it shipped to her and installed before they even returned from the continent. It was a surprise, and apparently she loved it. A member of the family had done the history on it even before the house was sold, so they gave Charlene a packet of historical documents on it at the sale of the house."

"Charlene?" Ann asked.

"She's the new owner," Sadie told Ann. "She and her husband. I do hope you'll have a chance to meet her while you're here. They're making a real contribution to Silver Peak history already. It's going to be a beautiful renovation, and not just anybody would have done it like they have."

"Oh," Ann said, as if she was trying to pay attention in a class, although her mind was thoroughly distracted by something else.

Sadie realized that, no matter how fascinated she might be by the history, she could hardly expect Ann to share her enthusiasm when Ann was seeking answers to such difficult questions about herself.

"So do you think it"—Ann hesitated, searching for the words—"has something to do with me?"

Sadie was slightly surprised that Ann hadn't recognized the similarity between the grate and the ornament she was wearing right away. But it was possible that Ann was so familiar with the ornament that she had almost forgotten what it looked like. To prompt her memory, Sadie circled around to the right side of the grate and gestured to the missing segment of the metal.

Ann's expression was so blank in response to this that Sadie doubted herself for a moment. Maybe the two kinds of metal weren't nearly as similar as she had thought. Maybe Ann hadn't recognized the similarities not because she had forgotten how her own ornament looked, but because she knew it so well that she could see immediately that it was really nothing like the fireplace grate.

"I'm sorry," Ann said. "I'm not sure what I'm supposed to be looking at."

"This fireplace grate," Sadie said, feeling more and more foolish. "When I looked at it, it reminded me of the ornament you're wearing."

"Ornament?" Ann asked, seeming puzzled.

"Your necklace," Sadie said.

Ann's hand rose toward her throat and closed around the delicate chain. A moment later, she had pulled the ornament that dangled at the end of it from the collar of her shirt. "This?" she asked, sounding baffled.

Now that Sadie had a good look at it, the sense of recognition pulsed through her again. She nodded firmly. "To me," she said, "it looks like it might have been part of this grate at one time. This part right here." She gestured again to the missing metal.

"But how would that be?" Ann said. "I never knew Josie Parker. How would I have? There were never any Parkers in school when we were there. She didn't have any children at all, did she?"

As Sadie stared back at her, Ann's eyes widened. "You don't think...," she began. "You don't think *she* could be my mother?"

"I don't think we have enough to go on to assume anything," Sadie said quickly.

"But then why would you think that my necklace has anything to do with this fireplace grate?"

"That's my question too. It just seems too coincidental. Do you know the story of the necklace?" Sadie asked. "Where did you get it?"

Ann fingered the filigree ornament again. “It’s a family heirloom,” she said. “My mother gave it to me.”

Sadie’s eyebrows rose, although she tried not to let too much excitement into her voice. If Ann had picked up the ornament later in life—if it had been a gift from her husband, for instance, it would have been much harder to believe that it had anything to do with the Parker House, despite the resemblance.

“So it may have actually come from somewhere here in Silver Peak,” Sadie said.

“I guess so,” Ann agreed.

“Did your mother tell you the story behind it?” Sadie asked. “How it’s connected with your family?”

Ann’s brows drew together in concentration, but after a moment, she shook her head. “I guess she didn’t,” she said. “All I remember her saying is that it was a piece of my family history. I should have asked her about it, but I was so young when she gave it to me. Only eight or nine. I barely knew what history was at that age. And then it became so much a part of my life that I guess I never thought to ask.”

“So have you always worn it so frequently?” Sadie asked.

Ann shook her head. “I did when she first gave it to me. Mom used to joke that I’d never take it off when I was a little girl. But I think I stopped in high school because it wasn’t like the jewelry the other girls were wearing.”

The two of them shared a knowing smile.

“I started wearing it again recently,” Ann said. “Maybe it has something to do with wanting to feel like I was really a part of the family. No matter what those tests say about me. Do you really think Josie Parker might have…?”

Sadie shook her head again. "I'll know more about her history when I'm done with this restoration," she said. "But for now I'd say it would have been very difficult in Silver Peak for a woman to go through a pregnancy and childbirth without anyone noticing. I mean, can you even imagine how that could have happened?"

"I guess that's true," Ann said slowly. "What about her family members? Is there anyone we could ask about it?"

Sadie shook her head. "Not anymore," she said. "That's the only way this house came on the market. Josie was really the last in her line. So after her death it passed into the hands of a distant cousin who had no interest in it. Luckily the Joneses fell in love with the history of the place, and want to preserve it themselves."

Ann stared into the fireplace grate, almost as if she were looking at a fire inside it only she could see. She turned the ornament on her necklace idly in her fingers.

"Would you let me try it?" Sadie asked.

"Try what?" Ann asked, with a questioning look.

"Well, there's one easy way to see if my hunch is correct," Sadie said. "We've got the necklace here with us now. We can see if it really does fit with the missing grate."

"Oh," Ann said quietly. Then she reached for the clasp behind her neck. She was obviously game to try Sadie's idea, but her hands wouldn't quite obey. After struggling for a few moments, she gave up, turned her back to Sadie, and leaned so that Sadie could reach the clasp to unfasten it.

When the necklace swung free in Sadie's hands, she moved quickly over to the fireplace grate.

5

ANN TOOK A QUICK BREATH. EVEN SADIE PAUSED FOR A MOMENT before she reached out to match the ornament to the grate. She wasn't sure what she would learn if it matched, or if it didn't. But she felt all the weight of what Ann must be feeling, along with her own curiosity.

Then she leaned down and tried to match the fleur-de-lis ornament from Ann's necklace into the missing part of the grate. Metal clanked against metal as she fumbled to find a fit.

After a few tries, the ornament fell firmly into place. For a moment, Sadie looked at the grate in confusion. The ornament had settled into the grate with such precision that she could barely tell which piece had ever been missing.

The piece from Ann's necklace fit into Josie Parker's fireplace grate perfectly.

Sunlight streamed through the open window of what had once been Josie Parker's second-story home office, where Sadie sat in the morning light, surrounded by stacks of papers and boxes. She'd made some good progress already that morning, identifying the original makers of some of the appliances in the kitchen, and even finding several sets of hand drawings by the decorator the original Mrs. Parker had worked with to furnish a number of the larger rooms downstairs.

But her mind kept returning to the moment when the ornament on Ann's necklace had fit so perfectly into the old Parker family fire grate. And Sadie couldn't shake a nagging thought about the large deposits and withdrawals she'd found in the old bank ledger. What could they have possibly been about? And could they have anything to do with the unexplained connection between Ann and the Parker family?

With a sigh, Sadie stood. When she'd started that morning, she'd done a quick look into every box in the office, making a general list for herself of what seemed to be in each. She'd thought, in the course of her explorations, that she'd be sure to run across a box of financial information that she might be able to compare to the mysterious ledger entries, and shed some light on the whole situation. But unless she had glanced right over it, she hadn't seen anything of the kind.

She pulled out her phone and dialed Charlene. She answered with a bright hello—obviously glad to hear from Sadie. "Have you got any good news for me?" she asked.

"I think so," Sadie said.

Sadie described the decorator's drawings to her. "That sounds amazing. More than I'd even dared hope for. I'd never heard of anyone unearthing a designer's original drawings before. Not from that long ago."

"We're very lucky to have them," Sadie told her. "She must have been a particularly conscientious designer, to make the drawings in the first place. Most designers at the time would have relied on, shall we say, something more along the lines of smoke and mirrors to make a sale. And the original Mrs. Parker must have been quite an unusual client to save the drawings. Not to mention the following family who preserved them for all those years."

"Well, we already knew it was a special house," Charlene said. "Why shouldn't it be a special family?"

Quickly, Sadie also gave Charlene a rundown of the original appliances she had identified in the kitchen, along with a few ideas of places Charlene might think about sourcing replacements among some of the better Denver antique stores.

"But I did notice something else that was interesting when I did a little catalog of what's in each box," Sadie added.

"Oh?" Charlene said, the interest in her voice evident.

"There don't seem to be any boxes of Josie's financial papers," Sadie said. "Was there any type of agreement that those would be left out?"

"Not that I remember," Charlene said. "Do you think they're important to the restoration project?"

"I don't know," Sadie said honestly. "But with the kinds of other records Josie kept, wouldn't she also have kept good records on her finances? It made me wonder if there was a set of papers that we had perhaps missed somehow. But she might have kept them separate if they were part of some separate project. And if we find the details of that project, whatever it was, it might give us even more clues to guide us in the restoration."

"*Hmm*," Charlene said. Then she broke out with an excited, "Oh!"

"Yes?" Sadie asked.

"You know what?" Charlene said. "I think there may be another set of papers in the house. The ones in the office are the ones Josie had left there, along with some more a family member brought over. But I think I remember them mentioning that there might be some more. In the attic. Does that seem like a possibility?"

"I'll definitely check it out," Sadie said.

"Well, you be careful," Charlene said. "I don't know what it's like over there, but I've seen some of these old-time attics that require a training in mountaineering to get into. We don't want you taking any risks with yourself. If you have any trouble at all, please ask one of the workmen to go up for you."

"I'll be careful," Sadie promised.

"And let us know if you find anything interesting," Charlene said.

"Don't worry," Sadie said. "You'll be the first to know."

Sadie hung up the phone, settled it back into her bag, then stepped out of the office onto the landing. Sometimes in these big old houses, the hatchway to the attic was just above the main stairs, but that didn't seem to be the case here—not unless the hatchway was almost perfectly hidden. And Charlene hadn't mentioned anything about a trick door to the attic. So the entrance must be more obvious—which must mean it was somewhere else.

Slowly, she made her way from room to room of the second floor. It was an interesting way to see the place. Usually, she noticed the contents of a room first, with her antiquer's mind. But other than the papers that the Jones family had asked the Parker family to provide them with, all the other Parker family furniture had been sold, or was in storage. And rather than even noticing the beautiful lines of each of the stately old home's rooms, Sadie wandered from one to the next studying the intricacies of the ceilings. Like everything in the Parker House, they were remarkable, with beautiful moldings, some simple and some ornate, decorating the upper corners of the rooms. Sometimes swirls or floral designs also graced the center of the ceiling, around a light fixture or chandelier. In one small room, a pair of angels reached their hands toward a beautiful frosted globe. *A child's room, perhaps*, Sadie thought, thinking back on Ann and her story.

Finally, Sadie stepped into a room in the back corner, with a staircase that led down into what she guessed must be the kitchen—probably a back way into the upper rooms, originally used by servants to carry linens or even food back and forth without being seen. She was right that the passage to the attic was often above a staircase. It just hadn't been the main staircase.

Here, there was a clear cut in the ceiling, bound by wooden molding, with a door and a pull line hanging down. A taller person might have been able to reach the pull line and just swing the door down, but for all her spirit, because of her shorter size, Sadie would never be able to catch that pull line on her own.

With a good-natured grumble, she pulled up a sturdy crate that a worker had left nearby, climbed up on it, and pulled on the line. The attic door creaked down from the ceiling, revealing a wooden staircase folded up within it.

A moment later, Sadie had the staircase unfolded and was climbing nimbly up it.

She'd thought that she might be climbing up into darkness, but she was pleasantly surprised to discover that the attic, at least in places, was just as flooded with light as Josie Parker's old office, which she had just left, had been.

The attic was formed from the peak of the roof, so some of the corners were indeed dim and shadowy, but several large windows let in an enormous amount of light that fell in large panes across the rough wooden floor. It was the kind of space that could easily have been made into a wonderland for children. It had all the potential for a giant playroom for kids, if the Parker House had had more of them.

As Sadie thought this, she wondered about Ann again. *What was her connection with the house? Was this somehow her rightful home? Why had Josie never married? Why had she spent all those years in this big old place, alone?*

The light and shadow in the attic didn't offer her any answers. But as Sadie's eyes adjusted to the change in the light, she did see that it looked like Charlene had been right. In one of the shadows stood several boxes. Sadie dragged them over into one of the bright spots, so she'd have no trouble reading them, then sat down cross-legged on the rough board and cracked the first box open.

It looked like the boxes downstairs might have been brought back from a storage unit—most of them dated back to much earlier than the ones Sadie was now looking at. These seemed to be Josie's own records, from several decades before. Most likely, Sadie guessed, Josie had stashed them up here at some point herself, and never had any occasion to bring them back down. Especially as Josie got older, it would have been harder and harder to make her way up to the attic, let alone bring them back to a lower floor on her own.

The first box Sadie looked through was full of personal mementos—a prize ribbon from a three-legged race, a trophy from a riding competition, birthday cards, newspaper clippings, letters from friends and relatives. But when Sadie opened the second box, her eyes widened. At the top was a bank ledger, very much like the one she'd first found the strange entries in. And below that were envelope after envelope of files from the bank, full of statements and canceled checks.

Could this be a clue to the big sums that had flowed into and out of Josie's account without explanation? Her heart thumped a bit harder, as it always did when she was on the trail of antique history. Her mind flipped through all the possibilities: Perhaps the accounts would reveal the provider of the original lumber for the house, so they could match it more perfectly, or the artist who had designed the beautiful stained glass in the back sitting room, so that they could better replace the missing pane that was now plugged with stout cardboard.

Quickly, Sadie pulled the ledger and envelopes out, sorting them into a rough chronological order as she did so. Her first question was whether these statements would go back far enough to shed any light on the entries in the old ledger downstairs. The ledger in this box began after the old ledger ended, so she tried to tell herself that this might be a dead end, as well.

But the bank statements predated the ledger that accompanied them by almost a decade. So they did cover the time of the first ledger, with all the strange deposits and withdrawals during the 1950s.

Sadie thought back to the first strange deposit she'd seen in the old ledger. When had it been? Late in 1949, she thought, and she flipped through the envelopes from the bank to see if she had any actual documents that corresponded to that time.

A moment later, she had pulled out envelopes postmarked in October, November, and December 1949. She sifted through the October envelope without finding anything unusual, either in the canceled checks or in the register of deposits. The November checks were unremarkable as well. But when she came to the November register of deposits, she stopped, eyes wide. There, at the top, was one of the large deposits she'd also found noted in Josie's handwritten ledger. But this time the bank had noted the source: the lumberyard where Josie had worked for so many years.

So the large checks were from Josie's place of employment. But why in the world would they have been giving her such large checks, equal to months and months of pay? It wasn't close enough to the end of the year to qualify as a year-end bonus.

As Sadie looked more closely at the entry, she saw another note, under a column labeled "Notes." It read, "Young Transportation."

What could that have meant? Sadie wondered. Was it a note of whom the check had been made out to? What would Young Transportation have to do with a construction project? In Sadie's experience, most of the useful antique documentation had to do with vendors who provided actual goods, like tables, chairs, and glass, rather than transportation companies. But this was a deposit, not a check Josie had written. And if it was a deposit that hadn't been made to Josie, why would the bank have deposited it into her account?

Sadie made a quick check of the last few boxes, which were full of other personal mementos—nothing that looked like it would be immediately helpful with the renovation—or the growing mystery surrounding Josie's finances and Ann's possible connection with the Parker House. Then she carried the box of financial papers downstairs, into Josie's old office.

With the help of the turquoise ledger that had first alerted Sadie to the large deposits, she combed through the bank statements. Sure enough, every time a large amount was noted in Josie's ledger, a large amount flowed into or out of her bank account, according to the bank records. And each time, the same words were noted in the column to the side: "Young Transportation."

Sadie had never heard of any such business in Silver Peak, but despite her deep knowledge of the town and its history, that didn't mean there hadn't been one. After all, most of these records were from a time when she had only been a very young girl—or even before she was born. And they were all so large that Sadie couldn't think of anything they would have been spent on other than the house. So they must have had something to do with the restoration, she reasoned, just as she'd told Charlene.

Well, what do You think of that? Sadie found herself praying, almost as if she was sharing the new discovery with a friend who was actually sitting in the room with her.

Then she smiled. She couldn't even imagine what God thought of that, she knew. Everything she didn't know about the situation, God already did. Including what would happen next. He even knew all the things she wasn't smart enough to know she didn't know. She laughed at herself for such a brain-twister of a thought. But somehow, she still felt like God might get a kick out of the moments when she forgot how much more He knew than she did, and spoke to Him like a friend. Jesus had told His followers that He didn't think of them as servants, but friends. And maybe, with all the things she didn't know, and all the things God did, that was one of the most important facts she could know, about God or about her life: that He wasn't up on some cloud somewhere, tossing lightning bolts. He had said that He was near to His people, just like a friend, and that He thought of His people as His friends too. And for Sadie, at least, knowing God was always near her was more important than everything else she knew, and everything else she didn't.

Still, for whatever reason, God didn't always share everything He knew. The world was still full of mysteries. And Young Transportation was another one.

6

Kimama Temoke, the Silver Peak head librarian, smiled as Sadie stepped into the library.

"Let me guess," she said. "You've got some important research to do on some member of the illustrious Silver Peak class reunion."

Sadie answered Kimama's smile with her own. "Have you been busy with reunion requests?" she asked.

Kimama nodded. "We always are, this time of year," she said.

"People checking out the old yearbooks for blackmail purposes?" Sadie guessed.

Kimama laughed. "Of course."

"Some of those old poses were pretty embarrassing," Sadie agreed. "I'm glad my mother talked me out of wearing my cat-eye glasses for my senior picture. I thought they were the height of style. Although I didn't even need them at the time."

"If you ask me," Kimama said, "your eyes still seem to have a lot of sparkle."

"Oh, you're sweet," Sadie said. "And I guess, on the other hand, some folks are coming in looking for old pictures to prove they ever could fit into one of those tiny-waisted dresses. Or lift a barbell over their head."

Kimama nodded. "Yes, we've had quite a bit of that," she said. "But in the past few years, there've also been some interesting advances in photo printing. You know, it's not all slides and snapshots anymore. So I've had a lot of folks trying to put together images for calendars. Or posters. One class had the option of making life-size cutouts of their former selves, if the class members wanted to pay the production fee."

"Is our class doing that?" Sadie asked, with a sense of dismay. She had loved her high school years. And she loved the woman she was now. But the idea of confronting a life-size cutout of her former self wasn't something she relished.

"No," Kimama said. "That was a few years ago. But because the files had to be so big in order to enlarge to the proper dimensions, the poor woman in charge of that reunion was in here for weeks, scanning and rescanning. They actually offered the library the cutouts for our historical collection, after the reunion was over."

Sadie glanced around. "Oh my goodness," she said. "How many of them were there?"

"Twenty-seven," Kimama said.

"All life-size?" Sadie asked.

Kimama nodded.

"And did you have to find a place to store all of them, then?" Sadie asked.

"The library regretted that we were unable to accept that generous donation," Kimama said, suppressing the faintest hint of a smile.

"Well," Sadie told her, "it is my reunion this year."

"This year?" Kimama said. "Impossible. I would have sworn that you didn't look a day over seventeen."

At this, Sadie laughed. "Oh, I'd have to question you on that," she said. "I earned all these laugh lines, through lots of good years. I wouldn't trade one of them. Not even to be seventeen again."

"That's a good way to think," Kimama said. "I hope I'll feel that way when I'm your age. I mean, when I'm thirty-five."

Sadie laughed again. "Well, in the meantime, I'm looking into a different part of Silver Peak history."

"Oh?" Kimama said.

"I'm interested in a business," Sadie said. "I think it may have something to do with a restoration I'm working on."

"What is it?" Kimama asked.

"Young Transportation," Sadie said. "Ring any bells?"

She watched Kimama's face for a flash of recognition. If anyone would know of an obscure Silver Peak business, it would be Kimama, whose grasp of local history was at least as deep as Sadie's, and constantly expanded and reinforced by her work as a librarian. But after a moment of thought Kimama just shook her head. "If I've ever heard of it, I don't recall," she said. "But there's an easy check for that. If the business has ever been registered in Silver Peak, it'll appear in the historical register. And I just finagled permission to access their files on behalf of library patrons."

She tapped a few keys on her keyboard and watched as the screen refreshed. Sadie read the results of the search for "Young Transportation" just as Kimama began to shake her head.

"It has no results for a Young Transportation," she said. "So no one's ever registered that name with the city."

"Is every business registered with the city?" Sadie asked quickly.

Kimama grinned at her. "An excellent question," she said. "Not that I'd expect anything less from you."

Sadie smiled. "Well, it just seems that some people might open businesses without even knowing that they needed to register the name."

Kimama nodded. "Yes," she said, "in theory, that could be true. But in practice, what you really get is many more businesses registered than actually exist. People get excited about a business name, go down and register it as the first step…"

"And then never get any further than that," Sadie said.

Kimama nodded again.

"I can understand that," Sadie said. Opening her antique shop, the Antique Mine, had been a great deal of work. And many times between the day she'd gone down to register the name and the day the doors actually opened, she'd been tempted to give up.

"Still," Kimama said, "I always like to check more than one source."

"I like the way you think," Sadie said.

"You said this was a historical question," Kimama said. "Do you have a time frame when this business would have been operational?"

Sadie thought back to the dates on the checks. "Starting in the late forties," she said. "Into the midfifties."

Her fingers sped over the keys once again. Then, suddenly, a small box flashed up on the screen, with only one letter inside: *O*.

"Oh?" Sadie repeated.

Kimama shook her head. "Zero," she said. "That's the number of mentions of Young Transportation during those years and before, even. So for a good chunk of the last century," she said, with a hint of librarian's pride.

Disappointment shaded Sadie's face. "Are there any other records we could try?" she asked.

"I'm sorry," Kimama said. "Not ones that are searchable. But you could always glance through the indexes of our titles on Silver Peak history. There aren't too many of them, so it might not take you too long."

"I'll give it a try," Sadie said, and followed Kimama over to the section she indicated. She had quite a collection of Silver Peak history books of her own at home, and she recognized many of the titles on the library shelves. But there was no harm in going through them here. And the library even seemed to have a few volumes she didn't.

"From here," Kimama said, "to here." She gestured to a few feet of books above a neat "Silver Peak History" label, perhaps about thirty-five in all. "Most of them are indexed, so you can just flip to the back, and see if there's any mention of Young Transportation."

"Thanks," Sadie said. She took the first book from the shelf and settled in.

But an hour later, she had worked her way all the way through the Silver Peak history collection, with the same outcome as the computerized searches Kimama had run for her: no mention of any Young Transportation.

She collected her things and nodded her thanks to Kimama, who was now busy with another library patron.

As she stepped out into the bright sun, she racked her brains, trying to think of anyone who might be able to give her any information on the obscure business. Would it make sense to give Edwin a call and ask if he'd ever heard of it? Or what about Roz?

But as Sadie turned these options over in her mind, she was struck with another idea. What about the business that had written the checks to Young Transportation in the first place? There might not be any traces she could find of Young Transportation in the town records, but the lumber company where Josie had worked was still a thriving business. And if Josie had had a business, maybe one of her former coworkers would still remember something about it.

When she got to her car, Sadie pulled out her phone, looked up the number of the lumber company, and dialed.

"Silver Peak Lumber," a man's cheerful voice answered.

"Hello," Sadie said, thinking quickly to see if she could recall the names of anyone at the lumberyard who might have worked with Josie. Then she had a flash of insight. While Edwin was working on the renovations to his home, she remembered him saying that Amanda Davis, the daughter of the lumberyard's original owner, still ran the company today. And she was probably in the best position to know something about the ancient history of the lumber company's finances, although there was no guarantee that she'd know about a detail as tiny as the handful of payments that had flowed into Josie's hands through Young Transportation. "I'm trying to reach Amanda Davis."

"May I ask what you're calling about?"

"I've just got a few questions about a former employee there at the lumberyard," Sadie said. "Josie Parker."

"One moment," the man said.

After a few seconds of silence and a series of clicks, a woman's voice came on the line. "This is Amanda Davis," she said.

"Amanda," Sadie said. "This is Sadie Speers. I'm a fellow business owner here in Silver Peak. At the Antique Mine?"

"Oh," Amanda said, "it's so nice to hear from you. I've heard wonderful things about your store."

"You should come in for a visit some time," Sadie said. "I'll give you a first-timers discount."

"Well, in that case, you can count on it," Amanda said. "But what can I do to help you? My assistant said you'd mentioned something about Josie Parker."

The warmth in Amanda's voice was evident. And Sadie could understand why. Josie had probably worked for the company since Amanda was a child, and for most of Amanda's life. She might even have felt like a family member to Amanda, who had obviously stayed close to the business right up to the present day.

"That's right," Sadie said. "I've been doing some work on the restoration of the Parker House."

"I was so glad to hear about that," Amanda said. "Everyone who worked with her knew how much Josie loved that place. She'd gone to such great lengths to keep it in good shape. It would have really stung to watch it be turned over to people who didn't see the historical value that she always saw in it."

"The Jones family is going to do a beautiful job," Sadie said. "And they're so committed to the history that they've asked me to work with them to make sure the restoration is as true to the house's original spirit as possible."

"That's wonderful," Amanda said. "Although I'm not sure I know much about the whole family. But Josie was always my favorite thing about Dad's office, from the time I was a little girl. She used to keep a jar of candy on her desk. I wasn't allowed to have much candy as a kid, but Dad didn't want to make her feel bad, so I was always allowed to take a piece when she offered one to me. At first, she kept butter mints. But eventually I worked up the nerve to ask her to stock Tootsie Rolls instead. I explained to her that it was very important, because I wasn't allowed to have candy unless she gave it to me, and Tootsie Rolls were my favorite. The next week, she had Tootsie Rolls. It wasn't until I was out of college and came back to the office to take my first job here that she told me that butter mints were actually her favorite. And she kept Tootsie Rolls all those years, just so I could have them.

"I tried to apologize, but she just laughed. She said I had done her a favor, and helped her watch her waistline, by not having her favorite candy on her desk. But that Christmas, I bought the entire drugstore out of butter mints, and wrapped up all twenty boxes and gave them to her."

Sadie smiled. It was a sweet story—and obviously Amanda wasn't just willing, but eager, to share her memories of Josie Parker.

"I always thought Josie was lovely, from what I knew of her myself," Sadie said.

"She was," Amanda said. "And it wasn't just an act. Some people seem nice enough until you really get to know them. But with Josie it wasn't just skin-deep, hi, how are you? She really cared about people. And she was kind, no matter what. Our company went through some hard times, but she never got hard herself, no matter how difficult the times were."

"That's rare," Sadie said.

"It is," Amanda said. "And now that I've been running the business myself for so many years, I know it's also priceless. So what can I help you with?"

"Well," Sadie said, "as I've been working through the records on the house, I've come across a reference to another business that Josie was apparently associated with. I wonder if it would ring any bells for you?"

"Another business?" Amanda said. "Perhaps, but I doubt it. Josie used to joke all the time about the fact that she'd taken her first job at Silver Peak Lumber, and just stayed."

"It was called Young Transportation," Sadie said. "Does that ring any bells for you at all?"

The silence on the other end of the line lasted for so long that at first Sadie thought her phone might have dropped the call. She glanced quickly at the screen of her phone. The call was still connected, the seconds still ticking off.

"Hello?" she said. "I'm sorry, were you able to hear my question?"

"I apologize," Amanda said. "Something's just come up. I need to let you go."

"Thank you for the time, Amanda," Sadie said. "Is there a better time for me to call?"

Amanda didn't say anything more. The only answer Sadie got was a droning dial tone.

Now what was that all about? she prayed.

But before she could even begin to ponder that question herself, her phone rang again.

7

"SADIE?"

The woman on the other end of the line obviously thought that Sadie should know who was calling. But although the voice was incredibly familiar, it took Sadie a long moment to place it.

"Hello?" she said, hoping for another clue.

"I'm so glad I caught you," the woman went on. "I've just been out to Jasper's. Sadie, it was awful."

Ann, Sadie realized. It wasn't just that she had finally recognized her friend's voice. Sadie also knew Ann's older brother, Jasper, who still lived in town. Or rather, out of town, still on the family ranch that he and Ann had both grown up on.

"I'm so sorry to hear that," Sadie said. Ann sounded so upset that she obviously needed to talk, and Sadie's mind began immediately to run through places they might be able to meet, and to shift around the pieces of her own day to make time for her friend. But before Sadie could even suggest a place to meet, Ann dove right in.

"I don't know what I did wrong," Ann said, "but he was so angry. He actually wouldn't speak to me when I left the house. Not even to say good-bye."

Sadie's eyebrows shot up in surprise. She'd known Jasper for years. He was popular around town, not because he had a big, showy personality, but because he always seemed to have the time to spend a moment with everyone he met, and probably a kind word for them too. Looking back, Sadie couldn't think of ever seeing Jasper lose his temper—or even hearing about it. But then again, everything was different in families. They tended to bring out things in people that the rest of the world didn't always get to see—for better, or for worse.

"What had you been talking about?" Sadie asked.

"Well, I wanted to know more about my..." Ann hesitated. "My adoption, I guess," she said. "I don't even know what word to use for it." She made an attempt to laugh at this, but to Sadie it just sounded even sadder.

"Was this the first time Jasper heard about the results of the DNA test?" Sadie asked.

"No," Ann said. "I told him as soon as I heard. We've never been a family that keeps secrets. At least, I didn't think we were."

"So he's known for quite some time?" Sadie said.

"Almost as long as I have," Ann said. "And he didn't seem to have any problem with it when I told him."

"What did he say to you then?"

Ann fell silent. "He mostly seemed to be worried about how I was doing," she said after a moment. "He just kept saying that it didn't matter to him. That I was his sister, no matter what. That Mom and Dad were our parents. That nothing could change that."

Sadie nodded. That sounded like the Jasper she knew. So what had made him so angry today? Angry enough to let his sister leave the house without saying a word to her?

"And what were you talking about today?" Sadie asked. "Before you left?"

"It was friendly enough to begin with," Ann said thoughtfully. "For the first little while I was there, we were just catching up, you know? His family, my family, what had been going on for us, that sort of thing. We try to keep up by phone, but it's always different when you get to see someone in person."

Sadie knew this from personal experience as well. "Especially with family," she said. "I think it's because we're so used to living with them. It's hard to talk on the phone, or even give someone an update, when all you know is what it's like to just share life with them."

"Maybe that's it," Ann said. "I never thought about it that way. But Jasper seemed glad to see me. Very glad, really. He gave me one of his big bear hugs when I came in. And then we both just kept smiling and smiling. You know how he is."

"That's right," Sadie said. "So when did all that change?"

"I'm not sure," Ann said reflectively. "I guess it was when I started asking questions about the time I was born."

"What did you ask?"

"Well, I'd been thinking about it," Ann said. "Jasper wasn't too much older than me, but he was old enough to notice things. And one of the questions I had, when I got to thinking about it, was that if I wasn't really Mom and Dad's, where did I come from? You know? Did people in town think that Mom was pregnant? Or did I just appear out of nowhere? I figured Jasper might remember something that happened around that time. Something that might help me. But as soon as I started to explain what I was thinking, he just sort of—froze up."

"He didn't want to talk about it?" Sadie said.

"He didn't want to talk, at all," Ann said.

"Did he say anything?" Sadie asked.

"At first, he did," Ann told her. "When I said the part about me not really being Mom and Dad's, he got quite agitated. He kept asking, what did I mean, not really Mom and Dad's? He wanted to know how I could not be Mom and Dad's, since they raised me all those years, no matter who my biological parents were. It was like he thought I had forgotten everything they'd done for me. And then, when I tried to keep on explaining, he just got quiet. By the time I asked him if he remembered anything from that time, he didn't respond at all. He wouldn't even nod for yes or shake his head for no."

"It sounds like it's a very emotional topic for him," Sadie said.

"But it's an emotional topic for me too," Ann said, her voice quavering. "At least he knows who his actual mother and father are. How does he think I feel?"

"I don't think it's an easy time for any of you," Sadie said diplomatically.

"You always could see all the sides of a problem," Ann said. She gave a small laugh, but this time it sounded genuine. "It used to drive me crazy. I'd come to you wanting to complain about something that had happened to me, and you'd always be trying to help me see it from the other guy's point of view. I just wanted you to take my side."

"I was on your side too," Sadie protested.

"I know that," Ann said. "That's why I need you to go over to talk with Jasper."

"Me?" Sadie asked in surprise.

"I'm sure you're busy," Ann said. "I know it's asking a lot. And I'm so grateful for everything you've already done, all your patience and understanding. But this is so important to me. I'm only here for a few days. These answers would mean so much to me. They could help me understand so much about my life. But even more than that, I don't want to leave here still at odds with Jasper. No matter what the answers about my biological parents are, I don't want them to drive a wedge between me and my family. And he's the only family I have left now. I would never want to lose him, chasing after some phantoms I might never find. But I think if I go back there now, I'll just make the problem worse."

"It sounds like that might be true," Sadie agreed ruefully.

"But I think he'll talk to you," Ann said. "You always got along, even in high school. And you're still friends with him now, aren't you?"

"We're friendly," Sadie said. "I don't see him all that often. But yes, I'd say we're friends."

"Then you'll go talk to him," Ann said quickly. "Won't you? Just tell him I'm not trying to say I'm not part of the family. Or it's not that I'm ungrateful to Mom and Dad for everything they did, for both of us. It's just, there's something else I need to know. And Mom and Dad aren't here to ask anymore. So he might be the only person who can help me understand it."

Sadie didn't say anything right away. She didn't really relish the idea of getting into the situation between Ann and Jasper. But at the same time, she knew they were both good people. She knew that they didn't want to be in conflict, and she had seen other families where small conflicts built up to great rifts that stole years of happiness from everyone involved. If there was something she could do to head that off at the pass in Ann's family, she would be glad to do it. And she knew from her conversations with Ann how much it would mean to her to have any further information on why she didn't share DNA with the people she had always considered her family. Sadie couldn't quite imagine what that would be like—but she was pretty sure that if she were in the same situation, she'd be searching for answers, just like Ann.

"Please," Ann said, "it would mean so much to me."

Sadie sighed. "All right," she said.

"Oh, Sadie," Ann said, "I don't know how to thank you!"

"Don't thank me yet," Sadie said. "We don't know how it'll go. But I'll go out there and see if I can talk with Jasper."

"Will you go right now?" Ann said. "I just left, so I know he's still there. But I'm afraid if you wait till the afternoon he might be out on the ranch, or come into town. And I don't have very much time left here in town myself. I'd hate to waste the time he and I have together. And the time I have to learn the truth about my history."

Sadie popped her car door open and settled into the front seat. "I'm on my way," she said.

8

As Sadie pulled away from the curb, her phone rang again. Keeping her eyes on the road, she picked up the call.

"Hello?" she said, expecting to hear Ann's voice, with some kind of last-minute addition to the conversation they had just had.

"Sadie," said Roz. "Am I glad to hear your voice."

Her voice was friendly, and Sadie could tell she was trying to keep their conversation light, but she could also hear a strain there. Something was going on.

"What's up?" Sadie asked.

"It's just nice to talk with another sane human being," Roz said. "After spending most of my morning trying to negotiate with Ann Cartwright. Who, I might add, does not fall into the category of sane human being. At least not according to *my* definition of sane human being."

Sadie was glad that Roz wasn't there to see her. She would have had trouble keeping a straight face, even though she knew her friend was genuinely upset by whatever had happened.

"So it wasn't the world's greatest meeting," Sadie said.

"I think it might be in the running for world's worst," Roz said. "I'm pretty sure it was actually a lifetime low for me personally."

"But we've been friends with Ann for so long," Sadie said, trying to remind Roz that there might be something more important than the details of the upcoming reunion that was causing so much conflict.

"You know, I think that makes it even more frustrating," Roz said. "Because you go into the meeting thinking you're going to meet with a friend. You know, someone you understand. Who has something in common with you. Who understands you."

"But that wasn't how the meeting went," Sadie said.

"Nope," Roz said. "Listen to this. You won't believe it, but I'll tell you anyway. Do you know what she suggested this time?"

The idea of trying to guess the many ways that planning on the reunion could have gone awry made Sadie's head hurt. Especially with all the other moving pieces she was currently trying to keep straight in her mind.

"No?" she said cautiously.

"This is her newest idea," Roz said. "Which she apparently doesn't think of as a terrible joke. Which is the only reason I can think of that someone would make a suggestion like this. She said, since we both feel so strongly about our different visions of the reunion, that maybe we should just go ahead and plan them both separately, and let the people who are coming choose between her more sophisticated take, or my bohemian ideas. Can you believe that?"

Actually, Sadie could. "Well, you know Ann," she said. "From her point of view, it probably seems sensible. It would end all this conflict the two of you have had to deal with. It might even seem like it's fair. You know, giving people a chance to choose."

"But it's also crazy!" Roz exclaimed. "The whole point of a reunion is that it's a reunion! Who wants to go to a reunion where half the other people who came across the country and got themselves all gussied up are holed up on some ranch outside town? Or sit out under the stars on some ranch while half your class is back in Silver Peak?"

"I would have thought you'd like to sit out under the stars," Sadie said.

"My idea has stars," Roz said. "It's just the stars of Silver Peak. Stars surrounded by our own hometown, which is what everyone is really coming to see. I don't want to have some expensive fake ranch experience. I want to re-create our high school days. Like a kind of living time capsule. You know I've got a flair for drama."

"Maybe a small one," Sadie allowed with a smile.

"Well, I'm thinking of the whole town as our set. So nothing about my idea will work, unless it happens in Silver Peak. And not much matters but that. I'd like the food to be good, but that's not the most important thing. The most important thing is the people, and the place.

"I mean, what could be more important?" Roz went on. "I can't believe Ann *doesn't* see it." For a moment, Roz was silent. "But I'm afraid our negotiations have already broken down too far. We've only got a few days until people start coming into town. And they're not going to be attending two different reunions, I can tell you that much. So we have to find something we can agree on, and soon."

Sadie, who had known this all along, was relieved to hear Roz come to that conclusion for herself. No matter how big Roz and Ann's disagreements, the two of them did have a responsibility to everyone who would be making trips, short or long, to come to Silver Peak for the reunion. When their classmates got there, there needed to be some kind of a reunion ready for them.

"Well," Sadie said, "that sounds good to me. And I know you and Ann don't agree on anything, but I'm sure you'll come up with something great. I wouldn't be too hard on her. You never know what people have going on. I know sometimes I must drive the people around me crazy, just because something else is weighing on my mind."

"What could she possibly have on her mind this week that's more important than this reunion?" Roz asked in a tone of incredulity. "Does she have some job I don't know about, advising the president on foreign policy?"

"I'm just saying," Sadie said. "We don't always know everything a person is dealing with."

"Well," Roz said, "that might actually help. I should pretend she's dealing with some great crisis. Maybe I'd have a little bit more patience with her then, myself."

And it wasn't far from the truth either, Sadie thought. But it wasn't her secret to tell. "It's worth a try," she said, encouragingly.

As she'd spoken with Roz, she'd driven out of town and made the handful of turns that took her out toward the Cartwright ranch. Now she could see the familiar buggy wheel that marked the long private road that led out to the house where Ann had grown up. She remembered vividly kneeling in the grass beside the side of the road to decorate it with Colorado wildflowers when she and Ann were girls. And another day, when it had been festooned with blue balloons in order to show the way to Ann's sweet-sixteen birthday party.

"Listen," Sadie said. "I need to let you go."

"Oh?" Roz said, curiosity sparking in her voice. "Up to anything interesting?"

Sadie was actually sure that Roz would find it very interesting that she was about to pay a visit to the Cartwright home. But she wasn't sure that now was the time to mention it. And, after all, she wasn't working on finding out something for herself. If she was, there was nobody she'd be more willing to share with than her best friend. But this was Ann's secret, not Sadie's. "I'll let you know if it turns out to be," Sadie said, to sidestep the issue for the time being.

"Well," Roz said, "I've got to get back to this planning anyhow. Do you think she'd go for the parking lot idea if I agreed to laying linen tablecloths on our trunks?"

Sadie laughed. "Let me know how it goes," she said.

She settled her phone back in her purse as she turned past the wagon wheel and onto the Cartwrights' private lane. A few moments later, she'd driven through the scrub pine and fields that lay on either side of the lane, and pulled up in front of the house.

She'd hoped to have a moment to collect her thoughts before she knocked, but Jasper was already standing out in the front yard, carefully repairing a stretch of damaged wire on the fence line that defined his yard from the larger pastures and fields of the ranch. He looked up curiously when her car rolled into the gravel parking area. Then his face brightened when he recognized her.

"Sadie Speers!" he said, leaving the fence line to come over and greet her, pushing his white hat back on his forehead to beam with blue eyes that sparkled just the way they had way back in high school, although his friendly face was now creased by years more of living. "I can't say I expected you to come up the drive today," he said. "What brings you out our way?"

Sadie tried to collect her thoughts as she shut the door of her car and settled her handbag on her shoulder. But she couldn't think of any good way to approach the touchy subject of Ann with Jasper other than to dive right in. She started by returning Jasper's smile.

"Well," she said, "I know that Ann's in town for this reunion."

At the mention of Ann's name, Jasper's smile vanished. "She's not here," he said. But as Sadie searched his face, she didn't see the anger that Ann had been so worried about. More than anything, Jasper seemed sad to her. Sad, and somehow worried, or uncertain.

Suddenly, Sadie was glad she had come. It could be tricky to try to help people understand each other, especially within families, where the dynamics were so deep and complicated. But sometimes the people who knew each other the best just weren't able to see themselves for what they were—maybe because they were so close.

"I wasn't looking for her, actually," Sadie said gently. "I was hoping to talk with you."

This didn't seem to put Jasper at ease. "Oh?" he asked warily. "*Hmm.*"

"About Ann, in fact," Sadie continued. "You know we were good friends in high school, she and Roz and I."

"Yep," Jasper agreed, but without really meeting her eyes.

"So she's told me a little bit about this search that she's been on. About her own history."

Jasper stared steadily at the gravel of the driveway, without giving any indication that he'd even heard her.

"She let me know about the results of the DNA test she got earlier this year," Sadie added quietly.

At this, Jasper looked up, his eyes almost flashing now with emotion. "Family is family," he said. "Whatever some blood test might say. In fact, if you ask me, I don't even see what a blood test has to do with it. Ann is part of our family. From the time she was born, just like me. And that's all there is to it."

He raised his chin defiantly, but Sadie thought she could still see that same hint of uncertainty in his eyes. Did he know something he wasn't telling her? Or was he just starting to realize all the things he didn't know about his sister's history—and perhaps his own?

"Ann will always be your sister," Sadie said. "Nothing can change that. And in fact, she cares about you so much that she's quite upset to have caused any problems between the two of you over this."

A flicker in Jasper's eyes gave Sadie the sense that he was grateful to hear this, even though he didn't say anything out loud to admit it.

"But there are some reasons for knowing about her history," Sadie pointed out gently. "In fact, medical emergencies like the one your daughter is facing are a good reason to understand our genetics and history. That's how she found out about all these questions in the first place. And I'm sure that she'd like to be able to pass on an accurate medical history to her own daughters."

"God forbid either of them ever has a problem like my little girl," Jasper said, his voice thick with emotion.

"Of course," Sadie said. "It sounds like your family has had more than enough to deal with in the past year. And I hope your daughter makes a full recovery and that nobody has to deal with an issue like this for quite some time. But even if that's the case,

Ann has questions she'd like to have answered, even just for herself. I can understand why that might be hard for you to think about. But I also know you love Ann. And you can understand where she's coming from."

She waited while Jasper swallowed, staring at the ground. After a minute, he looked up at her.

"Do you remember anything about the time that Ann was born?" she asked quietly.

Jasper took a deep breath. To Sadie's surprise, a brief smile flashed across his face. "It was a good time," he said.

"A good time," Sadie repeated.

He nodded. "A real good time," he said. "What I remember most about it is how much time I got to spend playing with our mom. She was always a great mother," he said quickly. "But she was busy too, you know. Things to do in town. Out and about. But before Ann was born, she stuck pretty close to home. So we got to play a whole lot, for those last couple of months. We had a whole fort out back, that she let me make out of old sheets and Brillo boxes. I'd be a pirate, and she was either my crew, or the whole navy, come to track me down."

"How long was she around home for?" Sadie asked.

"Oh, awhile," Jasper said. "I'd say…about three months."

Sadie smiled along with him. But inside her head, she was calculating what all of this might mean. Three months was a long time for a woman to spend most of her time at home. Had Ann's mother had a difficult pregnancy? That would be one reason for her to stay near home in the final months. But had Ann's mother actually been pregnant? Sadie had assumed that if Ann was adopted, Ann's mother hadn't had a child of her own. But suddenly she realized there was another possibility: that Ann's mother had delivered a child, but that child had not been Ann.

"What about the day Ann was born?" Sadie asked. "Do you remember anything about that?"

Jasper shook his head. "Aw, no," he said. "I don't think they really wanted a little feller like me running around the hospital. I think I'd have been a lot more trouble than help. Even though I would have done anything to help I could," he added.

"So when did you meet baby Ann?"

"Not for a little while," Jasper said. "They packed me off to Grandma's house. And when I came back, there was Ann. I don't think I ever loved someone so much before I met her. And I never loved anybody exactly that same way, ever since."

Sadie smiled. She was an only child, but she still had some sense of what he was talking about. She had gotten hints of it in her own childhood, longing for a little brother or sister. And although she knew from the experience of her friends, and her own children, that relationships with siblings could sometimes be complicated, she could see that it was a kind of love like no other. No wonder Jasper got so emotional over the idea that Ann wasn't truly family to him.

But still, she got the sense that there was something he was keeping from her as he'd told the story. He might have been young, but it had been an important and emotional time for him, and obviously many of the details were still vivid in his mind.

"Do you remember anything else about that time?" Sadie asked. "Anything at all? It might not have seemed important at the time, but anything we can find out now might help Ann better understand her own story."

Jasper took a deep breath. He squinted up at the blue and lavender mountains, with their tiny trees and sharp peaks. Then he looked down at the gravel, as if hoping it might give Sadie an answer, so he wouldn't have to.

"I never like to dwell on the past," he said.

"Of course not," Sadie said. "But sometimes there are good memories there. Or important ones."

"I was only a boy myself," Jasper said. "I'm not even sure whether I was old enough to know what I was seeing."

The hair on the back of Sadie's neck pricked. "What did you see?" she asked carefully.

"It's more what I didn't see," Jasper said.

Sadie waited.

As he stared down at the gravel, Jasper's brow knit. "I don't think I even realized it until my own wife was pregnant," he said. "With our daughter, actually," he said, his mouth twisting in a slight smile at how inextricably all these stories, old and new, were linked. "That's when I realized."

"Realized what?" Sadie asked.

"Well, it's not a minor thing for a woman, when she has a baby," he said. "It affects her, if you know what I mean."

Sadie suppressed her own smile. After having a child of her own, he didn't need to tell her that.

"And not just when she has the baby," Jasper said. "All the time leading up to it. My Alma was a trouper," he said. "But when she was pregnant, she couldn't do all the things she was used to doing. Especially not in those last few months. I think maybe that's when I started to realize."

"Realize what?" Sadie prompted.

Finally, Jasper's eyes met hers. "I never saw my mother like that. Not in any of the time before Ann came home. I mean, in those days, ladies wore those dresses with the big skirts. Maybe it was harder to see. I might have been just too little to understand. But my mother was running and playing with me just the way she always had, right up to the time Ann was"—he hesitated for a few moments before finishing his sentence—"born."

"You're not sure your mother was ever pregnant at that time," Sadie said quietly.

At this, something in Jasper's eyes flashed again. "Not that it would matter to me, one way or the other," he said. "Not one bit. My parents, whatever their reasons were, I'm sure they had good ones. They were good people. And Ann is my sister. No matter what. Especially now that Mom and Dad are gone."

At this last bit, his eyes turned sad again.

"I'm sure they had their reasons," Sadie said. "And they obviously loved you and Ann very much. Just like you and Ann love each other."

At this, Jasper gave a curt nod. Sadie could see that he was struggling to hold back what was probably a tangle of very strong emotions. But now that he'd begun to tell the truth about the time surrounding Ann's birth, she didn't want to lose the chance to learn everything she could.

"Do you remember anything else about that time?" she asked. "Anything at all?"

With his defenses down, Jasper was almost childlike, as if he'd gone back in his memory to that time and part of him was still there. "What would I remember?" he asked.

"What about the day she was born?" Sadie asked. "When you went to your grandmother's house? Do you remember anything about that day?"

Jasper's brows knit. Then his eyes widened. "Someone came to the house," he said.

"That day?" Sadie asked.

He nodded. "And as soon as they left, Mom scooped me up and put me in the car to Grandma's."

"Did you see who it was?"

Jasper nodded again. "I did. Mom looked out the window when she saw the car coming up the drive, and she told me to go upstairs to my room. I did as she said, but I was curious too. Usually I got to greet the guests with her. So I looked out my window, to see who it was."

"Who did you see?"

"A woman," Jasper said. "Two of them, actually."

"Do you remember anything about them?"

"One of them was pretty," Jasper said. "At least I thought so, at that age. She had short dark hair. And she seemed taller than the other one."

Sadie's mind skipped back to the snapshots of Josie she'd seen among her things at the Parker House. Around the time of Ann's birth, Josie had had short dark hair. And it would have been an unusual style for the time. But she might not have been the only one in town to wear that hairstyle.

"How well did you see her?" Sadie asked.

Jasper grinned. "I guess I took a big long look," he said. "I always was real interested in a pretty girl. Even at that age, I guess."

Sadie thought back to any other identifying information about Josie that a young boy might have remembered. It wasn't just that Josie had dark hair, she realized. She also had a distinctive mole on her cheek, almost in the shape of a tiny butterfly, on the left side of her face.

"Do you remember anything else about her?" she asked.

Jasper's eyes widened. "You know, I did see a mole, actually. A real pretty one," he said. "Right high on her cheek."

That was where Josie's mole would have been, Sadie realized with a jolt.

Sadie struggled to hide her excitement. So Josie had had something to do with Ann's birth, it sounded like.

"What about the other woman?" she asked.

Jasper shook his head. "It was all so long ago," he said. "And I guess the one with short hair must have had my attention. I don't really remember anything about the other woman."

His eyes met Sadie's. "Do you really think any of this will help Ann?"

"I don't know," Sadie said. "But I think the fact that you were willing to help her will mean more to her than anything else."

"I guess I was pretty hard on her," he said. "I don't know what was wrong. I guess it was a lot to take in, all at once."

"It is a lot," Sadie said.

"Is there anything else I can help with?" Jasper said. "Because if not, I think maybe I better go give Ann a call."

"I think that's a wonderful idea," Sadie said.

With his customary friendly wave, Jasper turned and headed for the house.

Sadie watched him go with a sense of satisfaction. No matter what the answers were to the mysteries surrounding Ann's birth, this was the most important thing of all: that Ann and Jasper stayed close no matter what happened.

But even as she thought this, new questions still tugged at her mind. She was pretty sure that Josie had been one of the women who visited the Cartwright home around the time of Ann's birth. Was it possible that Josie hadn't been childless, as everyone in Silver Peak always thought? Was there some chance that Ann was Josie's daughter?

9

Sadie sighed.

No matter where the questions about Ann's story took her, she always seemed to wind up back here: sifting through Josie Parker's old papers, at the Parker House.

Lord, she prayed, *please help me not to keep going over the same ground every day, without ever seeing anything new.* It was a prayer, she realized as she prayed it, that could also apply to all of life. *This all looks so familiar. But if there's something here I'm supposed to find, please give me new eyes.*

She shifted to a more comfortable position on the floor of the Parker House attic. Up till now, the focus of most of her research on the house had been to support the Jones family in their painstaking renovation, with a few forays into Josie's financial details. But she now was interested in the few boxes of Josie's personal effects, which she had once pushed aside as she sought for other details. They wouldn't contain the construction receipts, ancient home catalogs, or architectural drawings that might help with a renovation. And they probably wouldn't contain many financial details. But they might actually contain the best clues about who Jasper had seen with Josie the night his sister was born—if it was truly Josie who he had seen from the upstairs window of the Cartwright home. More and more, though, she was thinking it must have been Josie that night. Even the fleur-de-lis necklace that Ann still wore seemed to indicate some kind of connection between Josie and Ann. So what exactly was that connection?

Sadie opened the first box and glanced through it. For all her experience dealing in antiques, it was always bittersweet to look over the items that a real person had collected over the course of a lifetime. In some ways, to look at a collection of a single person's things was one of Sadie's favorite ways to enjoy antiques. They didn't just take you back to another time or place, like so many antiques. All together, a person's valuables could teach you a great deal about them. Even a single item, like a well-worn comb, or a well-used satchel, could give insight into how a person's life might have been. But there was always a tinge of sadness in looking over a person's things after they were gone, as well. No matter how much they told about a person, the main thing the items always spoke to was the fact that that person was no longer there to speak for themselves. And Sadie could never help recognizing that, no matter how little, or how much, a person had collected in the course of a lifetime, it never came anywhere close to equaling the value of that person .

In the boxes Josie had collected, Sadie found many of the things she'd come to expect in collections of personal effects. A favorite sweater, probably hand-knit decades ago by a loved one. A handful of costume jewelry, probably left behind after anything of real value had been disposed of. But at the bottom of the box, she found a collection of photograph albums, dating back to the cracked leather and paper-frame pages of the nineteenth century, through an album whose bright orange and green flower print announced it as an artifact of the 1970s. In the midst of the stack was a simple volume, bound in dark leather. Sadie recognized the simple lines as a product of the austerity measures around and just after the Second World War.

She pulled it out and flipped it open. Just as she had guessed, it seemed to begin in the mid-1940s, and even included several pictures of Josie with a handsome, smiling young man in uniform. To Sadie, it looked like some kind of romance. *Had he survived the war?* she wondered. *Could this be one of the answers to the question of why Josie had never married?*

She flipped to the back of the album. Josie had kept it far past the time she first bought it. In the pictures at the end, she was a grown woman, not just a girl, and the fashions and surroundings showed clear indicators of the late 1950s. As Sadie leafed backward through the book, she began to recognize another face besides Josie's: a young woman with blonde curls who seemed to have a mischievous grin on her face more often than not in the moment she was captured by the photographer's lens. The girl appeared all the way through the book, even on some of the early pages, before the possible romance with the soldier, who never appeared again himself after the war.

In a few places, someone had marked the photos with initials: a loopy *L* below a snapshot of the blonde, and a *J* below Josie. She was clearly a big part of Josie's life. Could she have been the person who came with her on Josie's mysterious visit to the Cartwright home? Or, if not, would she have been close enough to Josie to know what Josie had been doing, all those years ago?

Starting at the front of the album, Sadie worked her way through it again, studying each picture carefully, instead of skipping through looking for the broader patterns. Frustratingly, in most places, Josie seemed to keep her notes to a kind of personal code, mainly composed of the initials Sadie had already identified, but sometimes supplemented with nicknames. In one place, the spirited blonde was labeled "Salt" while Josie had labeled herself "Pepper."

But then, a few pages toward the end, was what looked like a portrait photograph of the blonde, perhaps for an engagement announcement, Sadie guessed from the romantic pose and the display of a diamond ring, with no wedding band, on her left hand. There was writing on it too, but not in the same handwriting in the rest of the album—probably a note the blonde made before sending it off to Josie, Sadie guessed. "Yours, Lyd," it read.

"Lyd," Sadie mused. "Short for Lydia?" She couldn't think of many other common women's names that nickname might stand for. But flipping to the end of the album didn't give her any confirmation: just a handful more pictures, and a few more of the familiar identifying initials.

She settled the album back in the box, then moved to the next one. This one seemed to be full of paper, rather than things. But not the financial papers Sadie had been sifting through for the past few weeks. Instead, these were greeting cards, Christmas letters, personal notes. Josie seemed to have sorted them carefully according to the sender: a batch in the shaky hand that might have indicated a grandmother, mostly sent during the years when Josie would have been a child. A collection of old-timey Christmas cards that covered Sadie's hands with glitter. A batch of letters on army-issued airmail paper in masculine handwriting. These broke off before the war ended, in the winter of 1945, whether from a misunderstanding or a more permanent loss, Sadie didn't know.

It was as she laid that packet gently aside that she picked up the thickest batch of letters she'd encountered yet. It seemed to be almost a foot thick, and tied with a length of yarn, since no rubber band would be able to manage it. And the top letter, written in a clearly girlish hand, had been sent from an "L. Devine."

Quickly, Sadie freed the stack from the bright knotted yarn, and began to flip through it. Just as she'd suspected, one of the following letters was showily addressed from a "Fabulous Miss Lydia Devine."

At first the letters seemed mostly to have been written in the summers, probably when the two friends were separated by travels or camps. Then they trickled in from a university campus where Lydia had apparently been a student. And after several years of reporting from the university, Lydia's last name changed, to Cameron.

This first batch of letters Sadie looked at were in rigorous chronological order. Sadie flipped quickly to the end, through everything from thick letters to holiday cards to postcards from Italy and Belize. Lydia and Josie obviously had a strong friendship, years long. But Josie had already passed on. There was a possibility that Lydia had as well. Or that, at her advanced age, she wasn't able anymore to send the letters and remembrances that she'd sent so steadily through the rest of their lives.

But the last envelope, at the very bottom of the stack, had a quite recent postmark, from the past year. Sadie calculated quickly: It was only a few months before Josie had passed away. There was a good chance, she suspected, that the correspondence had ended because of Josie's passing, and not because anything had happened to Lydia. She felt a faint sadness as she held the thick wedge of letters, the evidence and the actual weight of such a long, lifetime friendship. *It must have been a great gift and comfort to them both*, she thought. But at the same time, if Lydia was still living, it must have been very hard for her to let go of Josie. After all those years, Sadie guessed she still probably picked up a pen or a phone, wanting to be in touch with her friend—and then had to realize all over again that there was no number that could reach her with a call, and no address where to direct a letter.

Sadie scanned the last envelope. From its weight, she suspected it was a greeting card, rather than a letter. But she wasn't after the contents. She was far more interested in the return address, which she found when she turned it over to read the flap of the envelope. The handwriting was neater now than it had been when Lydia and Josie were girls, and perhaps a little less bold. But it was still perfectly recognizable, as was the name: Lydia Cameron. And the address: a nearby street in Silver Peak. After all that time, and despite all of Lydia's many travels, it looked like she had landed back in Silver Peak.

And perhaps, Sadie guessed, in her own childhood home. She calculated quickly. The address on Lydia's envelope was so close that it was almost laughable that she had put it in the mail instead of carrying it over herself. Probably the habit of a generation that had a much stronger belief in handwritten greetings and thank-you cards, Sadie thought. But also a clue to how the friendship between Josie and Lydia might have started.

She pulled out her phone, called up the navigational app, and typed in the address on the envelope. After a moment's hesitation, her own location appeared as a familiar dot, at the Parker House address. Then another dot appeared, almost on top of the dot indicating Sadie's own location.

Surprised, she enlarged the screen in order to see more detail. Now she could clearly see both the street she was on, and the next street over, where Lydia's address was located. She smiled.

Lydia and Josie had been almost back-to-back neighbors. Lydia's home wasn't directly behind Josie's, but it was one house over, just kitty-corner across the backyard. In fact, because of the way the homes were situated on their lots, Lydia's home was almost as close to the Parker House as its next-door neighbors on either side.

Sadie double-checked the address on the envelope against the one she'd typed into her phone. Then she wrapped the yarn back around Lydia's large stack of letters.

She climbed down from the attic, but she didn't stop there. Instead of returning to what had become her customary spot among the papers collected around Josie's old desk, she trotted down the front stairs and headed out the back door, with the interesting feeling that she was following an invisible path that Josie herself must have taken many times before.

When she stepped out into the sunlight of the backyard, she took a quick look around. It had been well cared for, and probably not just by Josie. All around were the telltale signs of generations of gardening: well-established bushes and flowering trees, and gardens that weren't sparse with new planting, but full of lush, mature plants, growing in a happy profusion of summer pinks, orange, red, and blue.

Sadie's heart flooded with a sense of gratitude. *Good job!* she prayed. The words poured out of her heart without her really thinking about them. And when she did think about them, they seemed so strange that she felt a little bashful. Mothers told children and teachers told students that they'd done a good job. So it was an odd thing to want to say to God. But it had been the honest response of her heart to all the beauty around her. And somehow, she had the sense that God understood what she meant by it—and even that He might be pleased. *It's all so beautiful,* she prayed. *Everything You make.*

Then she glanced to the left of the yard, where her map program had told her Lydia's house ought to be. Sure enough, the peak of another Victorian home rose just over the line of trees and shrubbery that separated the neighborhood lots.

Sadie set off down the slight rise that the house stood on, enjoying the play of the sunlight through the trees on the dappled lawn as she took a diagonal path, the quickest route from the backdoor to the neighboring yard. When she reached the corner of the yard, she discovered that she was, indeed, walking in someone else's path, whether it was Josie's or not. In the far corner of the yard, the ground had been worn down and branches broken back through the shrubbery that stood between Josie's yard and Lydia's. And it didn't look like it was just the artifact of a decades-old friendship. It was a bit overgrown, but still so fresh that it seemed to be the evidence of far more recent travelers from yard to yard.

Sadie put up her hand to guard her face from the brushing branches, ducked her head, and pushed through the little break in the trees. A moment later, she found herself standing in another yard. This house was a big old Victorian, like the

Parker House. But it showed much more evidence of modern inhabitants. The gardens were edged with neat plastic, instead of brick. A recent swing set took up one corner of the yard. And a classy leisure tent sheltered a set of trendy garden furniture, with dark wicker backs and cream-colored cushions, probably for the adults to get some much-needed rest while the kids were enjoying the swings.

Striding through the yard of the Parker House, where Sadie knew she was welcome, hadn't given her any pause. But now that she found herself boldly standing in the back of a stranger's yard, she felt a bit sheepish. She hurried as fast as she could past all the furniture, to the sidewalk that ran along the street in front of the house. From there, she turned up the front walk, went to the front door, and knocked.

A moment later, a pretty blonde with a broad smile opened the door. Sadie had to hold herself back from giving a visible start. She looked so much like Lydia had in the pictures of her as a young woman that it was almost like seeing those pictures come to life, all these decades later. But despite the incredible resemblance that this woman bore to Lydia, Sadie managed a friendly smile.

"Hello," she said, not quite sure where to start. "I'm Sadie Speers. I run the Antique Mine, downtown in Silver Peak?"

"Oh yes!" the woman said. "I'm Carol. I love looking in your windows. Your store always seems to be full of such wonderful things." She seemed friendly, but also a little bewildered, as if she was wondering why exactly that would mean that Sadie should show up on her doorstep.

Sadie smiled. "Oh, thank you. We do our best. And I'm also working with the Jones family on the Parker House renovation."

Carol's face lit up. "Oh, we are so grateful to them," she said. "It was so good to hear that the place had been bought by people who really care about the history. I know my mom was trying not to worry about it, but that house was almost as much hers as it was Josie's. And this place was almost as much Josie's as it was Mom's, I guess," she added.

"I understand they were very good friends," Sadie said.

"The best," Carol said. "And all their lives, since they were little girls."

"That's lovely," Sadie said. "I was actually hoping to talk with your mother, if she's around. I thought maybe she could give me some perspective on the work I'm doing."

"Oh, she would absolutely love that," Carol said. "She doesn't get as many guests as she used to, at her age. And I don't think there's anything she'd like better than reliving some of the glory days of her friendship with Josie. I have to warn you, you might get even more stories than you bargained for."

Sadie smiled. "I love hearing stories," she said. "That's why I'm interested in antiques. Things don't have too much interest for me in themselves. I love them because of the stories they have to tell."

"Well, you've come to the right place, then," Carol said. "Are you around the house pretty frequently with your help on the renovations?"

Sadie nodded.

"Well," Carol said, "you can come back anytime you like. It's pretty unusual for Mom to be out. But this is her quilt club day. They've been piecing this one for a month, and they've finally got the back on so they can get down to quilting it. It wasn't to be missed!" she added with a wink.

"Under no circumstances," Sadie said, playing along. "Well, if you wouldn't mind letting her know that I'm looking forward to talking with her, I'd be grateful."

"Absolutely," Carol said, and stuck out her hand. "So nice to meet you."

"It's lovely to meet you."

"And Mom will love meeting you too," Carol said. "See you soon!"

"See you soon," Sadie said.

10

WHEN SADIE FIRST PUSHED THROUGH THE NARROW HEDGE THAT separated Lydia's yard from the Parker House, she glanced up at the beautiful old building, with every intention of going back inside and picking up her research among the papers where she'd left off.

But after she took a few steps up the hill, she stopped.

She wanted to meet her commitment to Charlene. And she loved doing the historical work that required. But there was another kind of historical work, and with immediate real-life consequences on her mind: helping her friend learn whatever the truth was about the circumstances of her birth.

After a few moments' deliberation, she struck out in a new direction, cutting through the side yard toward her car, which was parked on the curb in front of the house. So far, her search through the papers had yielded as many questions as it had answers. It was time, she thought, to go ask a few of those questions to someone who might know. It had been clear to her that Amanda at the lumber company knew something she wasn't sharing with Sadie. There could be all kinds of reasons for that. And the secret could shed light on Ann's situation—or Amanda could simply be reluctant to share some kind of business at the lumber company that had very little to do with either Josie, or Ann. But Sadie knew one thing for sure: It was a lot easier to ignore questions a person asked over the phone than it was to put off someone who was actually visiting you in your own office. And as far as Sadie could see, there wasn't anything to stop her from paying a friendly visit to Amanda at the lumber company.

Just a few minutes later, Sadie had made her way through Silver Peak's neat historic streets, to the outskirts of town, where the lumberyard, with its wide lots of prime lumber, was situated. She smiled as she got out of the car at the scent of fresh-cut wood in the air. She'd always loved that smell for itself, but she also loved the association it had with building—making old things new, fixing what was broken, or making something that had never been built before real. And now that she was spending so much time with Edwin, it had started to remind her of him and her warm feelings for him, as well. Ever since they'd been together, he'd been working on his own painstaking renovation of his parents' Victorian home, so their entire romance had been "perfumed" by the smell of fresh-cut wood, new paint, and the comforting scent of sawdust.

The Silver Peak Lumber Company had started out as little more than a tent surrounded by piles of logs and planed wood, which Sadie knew because of all the historical photographs the company still displayed proudly in the current office. It had come a long way from that original tent, and now supplied lumber for homes and building projects not just for Silver Peak but for several other nearby towns in the surrounding area. But it still had an unmistakably humble, small-town feel. The current office was decades old itself, built in the 1940s to accommodate the boom in building as men returned home and started to set up households after the end of the war. In honor of Colorado's old-time history, the lumber office itself was a log cabin structure, with big, exposed golden beams making up both the walls and the roof. Just inside was a counter full of staff ready to do anything from help a teenager pick out two-by-fours to brace a parade float, to sourcing the best and best-priced lumber for an entire home.

When Sadie came through the door, she immediately recognized Frank Avery behind the counter. Frank was a husky redhead with a long red beard who looked like he had been sent from central casting to play the part of a Wild West lumberjack. In fact, with his red-and-black plaid shirt, he fit the part of a lumberman of the past century so well that it seemed a little surprising that he was able to briskly navigate a modern computer, as he was doing when Sadie walked in.

When he looked up, his face broke into a wide grin. He and Sadie knew each other well from Campfire Chapel, where they had worked together the previous year on a charity dinner. Sadie had been in charge of wrangling all of the volunteers in the kitchen, and to her surprise, Frank, whom she had had her doubts about at first, had turned out to be by far the most efficient member of her kitchen staff—and able to make a homemade ranch dressing that was the hit of the entire night. Sadie had been delighted, but her surprise at his skills in the kitchen had been so evident that Frank had teased her mercilessly, pretending to be wounded at the unfair judgments she had made about him when they first met. That teasing had developed into an easy friendship, and each time they met, Sadie enjoyed catching up with him about his grandchildren, ages seventeen to three, all of whom were just as redheaded as Frank, and about the always-expanding play area he was constantly building for them in his backyard, turning unwanted lumber from the company's scrap heap into a childhood fantasyland.

"Well, Sadie Speers," he said, "this is a pleasant surprise."

"How are you doing?" Sadie asked as she went up to the counter. "Any new additions to the Avery family backyard?"

"As a matter of fact," Frank said, pulling his phone out of his pocket, "I did some work on it this weekend. It's not an easy thing, keeping a seventeen-year-old interested in playground equipment. But I think I finally did it. Here, look at this."

He handed his phone over the counter. It was a picture of the play area, which Sadie by now was very familiar with: a kind of wooden castle that sprawled over the back of Frank's yard. But now it had some kind of large turret, supported by the structure, but also nestled in the low branches of a nearby tree.

"You've built a second story!" Sadie exclaimed.

"It's a private clubhouse," Frank said. "I even gave him a rope ladder he can pull up, to get some time for himself."

"That's amazing," Sadie said. "He's lucky to have you as a grandfather. But how do the other kids feel about that section being off-limits?"

Frank winked. "Well, that's the thing of it," he said. "He hasn't really kept it off-limits. Turns out, it's now the favorite play space for all of them. He even carried the three-year-old up there on his back on Sunday afternoon."

Sadie grinned.

"They still want to play, even at that age," Frank said. "They just need an excuse."

"I think all of us always want to play, at least a little bit," Sadie said. "Our kids and our grandkids just give us the reason to."

"Now you've got my secret too!" Frank said with a laugh. He leaned forward on the counter. "So tell me, what brings you in here? One of those renovations you're always working on? We've got a new partner now who can match the profile of any molding you've got. You don't even need to bring us a sample. It scans your existing molding, right in place, wherever you've got it. I've been dying for a customer to try it out."

"I'm glad to know about that," Sadie said. "But I'm actually here to see Amanda."

"I just saw her a minute ago," Frank said. "I'm sure she'll be more than happy to give you any help she can. Just a second."

He hopped down from his stool and disappeared into the management offices behind the main business counter. A moment later, he reappeared, grinning, and waved for Sadie to come in.

When she followed him through the glass door into the offices, Sadie could see at once that Amanda was actually quite a bit less than happy to see her. But in the face of Frank's cheerful certainty that there couldn't be any reason in the world two such delightful people wouldn't want to meet, she couldn't seem to come up with a way to excuse herself from at least a brief interview with Sadie.

"Come on in," she said reluctantly, only taking the slightest step aside from the door to her office, as if her real instinct was still to block Sadie from entering it.

Frank gave Sadie a broad wink, then disappeared out into the service area.

"Thank you so much for making the time to see me," Sadie said, hurrying past Amanda and into her office before Amanda could change her mind. "I'm sure you must be very busy."

"Yes," Amanda said bluntly. She circled behind her desk, where she stood, not inviting Sadie to sit down.

Sadie took a deep breath. *Lord,* she prayed, *help me think of the right thing to say.* Then a new thought struck her. Instead of asking Amanda more questions, why not tell her something about what she was working on? That might help her understand what was going on and ease any fears she had, either about revealing too much about Josie, or revealing too much about the lumber company business.

"I feel like we might have gotten off on the wrong foot," Sadie said. "I didn't mean to give you the impression that I wanted to pry at all into your business. Or into Josie's business. It's just that I've been helping a friend who is looking for her birth mother. Somehow, Josie seemed to be involved with the circumstances of her birth. And since I've been working through her files to help the Jones family with the renovation of the Parker House, I couldn't help noticing that some big deposits in Josie's accounts happened right around the time my friend was born. I don't mean to cause any trouble for anyone."

Across the desk, Amanda sank down into her chair. She nodded for Sadie to join her, which Sadie did, taking the seat across from her. Amanda looked a little baffled by everything Sadie had just told her. But for some reason, she also seemed—was it relieved?

"A secret child?" she said wonderingly. "Are you saying that Josie had a daughter that none of us ever knew about?"

Sadie jolted forward a bit in alarm. "Well, no," she said. "I'm not sure I'd be ready to say something like that quite yet. I'm just trying to understand how Josie was connected with my friend's birth."

"But that would be one way?" Amanda asked. "I mean, that would certainly be one obvious reason she would have had to be involved in the birth. If your friend was actually hers."

"Yes," Sadie admitted reluctantly, "but if you could just help me understand a bit about Young Transportation, before we…"

"That would explain so much," Amanda broke in, almost as if she were talking to herself.

"Explain what?" Sadie asked.

To her surprise, when Amanda's eyes met hers, they had tears in them.

"Young Transportation doesn't exist," Amanda said. The words came out in a rush, as if she'd been bottling them up for years and couldn't hold them in a second longer.

Now it was Sadie's turn to wonder. "Doesn't exist?" she said. "But I saw the checks."

"Yes," Amanda said, with a strange smile, "the checks were real enough. It's just that the company wasn't."

"I'm afraid I don't understand," Sadie said.

"Neither did I," Amanda said with a sigh.

In response to Sadie's inquiring look, she squared her shoulders. "I love Josie," she said. "A lot of businesses like to say they treat their people like family, but with Josie, it was the other way around. She treated me like her family. From the time I was a tiny girl, she always seemed to care about anything I cared about. She always remembered anything I told her. Even when I was a teenager, and

I thought I was much too mature to have anything to do with the old lady at the family business, she was always so sweet and patient with me. When my first boyfriend broke up with me, I was too sad and embarrassed to tell anyone else. But somehow, Josie knew something was wrong. She asked me what had happened to me, and she was the first shoulder I cried on. It was like that all my life, until we—lost her."

"She was an amazing woman," Sadie agreed.

Amanda blinked back her tears and fumbled a bit with the papers on her desk, until she seemed to realize that they had no answers to give her to the questions she and Sadie were talking about. "Well," she said, "after Josie passed away, I hired an independent accounting firm to go over the books. I didn't expect to find any problems at all. She'd always kept them in beautiful shape, and if anything, she was conscientious to a fault. I remember Dad joking that she was liable to leave him memos over a lost nickel that had been found."

"But they did find something," Sadie guessed.

Amanda nodded. "They said the books were in fantastic shape," she said. "Some of the best they'd ever seen. But there was one irregularity. And because everything else was in such good shape, they didn't think it was a mistake."

"Young Transportation," Sadie said.

Amanda nodded. "It would have been easier to believe that it was all a mistake," she said. "After all the years that Josie worked for us, nobody would have blamed her for having made one or two along the way. But according to the accountants, these transactions were handled with exactly the kind of speed and care Josie always brought to everything. Every *i* was dotted and every *t* was crossed. It's just that the money never flowed into anything called Young Transportation. It flowed into the same bank account as Josie's regular payroll checks."

"That's what I saw too," Sadie said, "in her private accounting."

"I just couldn't understand why she would have stolen from us," Amanda said. "It wasn't so much that she took the money. We would have given her anything she wanted. It was that, whatever she was facing, she hadn't come to us with the problem. If she needed something, why didn't she just ask us?"

Tears had sprung into her eyes again, but now she smiled. "I couldn't stand to think about it," she said. "So I didn't tell anyone else in the company about what the accountants had found. I didn't want to hurt Josie's name. And I just couldn't believe she was actually stealing from us, no matter how much I thought about it. She never seemed to care much about money. She didn't wear fancy clothes, or jewelry, or drive a luxury car. Or even take many vacations. So I couldn't even think what she would have spent the money on, *if* she did steal it. Remember, we worked side by side, every day, until the time she passed.

"But this could explain everything," Amanda said hopefully. "Maybe it was a secret she didn't think she could share with anyone. The money wasn't for her. It was for her baby girl."

Sadie hadn't been able to ignore the possibility that Josie was Ann's mother either, but she was uneasy with the way Amanda jumped to that conclusion so quickly. To Sadie's mind, nobody had enough facts to be sure of something like that. And leaping to conclusions in this case wasn't just a minor error. She'd seen how deeply all this was affecting Ann. It had shaken her to the core. And Sadie was hoping to find something truly solid for Ann to rebuild on: the truth, not just more guesswork and missing information.

"I'm not sure we know enough to come to that conclusion yet," Sadie said.

"Well," Amanda said, leaning forward, "how do we find out?"

"Right now," Sadie said, "I'm just trying to understand what Young Transportation meant to Josie."

"But it must have had something to do with her daughter," Amanda said. "There can't be any other reason."

Sadie tried to smile politely. If she'd learned one thing in life, it was that it was *always* possible there was another reason. "I think the first step is probably to understand everything we can about Young Transportation," she said. "Even if it was never a real business, what did that name mean to Josie, and what did she use it for? I've looked through Josie's records. But I'd like to check them against your own books."

Amanda glanced down. She opened a side drawer of her desk, rifled through a few papers, and drew out a brown file folder. Then she dropped it on the desk and pushed it over to Sadie.

"There you go," she said.

"What's this?" Sadie asked, flipping it open. Inside was a single piece of paper, with a list of dates and dollar amounts.

"That's everything we've got on Young Transportation," Amanda said. "The entirety of the accountant's report. I pulled it from the general report before we duplicated it for our board. I think I had an idea that I was going to shred it, but I could never bring myself to do that either. I just…kept it. I guess I'm glad I did, now. And I'm so glad that it might actually help someone."

"Thank you," Sadie said, slipping the file into her handbag.

"Sadie," Amanda said. "Promise me one thing."

Sadie met her eyes.

"I'd really like to meet Josie's daughter," she said. "I miss her so much. It'd be wonderful to meet someone who carries even a little part of her. And maybe she'd like to know something about Josie's life too. I'd tell her anything she wants to know."

Sadie took a deep breath. She was touched by Amanda's evident love for Josie, but it wasn't her promise to make. "I think that decision's still a ways off," she said. "And it wouldn't be my decision, even if we do discover that Josie had a daughter. But I can promise you one thing," she said. "If we discover anything that I'm able to share, you'll be the first to know."

"Well, you've already helped me," Amanda said. "Even if we don't know the reason yet, I'm glad to hear someone is working to find an explanation for these irregularities in her bookkeeping. It's been haunting me ever since the accountant discovered them. I'll be very grateful for any answer you're able to find."

Sadie smiled. "I'll do my best," she said. "That's all I can promise."

Amanda smiled back. "Somehow, I think that will be more than enough."

11

Sadie had just pulled up in front of the Parker House again when her phone began to ring. When she pulled it from her purse, Ann's number flashed on the screen.

"Ann?" Sadie said, after picking up the call.

"Sadie," Ann said. "I'm glad to hear your voice." She sounded agitated: rushed, or frustrated, or worried, or all of them.

"How are you doing?" Sadie asked.

Ann heaved a sigh. "It's this reunion," she said. "I can't believe how difficult it's been to plan."

Sadie suspected that what she really meant was, *I can't believe how difficult it's been to work with Roz.* But she held her tongue for the time being. "Oh?" she said, simply.

"It's so frustrating," Ann said. "The whole point of this event is to connect with old friends. And Roz is one of my oldest. I was so looking forward to getting the chance to reconnect with her again after all these years. In fact, working with her was one of the things I was most excited about, out of all the reunion events. But now I've upset her. I'm sure of it."

Sadie couldn't contradict her on this point, but she didn't want to stir the pot by agreeing with her either. That would just give her the feeling that Roz had been talking about her behind her back. And even though Roz had only talked to Sadie, who was her best friend, that could make matters worse.

Lord, Sadie prayed, *is there some way to bring good out of this mess? I can't see how. But You can. So please do.*

"I'm sorry to hear that," Sadie said.

"She keeps saying, 'but don't you agree that' her ideas about the reunion would be the best way to go. But I can't say that!" Ann said, her voice rising. "Because I don't agree! People are coming from all over the place. Some of us may never see each other again. I think we should celebrate that with something a bit more than a slice of pizza on a park bench. And I don't think that's wrong. She seems to think I want to make this into some big-city shindig. But I only want it to be something more special than just another day in the park."

Sadie didn't have strong feelings of her own about the reunion, but it was interesting, she thought, that whenever she listened either to Ann or to Roz, she sympathized with both of their points of view. And they did seem to have one thing in common: They were both far more passionate about the reunion than anybody else Sadie knew in their class. It was such a shame that they hadn't been able to find a way to agree and move forward together yet.

Still, because of her friendship with Roz, and because of all the things Roz had already told her in confidence about the spat between Roz and Ann, Sadie didn't feel she could weigh in much. Instead, she changed the subject.

"I did get a chance to talk with Jasper," she said.

"He called me after he talked with you!" Ann said. Her voice, which had been so strident just moments before, now sounded childlike and unsure, as if the mention of her family sent her back to her own younger days—even before she'd been a part of the high school class she was wrangling with Roz over now.

"Oh, Sadie," she said. "Thank you. That's much more important than this whole—reunion." A note of exasperation, with herself, or with the whole project, crept into her voice as she said the word. "It was so good to talk to him, but I'm afraid I didn't get much of what your conversation with him was about. I was so glad to talk with him that I didn't want to upset him by asking about our parents. What did he say to you?"

Sadie thought for a moment. "Where are you?" she asked. "I'm at the Parker House. Would you be able to come over?"

"Is everything okay?" Ann asked.

"I think so," Sadie said. "It's just that I think it'd be good to talk in person."

"I'm just downtown," Ann said. "I'll be right there."

A few minutes later, Ann sank down on the spare chair in the room Josie had once used as her office. With a quick glance, Sadie noticed that she was still wearing the unique fleur-de-lis ornament on its delicate chain. Her mind flashed to the missing piece of the decorative fireplace screen downstairs. But Ann had other things on her mind, for the time being.

"I can't thank you enough," she said. "I don't think I realized until after I got off the phone with you what a big request I was making of you. I thought it would just be a quick conversation for you with a friend. But really"—a far-off look appeared in her eyes—"it was so much more than that." She searched Sadie's face anxiously. "How is Jasper?"

Sadie gave Ann's hand a squeeze. "Jasper loves you very much," she said. "I think that's the most important thing for you to remember about this whole conversation. And probably about all the conversations you have with him."

Tears sprang to Ann's eyes. "I know that," she said. "I love him too."

Sadie smiled.

"But why is it so hard for people who love each other so much to have a simple conversation?"

"The thing is," Sadie said, "I don't think it was really all that simple."

"No?" Ann said.

Sadie shook her head. "And I know this is an emotional issue for you," she said.

Ann nodded. "I don't even know who my parents were," she said, her voice cracking. "He doesn't seem to understand that. Or else why wouldn't he help me?"

"Well, there's another way to think about it," Sadie said. "The other thing I heard from Jasper is that the facts you've been discovering don't just affect you. You might think that you're looking for your birth parents. But the things you're finding out don't just tell you about them. They tell both you and Jasper things you never knew about your own parents. So in some ways, he's going through some of the same things you are. His whole world probably feels pretty shaky right now too."

Ann nodded. "I guess I was so wrapped up in how this was affecting me that I didn't think of how it must be affecting him," she said. "But I'm the only family he has. It must be a little scary to hear me say I'm looking for another one."

"I think there might be something to that," Sadie said. "But he cares about you a lot. That's the main thing. And he is willing to help. In fact, he told me everything he remembered about the time surrounding your birth."

"What did he say?" Ann asked, leaning forward.

Sadie filled her in on the details of her conversation with Jasper. When she was finished, Ann looked around Josie's office, her eyes wide, as if she expected Josie herself to step into the room at any moment. "So Josie was my mother?" she asked.

"I'm not sure we have the evidence to be sure of that yet," Sadie said. "After all, I've never heard any stories around town that might suggest Josie hid a pregnancy for all that time."

"Yes," Ann said, "but somehow my mother was able to hide the fact that she was never really pregnant with me. It was a different time. Women didn't spend as much time in public."

"Perhaps," Sadie said. "But Josie would have been working at the lumber company even then. She was a trim woman, so it would have been difficult to hide a pregnancy from her fellow employees. And I'm almost certain that Amanda would have mentioned any large leaves of absence. But she said Josie rarely ever traveled, and not for long."

Ann looked almost disappointed. Sadie felt for her. It was so difficult not to have the answers to such a big question. But then Ann squared her shoulders. "Well," she said, "how do we find out? What can I do to help?"

Sadie drew the folder that Amanda had given her at the lumber company out of her bag and opened it on the desk.

"What is that?" Ann asked.

"It's a list of checks that Josie wrote to herself from the lumber company account," Sadie told her. "They were written to Young Transportation."

"I've never heard of that," Ann said, glancing over the list.

"That's because it never existed," Sadie said. "The money flowed straight into Josie's own accounts. What I'm interested in is when. And where it might have gone afterward. Are you up for spending some time combing through old ledgers?"

"I'm up for anything," Ann said.

Sadie watched as Ann scanned the list. "Does anything pop out at you?" she asked.

Ann shook her head. "No," she said. "This here, it's about three months before my birthday. But then there isn't another check to Young Transportation for almost another year. And there are checks from well before the time I was born too." Her finger traced down the page. "This one is for more than a year before."

Sadie's brow furrowed. Part of her must have hoped that the Young Transportation checks would offer some instant clue that would give them some of the answers Ann was so eager to find. But it looked like, as was true with much of life, it would be a matter of slow, steady work to arrive at any answer.

But Sadie was ready to do it. And Ann was there to help.

She cracked open a ledger and handed it to Ann.

"What am I looking for?" Ann asked.

"I'd like to start from the date the Young Transportation checks were deposited to Josie's account," Sadie said, opening the turquoise ledger from the 1950s, and showing Ann the numbers as she spoke. "Quite frequently, there are debits that match those amounts at some point after the deposit. But Josie made no notes about where those debits were directed. I'd like to search through the canceled checks themselves and see if we can find any clues."

She settled a box of canceled checks on the desk between them, pulled out an envelope stuffed with old checks and bank documents, and checked the date on it. "I'll start from the bottom of the list of Young Transportation deposits," she said. "You start from the beginning."

"You've got it," Ann said. She checked the list for herself, and then began to sort through Josie's box of checks and documents, searching for the corresponding date range of checks.

For several minutes, the two of them sat in companionable silence, the gentle swish of paper against paper the only sound as they leafed through the piles of checks. Then Ann sighed and settled one envelope of checks back in the box. "She's incredibly organized," she said. "If she is my mother, I wish I'd inherited that from her."

Sadie smiled. "Any luck?"

Ann shook her head. "No. I can see the record of the large debit, but there's no corresponding check. At least not for this first date."

"Then I guess we check the next one," Sadie said.

"That's the one that's closest to my birth," Ann said quietly, as she took the next batch of checks from the well-ordered box.

A few minutes later, she put that one away, as well. In the meantime, Sadie had checked several dates of her own, with similar luck.

"There's nothing that matches these debits," Ann said. "I might be tempted to think that she had just lost a check here or there. But Josie doesn't seem like the type of woman who ever lost much of anything."

"And in the stacks I've been looking through, all the checks are in order by number," Sadie said. "And all the numbers are there."

"But there is always a debit in the ledger," Ann mused, turning the pages of the old turquoise book. "For every single one of the Young Transportation checks. Usually within a week. Whatever she was doing with that money, she never kept it for long."

Sadie put another envelope back in the box. As she did, she tried to straighten the checks back into the neat order Josie had left them in. A few, at the back, wouldn't settle down with the others. When she pushed them aside to see why, she discovered a crumpled piece of blue onionskin paper.

She spread it flat on the desk, pressing with both hands to get rid of some of the creases.

"What's that?" Ann asked.

Sadie read the printing on the upper corner. "It's a receipt," she said. "For cash."

Ann's eyes widened as she looked at it. "That's a lot of cash," she said.

"Check the list," Sadie said. "I think it's close to one of the dates."

"It's close to my birthday," Ann said, quietly.

She scanned the list that Amanda had given them of checks written from the lumber company to Young Transportation. "And it's for just a week after the Young Transportation check was written."

Her eyes began to fill with tears.

Sadie laid a hand on her shoulder.

"I'm sorry," Ann said. "You have been nothing but helpful. I'm so thankful. I don't know what's wrong with me. It's just so frustrating, to have all these clues, but not be able to understand what actually happened. And this—it just makes me realize, maybe there's even more I don't know. If Mom wasn't my mom, who's to say when I was even born? Maybe my birthday isn't even my birthday."

"That might be true," Sadie said. "But that wouldn't matter at all to anyone who already loves you."

"It matters to me!" Ann said, her voice breaking.

"I can understand that," Sadie said, squeezing her shoulder. But a new idea had begun to form in her mind. They'd been looking through the documents in Josie's house. But there were other documents that related to Ann's birth. What part of the story did they have to tell?

"Ann," Sadie said. "Do you have a copy of your birth certificate?"

Ann took a deep breath to steady herself. "Of course," she said.

"Where is it?" Sadie asked. "Is it in a place where someone back home might be able to take a look at it?"

"Better than that," Ann said, taking her phone from her purse. "I've got it in an online vault."

"An online vault?" Sadie asked.

"It's a special app," Ann told her, swiping quickly over her phone. "I've actually never had to use it before. But my husband set it up recently. It's got digital copies of all our important records in one place online, so that if anything ever happens to either of us, we know right where to look. And we don't have to go back to the house to search for documents in the middle of any kind of an emergency."

Sadie watched with interest as Ann drew up a list of documents, then selected her own birth certificate. After a single tap, a facsimile image of it appeared on the screen, a birth certificate clearly labeled as being issued from the local Silver Peak hospital.

"I don't think I've ever read the whole thing," Ann said, scrolling through it.

"Do you see anything that seems unusual now that you're looking at it?"

As Sadie looked over her shoulder, Ann glanced over everything, including her description, her parents' names, the delivery doctor, and the date. "It all lines up with everything I ever thought was true about my birth," she said. "The only thing that's unusual is that I know now that the people it lists as my parents weren't really my parents."

"Well, sadly, they're no longer here to ask," Sadie said. "But they aren't the only people mentioned here on the certificate."

"I am," Ann said.

"Yes," Sadie said, "but there's someone else. The doctor."

Ann scrolled down to the signature of the physician who had signed as having attended her birth. "Dr. Kirchener," she read.

Sadie nodded.

Ann looked up. "Well, yes," she said. "But if he was old enough to be a doctor at the time I was born, I doubt that he's still living."

"If he is living, though, he'd be an excellent person to talk with," Sadie said. "And even if he's not, we might be able to find out more about him." She rose, picked up her bag, and slung it over her shoulder.

"Where are you going?" Ann asked, looking up at her.

"I'm going over to the hospital, to see if they can tell me anything about Dr. Kirchener," Sadie said. "Do you want to come?"

12

"Dr. Kirchener?" The woman at the hospital records desk repeated. Then her face broke into a wide smile. "Well, of course. Everybody knew him."

"Did you work with him?" Sadie asked. Ann stood by Sadie's side silently, but her eyes were alert and searching as the woman at the records desk nodded.

"Not for very long," the woman said. "He had a long history with the hospital. He came here straight after the war, after doing his first service as a doctor in combat hospitals. I heard him tell stories about how he had to get used to saying 'please' and 'thank you' to the nurses instead of just barking orders all the time.

"I may be getting along in years," the woman said, running her hand through her short blonde hair, "but I hope I don't look like I've been around here *quite* that long."

"Let me guess," Sadie said. "You're nineteen."

The woman laughed.

"Twenty?" Sadie tried.

The woman laughed again. "Thank God I'm not twenty anymore," she said. "I know everyone wants to look young, and I try to keep myself up as well as I can. But you couldn't pay me enough to *be* young again. I'm glad for every last year I've lived, and every last thing I've learned in each one."

"Amen to that," Sadie said. "But you did work with Dr. Kirchener?"

The woman nodded. "My first few years here were his last," she said. "He retired just after I came."

"And do you know how he's spending his retirement?" Sadie asked.

The woman's face clouded. "He always talked about how he was going to go on a trip around the world with his wife. Every time somebody came back from vacation, talking about some new place they'd been, he'd say, 'Well, we'll just have to go there too.' And they did do quite a bit of traveling, I heard, in the early days. But he waited a long time to retire. He just loved the work so much, I guess. So we lost him just about a year after he left the hospital."

"I'm sorry to hear that," Sadie said.

The woman sighed. "He had a good life," she said. "A full life. He touched a lot of people. You should have seen the funeral. I think pretty much the entire hospital staff was there. And from the looks of it, just about everyone who had ever been in the hospital here in Silver Peak." She glanced from Sadie to Ann. "I'm actually surprised neither of you ever met him," she said. "Can I ask why you're interested?"

Sadie leaned on the counter. "My friend and I are just doing some research on her family history," she said. "And we noticed that Dr. Kirchener was listed as the delivery doctor on her birth certificate. We were wondering if there were any other records at all surrounding her birth."

The woman pursed her lips. "Well, I'd need to see some ID and have you sign a privacy waiver," she said. "All those records are protected under the patient confidentiality act."

"I can do that," Ann said, stepping forward.

The woman leafed through a few files on her desk, pulled out a copy of a privacy waiver, and handed it to Ann, who glanced over it quickly, then signed.

The woman placed it on the desk beside her and read carefully from the information Ann had given.

"Ann Cartwright," she said, then typed a flurry of strokes on her keyboard. She glanced up after she did. "This may take just a minute. We've only just now digitized the hospital's original records, and it can take a moment for the search to complete. Yep, there we go."

She glanced back at the screen. Then she frowned, and hit a few more keys. Then a few more.

"Is something the matter?" Sadie asked.

The woman gave her head a brief shake, as if she was trying to be patient, but having to answer Sadie's questions was just slowing her down as she tried to solve the problem.

"Strange," she said.

"What's strange?" Ann asked, her voice rising.

"It's probably nothing," the woman said, shaking her head. "Your birth certificate isn't coming up when I search under your name. But I'm sure it's just yet another glitch in this new system. Nothing ever works the first time anymore. Just give me a second…"

She punctuated this with another burst of typing. "I can search by deliveries by Dr. Kirchener around that time. It's a little less elegant, but it should come up there, no problem."

"Smart," Sadie complimented her.

"I like to tell my husband I was with the CIA before I married him. That's why I'm so good at solving sticky problems in high-pressure situations." The woman winked.

Then she frowned again. "What is your birthday?" she asked Ann.

Ann told her.

"*Hmm*," the woman said, typing swiftly. Her eyes scanned the screen, but then she shook her head. "This may sound like a strange question," she said, "but are you sure about the date?"

Ann glanced at Sadie, her eyes almost haunted.

"Forget I asked," the woman said. "What are the chances that you'd be wrong about your own birthday? Back in the CIA, they always used to tell me that if I couldn't get out the door, I should try the window. And if there wasn't a window, I should make one."

"That's part of the official CIA training, huh?" Sadie asked.

"You bet," the woman said. "I'm going to search all the births on that date. Not only does the new computer system not work, some of the data wasn't entered with perfect precision, if you know what I mean. They may have it listed under Dr. Kentworth, instead of Kirchener. Or under somebody else completely. So we're just going to take a look through all of them until we find you. And that list will be right…"

She struck a key, but suddenly her face registered absolute astonishment.

She glanced up at Ann, the surprise on her face still evident. "I'm sorry," she said. "It may be some kind of a mistake. But…"

"But what?" Ann pressed.

"The hospital has no record at all of any babies being born on that day. Not to any of the attending physicians."

"None at all?" Sadie asked, just as surprised as the woman had been.

The woman shook her head. "As I've been saying, the record-keeping with the new system hasn't been a model of perfection. There's a lot that might take some persistence to track down. But in my experience, there's never been one that just went missing completely."

"But I have the birth certificate. From this hospital," Ann said. "We just looked at it this morning."

"I don't know what to tell you," the woman said. "If the hospital had a record of it, it would be in this system."

"Can you think of any reason the hospital would issue a birth certificate that it never recorded?" Sadie asked.

"I'm sure it's not something the hospital did as a matter of policy," the woman said. "But there is always the possibility of human error. If we still had the original document, it would be in this digital system. But a doctor or a nurse might have misplaced it. Or even a records clerk," she added with a smile. "Although in my experience it's much more likely to have been the doctor or the nurse."

"So it never would have had a chance to become part of the digital system," Sadie said.

The woman nodded. "That's possible," she said. "And there's another possibility, as well. I know we've already agreed that we're all quite young here, at least at heart. But it has been quite a few years since this document was issued. The records have been moved at least once that I know of during that time, and then digitized. And before they were digitized, all kinds of people were in and out of the records rooms. If it was ever part of our records, it might also have gotten misplaced, lost, or destroyed over the years."

"Who would have had access to the records rooms?" Sadie asked. "The whole hospital staff?"

The woman shook her head. "Just the records clerks," she said. "And we guard them pretty zealously, because you can't really trust the doctors and nurses with a patient's records. At least not for any longer than they have to have them."

When she finished her explanation, the woman's eyes returned to Ann's face. Sadie also looked over at her friend. Ann's eyes were wide and her expression stricken.

"I'm sorry," the woman said. "I wish there was more I could do to help."

Ann gave a quick nod, then turned and strode away from the records desk, toward the main entrance beyond the lobby.

"Thank you," Sadie said quickly. She glanced back over her shoulder at Ann's retreating figure. "I need to…"

The woman nodded and waved for her to go after Ann. "I understand," she said. "I can't say I'd like to hear that news either."

A few moments later, Sadie had followed Ann out of the lobby and onto the sidewalk outside the hospital entrance.

Ann's eyes were filled with tears. Sadie put her arms around Ann, and Ann cried silently for a moment. Then she tried to recover herself, and pulled away.

"I'm not sure why this seems so much worse than anything else I've found out in the past few months about my birth," Ann said, her voice still wavering. "I mean, I don't know what could be bigger news than the fact that I'm not really related to my own family."

"There doesn't have to be a rhyme or reason to the way we feel," Sadie said. "Sometimes we just feel things, and we never know why. And that's fine," she added.

"I guess I wasn't sure what it really meant, when I first found out," Ann said. "I didn't know what my parents had done. Why they'd never told me. I was hoping if I came back here to search, maybe I could find some of those answers. But all we seem to find is more questions. And now I don't even have a birth certificate!" she added. "It's like I don't even exist."

"You exist," Sadie told her with a smile. "I can promise you that. You're standing right in front of me."

Ann gave her a grateful smile. "Thank you," she said. "Everything you've done has been such a help." But then her concerns began to creep back in. "But who *am* I? Where did I come from? I feel guilty even asking these questions, because I love my parents so much, and I know they loved me. I don't even really understand why I feel like I need to know anything more besides that. But then I also feel as if everyone I trusted the most has lied to me. The entire time I knew them. About some of the most important things in the world."

"I'm sure they had their reasons," Sadie said. "And we haven't given up yet on finding some answers. At least I haven't."

Ann squeezed her hand. "I'm so glad you're in this with me," she said. "At first I thought I might be able to just do this on my own. Can you even imagine?"

"I'll just be glad if there's anything I can do to help," Sadie told her.

Inside Ann's purse, her phone dinged.

"Do you have a text?" Sadie asked.

Ann's brow knit for a minute, then smoothed in recognition. "No," she said. "Actually, that's a reminder I set for myself. I've got to get to another meeting with Roz." She sighed. "This reunion doesn't seem nearly as important to me now as it used to," she said. "But I don't want to let the class down."

Sadie felt a little surge of inward hope. Maybe if Ann could let go of her ideas for the reunion a little bit, she and Roz could finally come to some common ground.

"Well, you better get to the meeting then," Sadie said. "I know Roz is looking forward to working out all the details with you."

"Really?" Ann said, her eyes suddenly hopeful.

Sadie nodded. Roz might not be crazy about Ann's ideas, but she knew that, as the reunion was almost upon them, Roz wanted to come to some agreement with Ann just as much as Ann wanted to come to an agreement with Roz. And it couldn't hurt to give Ann a bit of positive feedback from Roz. Maybe it would keep them both more open in their upcoming conversations.

"And don't worry," Sadie said. "You can go ahead and concentrate on the reunion. I'll still be trying to find out anything I can about the truth about your family."

13

"WHAT ARE YOU WORKING ON, GRANDMA?" SARA ASKED, TRAILING into the back room of the Antique Mine, where Sadie kept treasures she'd discovered that still needed restoration before they could go out on the sales floor. And it was where she often did a bit of restoration herself, as she was doing now.

Sadie looked up from the workbench where she'd been carefully cleaning the gorgeous, tiny panes of glass that made up one of the stained-glass windows on the lower floor of the Parker House. Her mind was still working hard, going over all the details that she'd collected that had anything to do with Ann and her questions. But she'd found that sometimes the best way to solve a problem was to work on something else for a while. And she'd been looking forward to cleaning the Parker House glass ever since she saw it. Glass restoration was one of her favorite projects, because in general it was so simple: just a very careful window washing, with often truly spectacular results as water and a mild soap cleaned away years of grit and grime to reveal the jewel-like windows glinting beneath.

"Take a look for yourself," Sadie said, pulling over a strong light so that the color of the windows would glow brightest.

Sara, at fourteen, wasn't always easy to impress. But at the sight of the riot of beautiful colors the light revealed, she couldn't help but gasp. "Oh, Grandma," she said, "it's so beautiful!"

"Would you like to try?" Sadie said cheerfully, and handed the small soft cloth to her granddaughter.

"What do I do?" Sara asked.

"Just clean it, like you'd clean a window," Sadie said, then drew in her own breath at the eagerness with which Sara pounced on the antique glass. "But gently, gently."

"It's like an amethyst!" Sara breathed as a tiny triangle of deep purple glass was revealed by her careful wiping.

"You did a great job," Sadie said.

"Can I do some more?" Sara asked.

Sadie smiled. It looked like a love of restoring glass might run in the family. "Sure," Sadie said, relinquishing the table to Sara. "I was just thinking about going over to Arbuckle's to get a cup of coffee. Would you like me to get you anything?"

But Sara was already too absorbed in her work to do more than shake her head as Sadie slipped out of the back room and threaded her way through her own store, to the wide door that connected it to Arbuckle's.

Luz, the store owner, smiled at her when she came in. "The regular?" she asked.

Sadie grinned. "You must know me better than myself," she said. "I'm not even sure what my 'regular' is. But whatever it is, I don't want it today. I'm in the mood for something new. Have you got anything interesting on special?"

"Did you have your heart set on a hot drink?" Luz asked.

"Not necessarily," Sadie said.

Luz whipped a large glass pitcher full of a pale amethyst liquid out from under the counter. It looked strangely like the glass that Sara had just uncovered a few moments earlier back in the Antique Mine. "How about a glass of fresh blueberry lemonade?"

"Now, who in the world could turn down an offer like that?" Sadie asked with a smile.

As Luz poured the lemonade into a clear to-go cup, she raised her eyebrows at Sadie. "You just missed Roz," she said.

"She was in here?" Sadie asked.

"Just for a minute, though," Luz said. "She seemed to be in quite a hurry."

"Which way did she go?" Sadie asked, handing Luz a few bills in exchange for the lemonade.

"Thank you," Luz said, sliding the cash register closed. Then she nodded in the direction of Putnam Hardware, which faced the street on the other side of the Antique Mine from Arbuckle's.

"I bet she went over to see Roscoe," Sadie guessed. She waved the lemonade at Luz in farewell. "Maybe I can still catch her."

"Have a good day," Luz called after her.

As soon as Sadie walked into Putnam and Sons Hardware, she could tell that Roz had been there by the expression on Roscoe's face. Roscoe, Roz's husband and the proprietor of Putnam Hardware, wore the same expression Sadie suspected she often did when negotiating with her best friend: one of fondness and admiration, but with a tinge of bewilderment.

"Looking for Roz?" he guessed, as Sadie swung in the door, sipping her lemonade.

"I heard at Arbuckle's she had just come here," Sadie said with a smile. "Are my sources correct?"

"They were correct," Roscoe said with an answering grin. "But I'm afraid your suspect has already fled."

Sadie glanced down the street to see if she could catch a glimpse of her friend. She couldn't.

Roscoe gave her a rueful look. "She was in a bit of a hurry," he said.

Sadie searched his face. "*Hmm*," she said, "do you think our suspect has any nefarious plans up her sleeve? Anything we ought to worry about?"

"Only if your name is Ann Cartwright," Roscoe said.

Sadie rolled her eyes in commiseration. "So you've been hearing all about that too," she said.

"I don't hear about anything else!" Roscoe protested. "It's so strange. You'd think Roz would love the idea of a big party out in a barn, right?"

"It does seem to be right up her alley," Sadie said.

"But I guess this barn is too fancy," Roscoe said.

"My impression is that it's more like a four-star restaurant," Sadie said. "Disguised as a barn. And I guess the pricing is a little rich for Roz's taste."

"More than a little," Roscoe said.

"Do you think we need to send in a rescue party?" Sadie asked, glancing out the window.

Roscoe shook his head. "I wouldn't say we're on a red alert yet," he said. "But I will tell you one thing. I'll be darn glad when this reunion is all over and done with."

"I don't think you'll be the only one," Sadie said. Then, with a smile, she headed back out.

14

Sadie sighed and flipped back to the beginning of Josie's photo album, to start looking through it again. She'd returned to the Parker House after her conversation with Ann, determined to find any evidence she could of a pregnancy that Josie had hidden—or a romance leading up to it.

But if Josie had had a secret romance, she had hidden it well. Sadie had begun by sifting through the box of letters again, starting with the ones the soldier had sent Josie from the front in World War II. But when Sadie looked at them more closely, they didn't appear to be love letters at all. The young man had been a friend of the Parker family apparently—in a few of his letters, he referenced playing together with Josie when they had both been little tykes. He always sounded grateful to receive Josie's letters, but in the first few they were nothing more than affectionate, and in the third Sadie read, he mentioned how much he missed his Sarah, who was apparently a mutual friend of both his and Josie's. It seemed that Josie had just been writing him to keep his spirits up, as something she could do to support the men in uniform who were giving so much.

Sadie scanned through the rest of the dozen or so letters in the batch, to see if they ever took a romantic turn, but as far as she could tell, they never did. And then they broke off, hauntingly, well before the war ended. Sadie tried to tell herself that maybe he had been brought home, safe and sound, before the end of the conflict, but even as she did, she realized how unlikely it was. During World War II, the expectations about military service and leave were very different than in more modern times. Some men didn't see their families for over a year at a time. And when they did come home on a brief leave, they were expected to return to the theater of war almost immediately, and stay there until the conflict was over. If this soldier's letters had stopped before the war was over, it likely meant his own story didn't have a happy ending.

But even if he had returned from the war, the timing of his letters didn't match with Ann's birthday, which was almost ten years later. If he had been a secret romance of Josie's, and their relationship had still been intense enough to result in a daughter, why was there no further evidence of it?

Sadie had also sifted through the rest of the letters, but the vast majority of Josie's personal correspondence had been with women, both friends and relatives. Sadie's heart had beat a little faster when she detected masculine writing on another small pile of letters near the bottom of the box, but she quickly discovered that they were a batch of notes written by an elderly uncle after the death of his wife, when Josie had apparently begun to write him from time to time in hopes of letting him know he wasn't forgotten or alone in the world. After his initial grief, he returned to a boyish love of rocks and caving, and some of his letters were full of beautiful descriptions of cracking open geodes, or spelunking into easily accessible caverns. But they certainly weren't evidence of any kind of romance.

Sadie even sifted through the financial documents again, in case Josie had hidden away any romantic mementos separately from her regular file of correspondence. But just as she remembered, the financial documents were in close to perfect order, without any enlightening clues.

Finally, she'd had the bright idea of looking through the photograph albums again. If she could find any difference in Josie's body type around the time of Ann's birth—or even if there was a mysterious lack of photographs around that time, that might provide some indication that Josie was, in fact, Ann's mother.

Deftly, Sadie turned the pages of the old album, skipping quickly through the 1940s, and the familiar faces of the handsome soldier and a young Lydia, to the early 1950s. With the postwar boom, by the early 1950s, the skirts were wider and made from yards and yards of fabric, often supported by layers and layers of crinolines. Sadie remembered the feel of her own mother's, from when she was just a tiny girl, and the almost spooky way that the starched underskirts seemed to stand up on their own, even after her mother had taken them off for the day.

Just like other women at the time, Josie had adopted the new styles and appeared in the pictures in the classic 1950s skirts. *Could they have been wide enough to hide a pregnancy?* Sadie wondered.

But even as the 1950s skirts had become more and more extravagant, they still featured the same trim waist that had been favored in the wartime designs of the 1940s. And as Sadie flipped through the pictures of Josie, joking with Lydia, opening Christmas presents, standing in a summer garden, in almost every shot, she could clearly see Josie's nipped waist, even as the 1950s skirts billowed around her legs.

As Sadie arrived in late 1952 and early 1953, the months leading up to Ann's birth, she looked at the pictures even more closely. There weren't any outstanding gaps in them: Josie was pictured in a faded color photograph holding an armful of early fall dahlias, wearing some kind of ball gown with fairy wings and surrounded by neighborhood children dressed as ghosts, witches, and cowboys at what Sadie could only guess must have been a Halloween celebration. She stood by a table packed with relatives, proudly holding out a Thanksgiving turkey. She lifted handfuls of tinsel to decorate a Christmas tree. And she had apparently gone outside after what looked to be a record snowfall, to measure the height of the snow against her waist.

Not every shot of Josie offered a clear view of her figure, and whether it was expanding in any telltale way. But Josie's figure was clear enough in enough of them that Sadie was able to see that her figure did not seem to have changed significantly during the entire time leading up to Ann's birth. In a few of the winter photos, Josie had dressed up in men's overalls and a large barn jacket to participate in a snowball fight. But the record snowfall, according to the dates Josie had scrawled under many of the pictures, happened only a few weeks later, and less than a month before Ann was born. And in that picture, Josie had apparently run out of the house without putting on a coat. And she had turned to the side, clearly showing a narrow waist, with the skirt dropping in a flat line neatly to her knees.

Sadie shook her head and closed the photograph album. Then she picked up her phone and picked a favorite number from her list of contacts.

A moment later, Edwin's familiar voice came on the line. "Hello," he said, the pleasure at hearing from her evident in his voice.

"Hello," Sadie said. "I'm calling from the Silver Peak Reunion Committee."

Edwin laughed.

"Yes, I am," she said, keeping her voice brisk and professional. "I'm wondering if you have a few minutes to answer some questions for our class survey."

"Well, I'm not sure about that," Edwin joked, adopting his own businesslike tone to match hers. "I've been extremely successful since high school. So you see, I'm very busy."

"I'm sorry," Sadie said, matching him spar for spar. "Do I have the right number? Is this Edwin *Marshall*?"

"None other," Edwin said. "Why do you ask?"

Sadie ruffled some of the papers on the desk to give the sound effect that she was actually working from some kind of list. "It's just that, according to my notes, you weren't exactly thought of as 'most likely to succeed.'"

This wasn't true, in fact. From the time they were kids, everyone had recognized that Edwin Marshall was likely to do something special. The only question was, what would it be? And given his work ethic and his strong sense of right and wrong, Sadie wasn't even a little surprised that he had turned out to be a circuit court judge. She wouldn't actually have been surprised if he'd turned out to be governor. But it never hurt to give him a little bit of ribbing.

"Well," Edwin said, "you know what they say. Don't judge too soon. I apparently had some qualities that weren't immediately recognized by my fellow teenagers. Although I understand teenagers are quite discriminating judges of character and quality."

Sadie grinned at his barb.

"But I guess, in memory of those golden days gone by, I could spare you a minute or two," Edwin said. "What were your questions?"

Sadie had almost forgotten about her original joke. "Questions?" she asked.

"For your survey."

"Of course," Sadie said. "Our survey. Well, we were just wondering if you could tell us if you've stayed close with any of your class members."

"What do you mean by *close*?"Edwin said in a teasing voice.

Sadie felt herself pleasantly flustered at his teasing tone.

"I have to say," Edwin went on, "I enjoy being in touch with members from my class, *very much*. In fact, some much more than others."

Sadie began to laugh.

"Sadie?" Edwin asked. "Is that you? I had no idea!"

"It's good to laugh," Sadie told him, as her giggles died down.

"Well, that goes without saying," Edwin agreed. But then his voice became more gentle. "But I can tell something's going on with you. Why do you need a laugh?"

Sadie sighed. "It's just...," she said and hesitated.

"It's something you can't tell me about," Edwin guessed. He'd heard this before, and he sounded like he was starting to get used to it.

"I would if it were my secret," Sadie said. "I'd tell you in a minute. But it's not my story to tell. I'm sorry."

"Don't be sorry," Edwin said. "What you're really telling me is that you'll never tell anyone one of my secrets. And that means a lot to me."

"Wait," Sadie said. "You have secrets? Now you're going to have to tell them to me."

Edwin laughed. "Maybe not so many of the deep dark kind," he said. "But still. You don't always want everything you'd tell a close friend circulated all around town. And I know with you, that would never happen."

"I have many flaws," Sadie said, "but you're right. That isn't one of them."

"Well, whatever it is," Edwin said, "it sounds like it's got you down."

"I'm a little frustrated," Sadie admitted. "It's an important question. It matters a lot to someone I care about. And everywhere I turn seems to be a dead end."

"I wish I could talk it over with you," Edwin said. As Sadie took a breath to explain why that was impossible, he reassured her. "I understand that can't happen," he said. "And to be honest, I'm not sure how much help I'd be. You're pretty capable of figuring just about everything out on your own, in my experience."

"I don't seem to be figuring this one out very well," Sadie said.

"Well, it's late in the day," Edwin said. "Maybe you just need to take a break until the morning. Give your mind a rest."

Sadie sighed. "That sounds really good," she said. "It just feels funny to stop working on a problem when we still need an answer."

"Well, I bet your mind will keep working on it, anyway," Edwin said. "But it sure sounds like you've gone about as far as you can go based on what you know now."

"That's true," Sadie said.

"Has Scout been out for a ride recently?" Edwin asked.

Sadie smiled at the thought of her chestnut gelding. Edwin was right. She hadn't ridden him in a few days. And her golden retriever, Hank, hadn't been for anything but the most minimal of walks. Maybe all three of them could stand a break out in the fresh Colorado air.

"That's a good idea," she said.

"I'm full of them," Edwin joked. "It's how I've become such an important and busy man."

"Well, I have to thank you for taking our call today, then," Sadie said, slipping back into the businesslike tone she had used at the beginning of the conversation.

"I'm afraid I'll take your calls just about anytime," Edwin said. "They make my day."

"How is your day going?" Sadie asked him.

"Oh, so far it's great," Edwin said. "I'm setting some new tile in the bathroom. I should probably have left it for a contractor, but I've always wanted to try it myself. And to tell the truth, I got kind of mesmerized by the sight of all these beautiful pieces of glass. I didn't want anyone else to get to play with them. Now there's a secret that I wouldn't like to have spread all over town."

"It's safe with me," Sadie said. "So you're doing all right?"

"I'm doing great!" Edwin said. "I just got a call from the prettiest girl in town. And I'm thinking, if I play my cards right, that I'm going to be able to get her to go to this big dance with me at the end of the week."

"Well, don't let her know you're so sure about that," Sadie said. "Women don't like to be taken for granted, you know."

"Don't I know it," Edwin said. "Especially not this one. She always keeps me on my toes."

"*Hmm*," Sadie said. "That sounds like it might be a lot of work."

"No way," Edwin said. "It's a lot of fun. And even if it was a lot of work, she'd be worth it."

"That's pretty romantic," Sadie said. "Maybe if you tell her that, she'll agree to go to that dance."

"Interesting idea," Edwin said. "I'll try it, and let you know how it goes."

"You do that," Sadie said.

"And you take a break," Edwin said. "Go for a ride. I know you'll come home with a clear mind. And I bet you'll actually come back with a head full of new ideas."

"It's worth a try," Sadie agreed. "It's good to talk with you."

"It's always good to talk with you," Edwin said. "I'll see you soon?"

"Soon," Sadie promised.

Less than half an hour later, she opened the door of her car to let Hank, her rambunctious golden retriever, leap out into the driveway of the property of her friend Milo Henderson's property. Milo's place was only a half mile away from hers, and often she'd make the short walk over with Hank. But even though she needed a break, the sun was setting and time was still of the essence, so this time she'd just popped Hank into the car and made the short drive.

Hank gamboled happily around the car, then made a beeline for the stables, where he knew Scout was boarded. Sadie was never sure if Hank enjoyed her company more, or Scout's. But luckily, Hank never had to choose between them—he always saw plenty of them both. With a smile, Sadie took off after him.

Scout was just as glad to see them as they were to see him, although he was somewhat more dignified than Hank in the way he expressed his pleasure. While Hank practically danced between Scout's hooves, Scout neighed and nuzzled Sadie as she greeted and saddled him.

Shortly, all three of them were trotting along in the early twilight on one of the beautiful trails just beyond Milo's property, Scout with his ears pricked happily as he clopped along, Sadie riding comfortably on his back, and Hank keeping up along beside them, with periodic forays into the underbrush to investigate various points he deemed to be of interest, then galloping up behind them to catch up with horse and rider.

Sadie always felt herself calmed by the sound of the wind rustling through the needles of the Colorado pine, which on this trail surrounded them on every side. She had always loved the Bible verse about how God's Spirit was like the wind: Everyone could hear it, but nobody knew where it came from or where it was going. To Sadie, the sound of wind in the pines always sounded especially like God's voice. Of course, the wind in the pines never said a clear word that she could understand. But she always felt as if it held a special meaning for her anyway. It reminded her of things far beyond her own understanding, but at the same time it offered her a strange comfort—very much the way she felt God often did.

Thank You for this beautiful day, she said. *Thank You for Scout, and thank You for Hank.* And then, instead of asking God for the answers to all the questions surrounding Ann's birth, she remembered the letter in which Paul told the early Christians to be grateful in all circumstances. It wasn't wrong to go to God with her questions and her hurt, she knew. Sometimes that was the only thing she could do. But this time, she decided to thank Him for her problems for a change. *Thank You for all these questions about Ann's birth,* she prayed. *I don't understand why we seem to be running into so many dead ends. And I don't understand how Josie is connected with it. But I thank You that I have the chance to be Ann's friend through this, even if all it means is that she knows she isn't alone during this vulnerable time.*

As she rode Scout down the winding paths between the pines, her mind drifted back to all the questions surrounding Ann and Josie. Was there some chance that she'd missed a change in Josie's figure? She didn't think so, but it might be possible, especially with those big 1950s skirts. But in that case, who would the father have been? Would Josie not have kept even one memento of him? Had she really destroyed all the evidence of his identity?

Her heart tugged when she considered more fully the idea that Josie might be Ann's mother. Even if Josie had thought it was the best thing for Ann to give her up, she must have loved her a great deal. What would it have been like to have Ann grow up in the same town with her, but never be able to acknowledge that she was

Ann's mother? Or was there some other explanation? But what could that be?

At that point, Sadie got stuck again. Everything she'd found so far pointed to Josie's connection with Ann. She hadn't found anything that might connect her with anything, or anyone, else. She was back at another dead end.

Ever since Sadie had started on her work on the Parker House for the Jones family, she had wished that Josie was still around, just to answer this or that little question about what the house had originally been like, or where this or that little item had originally come from. Now she still wanted to talk with her, but for completely different reasons. The questions about the house that had seemed so important paled in comparison with the seriousness of Ann's questions about her identity and parents. If only Josie were still around to answer them. But she couldn't answer questions anymore.

Then, suddenly, Sadie had a flash of insight. Josie might not be around to answer questions anymore. But someone else was. Whom had Josie shared all her secrets with? Who had probably asked her all kinds of questions, and heard all kinds of answers, over the course of decades? Who had perhaps even been there on the very same night that Ann was first put into the arms of the Cartwright family?

Lydia Cameron. And according to her daughter, she was actually eager to talk.

Sadie whistled for Hank, who reluctantly turned back, then romped over to where she'd stopped Scout in his tracks. She wheeled her chestnut mare around and headed for home.

15

THE NEXT MORNING, INSTEAD OF PUSHING THROUGH THE BACK hedge of the Parker House, Sadie parked on the next street over, at the curb of the home where Lydia Cameron had grown up, just a stone's throw from her friend Josie.

As she walked up, Sadie looked at the rambling old home, with its wide Victorian porch, neatly painted gray wooden siding, red roof, and accents of marine blue at the doors and window frames. It wasn't quite as unique as the Parker House, but it was still a remarkable example of Victorian architecture—and even more important, it gave the feeling so many Victorian houses did, of being a haven for a family, a real home.

At her knock, she could hear footsteps inside almost immediately. Then Carol swung the door open with a questioning look. When she recognized Sadie, she beamed.

"Sadie!" she said. "It is Sadie, isn't it?"

Sadie nodded, but Carol was already going on, and pulling her into the house, as if she was afraid Sadie might escape if she didn't act quickly. "I'm so glad you came back, and so soon. I mentioned to Mom that you'd been here, and she's been worrying over it ever since. She can't think of anything she'd rather do than help you with the Parker House renovation, and she was concerned that if you didn't have her perspective, it would never be right. And she couldn't quite believe that I hadn't managed to get your phone number, or give you ours, when we met. So it's a very good thing you've come back to help me out of the doghouse, in her estimation."

"Well, I'm glad to do anything I can in that respect," Sadie said. "But I'm sure she'll be much more help to me than I can be to any of you."

"Carol?" a voice called from a nearby room. "Who is it? Did my new yoga pants arrive? I tracked them on the Internet this morning and they were scheduled to arrive by end of business today."

"Even better, Mom," Carol called, leading Sadie down a lovely Victorian hall.

"Better than yoga pants?" Lydia called. "I'll have to see that to believe it."

As Carol and Sadie reached a room at the end of the hall, Carol glanced back to welcome Sadie to follow her, then ducked in. Sadie stepped in after her.

It was a cozy sunroom, still decorated, Sadie noticed quickly, with what were likely some of the original furnishings: fine but not showy specimens of Victorian wing chairs, couch, and end tables, all surrounded by remarkably well-preserved pale green velvet-flocked wallpaper.

"This is Sadie Speers," Carol said with a smile.

Lydia, who had been sitting in one of the wing chairs, laid aside the magazine on her lap and stood spryly to greet Sadie. "Lydia Cameron," she said. "I'm awfully glad to meet you. Carol let me know that you'd been by, and I apparently didn't train her very well as a social secretary. We had no way to get in touch with you and let you know how much I was looking forward to any way I could help with your renovation of the Parker House."

Sadie took her hand and shook it warmly. "It's so nice to meet you," she said. "And I'm so grateful that you're willing to talk with me."

"You may not feel that way after I'm done," Lydia said. "I tend to have a lot to say." She winked and nodded toward the nearby couch, where Sadie sat down.

"Can I get either of you anything?" Carol asked from the door.

"I'm fine," Sadie said. "Thank you for asking."

Lydia shook her head and gestured toward a mug decorated with violets on the table beside her. "I've got my morning tea," she said. "Thank you, dear."

"Well, I've got a loaf of bread half-kneaded in the kitchen that won't be much of a loaf if I don't finish it," Carol said. "So if you two will excuse me..."

As Carol disappeared, Lydia took her own seat again, and leaned in confidentially toward Sadie on the couch. "Now, my dear," she said. "Tell me everything. What are you working on over there? I know that place just as well as I know my own, I think. Maybe even better. In your own home, you get so used to things that you barely see them anymore. But I bet I remember just about every detail of Josie's place."

At the mention of Josie's name, a flicker of sadness passed over her face. "You know, I still miss her every day," she said.

"I'm sure you do," Sadie said. "As I understand it, you were friends pretty much your entire lives."

"Well," Lydia said with a twinkle in her eye, "I used to tell Josie it was for *her* entire life. I was born almost six months before she was. So I was around for half a year before she even existed. When we were kids, I used to torment her with that mercilessly. But at some point, being the older one didn't seem like the winning card anymore."

She laughed, and Sadie laughed along with her.

"But I was born right here in this house. Since times were more 'modern' by the time Josie came along, she was born in the hospital, but she came home from the hospital right to the Parker House. And that afternoon, my mom brought me by with a basket full of warm rolls and peach jam. That was the first time Josie and I ever met. And I like to think we've been friends ever since."

The same shadow crossed over her face a moment later. "Even now," she said quietly.

"I don't think a friendship like the one you had with Josie ever ends," Sadie agreed.

At this, Lydia's customary smile reappeared. "You're exactly right," she said. "I might have beat her to the punch on being born, but she beat me to the punch on going to heaven. That's all. She's just going to have to find a way to amuse herself up there until I get there too."

She folded her hands in a "Let's get to work" gesture. "I told you I have a lot to say," she said. "But that's not what you came to talk about. I'm so glad the Jones family has taken such an interest in the place. It would have been terrible to see it go to neighbors who didn't realize what a treasure they had."

"They certainly understand that they've got a gem," Sadie said. "It's been a real pleasure to work with them. Charlene, in particular. I think she may know just as much as I do about some varieties of antiques. Sometimes even more. But they're not just collectors. They've got a real love for that house. And for the history of the Parker family."

"Well, it's a long history," Lydia said. "And an interesting one."

"That's what I've been finding," Sadie said, glad for the opportunity to delve into the Parker family history, instead of getting lost in the details of the restoration process. But she still knew she needed to tread carefully. Whatever secrets Josie had been hiding surrounding Ann's birth and the missing money, she believed she had carried to her grave. And Lydia was still clearly fiercely loyal to her longtime friend. She might not be too eager to spread around information that Josie had hoped to keep secret. If she even knew anything for certain.

"And as I've been working through the history, I've become especially interested in Josie," Sadie said.

"She was interesting, all right," Lydia said.

"She seems like such a remarkable woman," Sadie said. "She supported herself fully, working her own job."

"She loved that job," Lydia said. "She used to tell me that she liked doing the numbers so much that she would have paid them to let her do it. It was all like a puzzle to her. But it had some real-life consequences too. She loved finding ways to help people pay their bills over time, or make it possible for them to do projects they couldn't have done otherwise. You know how the lumber company will give people loans in order to complete their projects?"

Sadie nodded.

"There's almost no other lumber company in the country that offers anything like it," Lydia said. "But it was Josie's idea. She set the whole thing up, and she did it with just a few customers at first, to make sure it would really work. The way she saw it, in a town this size, she knew a lot of people they could trust to make their payments on time, even though it wasn't a very traditional loan. At first the owner was skeptical. But it turned out to bring a big increase in business."

"That's wonderful," Sadie said. "Now, I understand you lived in town for most of your life."

Lydia nodded. "I did quite a bit of traveling, with my husband, for business. That took us all over the world, for a while, until he retired. But this was our home base."

"And what about Josie?" Sadie asked. "I know she made her own way, even though she never married. But that was so unusual for her time. One of the things I've been curious about is why she never had a family."

Lydia nodded. "You know, I think she might have wondered about that herself," she said. "At least for a while. But it's interesting. Since she never had one of her own, she had some perspective on it. Families bring some people a lot of happiness. But they don't always. And Josie had plenty of love and friendship and meaning in her life, even if she didn't have a husband and kids. I wouldn't trade my own life story for the world. But I do have to say that sometimes, as a wife and mom, I was actually jealous of her, with all her freedom. I can say one thing, though. If she did wonder about it, she never let it slow her down. Or distract her from doing anything else she wanted to do."

"Did she ever have any kind of romance in her life?" Sadie asked. "Even if it didn't blossom into a marriage?"

Lydia smiled. "Oh, here and there. In high school, just like any girls, we both had our crushes. And Josie went out on dates, just like everyone else. But a big affair of the heart? Are you asking if she never married because of the one who got away? I wouldn't say so, no. It's just that the right man for Josie never seemed to come along."

"I'm curious about something else," Sadie said. "It doesn't have as much to do with the house, but it does relate to Josie."

"Oh?" Lydia said. "What is that?"

Help me know how to put this, Lord, Sadie prayed quickly, before she dove in. "Well, I have a good friend who is in town for the reunion this weekend," she said. "It's a little odd, but I'm trying to help her with some family history too, because of the research I'm doing on the Parker House. You see, it seems that she was adopted. And apparently Josie was somehow involved with that adoption."

Sadie could see recognition flash instantly in Lydia's eyes, but just as she suspected, Lydia still seemed very protective of her friend. Her face, which had been so friendly since Sadie entered the room, was suddenly wary and guarded.

Since Lydia was already on guard, Sadie thought, she might as well lay her own cards out on the table. "My friend is Ann Cartwright," she said. "The Cartwrights' daughter."

"I know the Cartwrights," Lydia said. That came as no surprise in a town this size.

Sadie nodded. "Good," she said. "Well, I spoke with Ann Cartwright's older brother, and he told me that he remembered a night around the time she was born. There was a woman there who fit Josie's description that night. She had short dark hair, which would have been unusual at the time."

"Yes," Lydia said, nodding, "she did."

Encouraged by Lydia's willingness to share even this small detail, Sadie pressed on. "But he also said there was another woman there," she said. "Since I know how close you two were, I thought she might have been you. Or at least that you might know something that could shed some light on all of this."

"I'm not sure that's something I want to talk about," Lydia said.

Sadie nodded to show she had heard and understood. "But you do remember it?" she concluded. "You were the woman who was there."

Lydia didn't say anything, clearly feeling torn by her loyalty to her friend.

"I know you don't want to betray anything that Josie wouldn't have wanted the world to know," Sadie said. "But I'm not asking you to tell the world. My friend only found out recently that she was adopted. It's been a big shock to her, and to her brother. I'm just hoping that having some answers can help them have some peace, and move on. I'm not asking you to tell everyone any secret of Josie's. I'm just hoping you might know something that might help this family understand their own history."

Lydia took a deep breath. "Are you thinking that Josie is Ann's mother?" she asked.

Sadie didn't nod or shake her head. "That was one of the possibilities that did cross my mind," she said.

"That's impossible," Lydia said decisively. "I saw Josie almost every day that winter. She never would have gone through something like that without telling me. And even if she had tried to, I would have noticed."

Sadie nodded. "Well, if you spent most evenings with Josie, were you with her that night? Did you ever go to the Cartwrights' with her?"

Lydia wavered visibly, glancing around the room and running her hand nervously through her neatly curled hair.

"Would you at least be willing to share with my friend why you two were there on the night she was born?" Sadie asked.

At this, Lydia's shoulders drooped in surrender. She shook her head and met Sadie's eyes. "I never knew myself," she said. "In fact, I didn't know that it was anybody's birthday, that day. And I promise you, I didn't see any baby."

Sadie's eyebrows leapt in surprise. "Would you tell me," she asked, still treading carefully, "what happened that night?"

Lydia sighed. "We were playing cards together," she said. "When my children were little ones, after I got them in bed, sometimes I'd leave my husband at home, to give him a little time to putter around on his own, and go over and play a few hands of cards with Josie. I just ducked right through the hedge, like we had done all our lives."

She smiled at the memory. But then her expression clouded. "It was so strange. We were right in the middle of a game. We'd just started, actually. And I had a great hand. So when she got a phone call in the middle of it, as she went to take it I teased her that she could delay the inevitable, but that she couldn't prevent it—no matter when she came back to the table, I was still going to win that round."

She flashed another quick smile. "But when she came back, she said she had to go."

"Was that unusual?" Sadie asked.

"Unusual? For her to give up in the middle of a card game, and wander out into the night at ten o'clock? I'd say so. But you want to know what was even more unusual?" Lydia asked.

Sadie nodded, prompting her to go on, and praying that she wouldn't stop now.

"She wouldn't tell me where she was going."

"No?" Sadie said.

"No!" Lydia repeated, still slightly incensed after all these years. "I'm talking about a woman whom I'd shared every secret with for the past twenty-odd years. Hers and mine. And all of a sudden, she couldn't be bothered to tell me the simple fact of what could possibly be so important that she needed to drop everything and rush out into the night."

"So you asked her?" Sadie said.

"I didn't just ask her," Lydia said. "I told her. I figured, if there was something she didn't want to tell me, it must be bad, one way or another. She'd gotten into some kind of trouble. And I tried and tried to get her to tell me what it was."

"What did she say?" Sadie asked.

"She told me it wasn't her secret to tell."

Sadie nodded. If Josie hadn't been Ann's mother, in fact, then it wouldn't have been her secret to tell. And at that time, it would have been a big secret to keep.

"Then how did you wind up going out to the Cartwrights' with her?" Sadie asked.

"I just wouldn't take no for an answer," Lydia said, her chin lifting with pride, and a hint at the fight she would have been able to put up as a younger woman. "I told her I could see she was in some kind of trouble. She didn't have to tell me what it was. That was her business. But it didn't matter to me what she was dealing with. Friends were friends, no matter what. And I wasn't about to let my friend go out into the night herself all alone. She could either take me with her, or I was going to stand in the driveway and she'd have to roll her car over me to get out."

"It sounds like you were...determined," Sadie said.

"That's one word for it," Lydia said. "But she didn't test it. She just let me in the car."

"And did you go right out to the Cartwright ranch?" Sadie asked.

"Straight there," Lydia said. "I might not have recognized it in the dark, but I recognized the Cartwrights when they came to the door."

"What did they say?"

Lydia shrugged and shook her head. "When they saw me, Mrs. Cartwright looked almost afraid," she said. "Josie asked me if I'd be willing to stay on the porch while she went in and talked to them. And since I didn't think she'd be in any danger from the Cartwrights, I agreed."

"So you didn't hear anything at all," Sadie mused.

Lydia nodded. "That's right," she said. "I asked Josie about it once more, in the car on the way home. She was adamant that she couldn't tell me. So I made her promise me that she wasn't in any trouble herself. She promised me that. I never asked her about it again. And she never told me."

"And you never learned anything more about it?" Sadie asked.

"I heard the Cartwright family had a little girl right around that time," Lydia said. "I always wondered if it might have had something to do with that. But Josie had made it very clear that it wasn't something she could talk about. So I never pressed. But now you tell me that Ann isn't the Cartwrights' biological daughter..." She trailed off.

"Do you remember anything else about that night?" Sadie asked. "Anything at all?"

Lydia shook her head. "Not about that night," she said. "I told you everything I remember. But I do remember something else."

Sadie raised her eyebrows, listening.

"The fireplace grate," Lydia said.

Sadie's ears pricked up. "With the fleur-de-lis decorations?" she asked.

Lydia nodded. "I don't know if you've noticed that one is missing," she said.

Sadie nodded. "In fact," she said. "I think I know where it went."

"You do?" Lydia said, surprised.

"My friend has it," she said. "She wears it as a necklace."

Lydia smiled, her eyes bright with something suspiciously like tears. "So she *was* telling the truth," she said. "I just couldn't believe it."

"Believe what?" Sadie asked.

"Well, that piece had been loose for a while," Lydia said. "It got broken while she was taking a big delivery of wood one winter. Snapped right off when a big log fell against it." She gave a wry laugh. "I think Josie must have tried just about everything to stick it back on again, but it never stayed for long. It was one of our running jokes, when we had our card games. And then one day, it was gone. Just after I made her take me out to the Cartwright ranch with her."

Sadie nodded. "That would make sense."

"I asked her about it," Lydia said. "Around that time, I was so worried about her, I wouldn't take any of her excuses for an answer. Finally, she told me there'd been a baby in the house who wouldn't stop crying. She was at her wits' end until she picked up the broken fleur-de-lis piece from the mantel and handed it to her. Then the baby settled right down. So she let her keep it.

"I didn't really believe Josie when she told it to me," Lydia said. "We didn't have any new babies in our circles. I would have known about it. And she wouldn't tell me whose baby it was. She was so vague about it. Just a 'visitor,' she said." Lydia looked away wistfully.

"So that's how Ann came to have that ornament," Sadie said. "Her mother told her it was a family heirloom."

"Well, I guess it was, in a way," Lydia said with a smile.

Sadie grinned back at her.

"And one other thing," Lydia said.

"What's that?" Sadie asked, leaning forward.

"That wasn't the only time Josie got a call she wouldn't explain," Lydia said.

"No?" Sadie said. "When else do you remember her taking a strange call?"

"Several times," Lydia said. "They were usually later in the evening. But whenever the phone rang, she'd jump right up to get it. Sometimes she'd stop the caller after a few words, and go take the call in the kitchen, out of my earshot."

"And she never explained them?" Sadie asked.

"It was just like with the visit to the Cartwright ranch," Lydia said. "I asked her the first time she got one, and maybe the second time. But she said she couldn't tell me, and I could tell it bothered her that I kept asking. So finally, I just stopped."

"Do you remember anything else about those calls at all?" Sadie asked.

"They didn't happen all the time," Sadie said. "Really only for a while after Ann was born. Maybe ten years?"

Sadie nodded.

"That's all I remember," Lydia said. "Oh! Except for one other thing."

Sadie watched her closely.

"After she made the calls," Lydia said.

"Did she do something special?" Sadie asked.

Lydia nodded. "Every time I heard her get one of these strange calls," she said, "Josie never came straight back to our games."

"What did she do instead?" Sadie asked.

"She always made a stop first," Lydia said. "In the conservatory. You must know it. The room with the fireplace."

16

"SADIE!" ROZ SAID. "YOU'RE NOT GOING TO BELIEVE THIS. HAVE you been praying for me and this reunion? Because I think God has been answering your prayers."

Sadie raised her eyebrows as she adjusted the phone against her ear, squinting in the sun. She'd just driven her car around the block to return to the Parker House after her conversation with Lydia, and Roz had caught her just as she pulled up outside it.

"That's great!" Sadie said. Roz was right: she had sent up a prayer or two for some sort of resolution to the snarl Roz and Ann had gotten into over the reunion. But she wasn't totally sure that Roz would be so happy over the kind of compromise Sadie had had in mind. "What's going on?"

"Well," Roz said, "I had a meeting with Ann earlier. And she wasn't nearly as hard to deal with as she had been. It was like some of the fight just...went out of her. I finally felt like she was actually listening to what I had to say."

Sadie felt a little twinge as Roz said this. Of course, she couldn't blame Roz for being glad that she and Ann seemed to be communicating at last. But since she knew so much more of Ann's story than Roz did, she was aware of how difficult the last few days—and even the last few months—had been for Ann. She knew of all the things that might have made Ann seem unreasonable to Roz, and also of everything that had gone on in the past day in Ann's life to distract her from the reunion. It made Sadie wonder how much she herself missed about what was going on in the lives of people around her. Although her life was full of good things and joy, it was also full of pressures and worries, and sometimes genuine trouble. The same was true for all of the people she knew and loved best. But so often, she forgot that it must be true for everyone else in the world too.

"I'm so glad to hear it," Sadie said.

"Yikes!" Roz yelped on the other end of the line.

"Roz?" Sadie asked. "Are you okay?"

"Yes, fine," Roz said, slightly out of breath. "I probably shouldn't be driving while I'm on my phone. Silver Peak isn't exactly Denver, but there are still some crazy drivers out there."

Sadie smiled. Knowing Roz's driving, that was probably exactly what the other driver she'd just passed was saying too. "You can't ever be too safe," she said.

"Listen, I'm sorry to call and run, but I'm about to pull up at the fabric store. You can pray that they've got a hundred yards of tulle on hand."

"A hundred yards?" Sadie said. "Of tulle?" This was quite a departure from Roz's vision of pizza in the parking lot, but she wasn't eager to fan the embers of Roz and Ann's argument back into flame by pointing that out.

"It's a small concession," Roz said. "In the larger battle. Trust me. I'm playing the long game."

"Okay," Sadie said, somewhat bewildered.

"Oh, here we are," Roz said. Over the phone, Sadie could hear her car purr into what was probably a parking spot, then shut off. "I'll call you later. I was just so excited, I couldn't wait to tell you the good news."

"Well, Ann's always been a good friend," Sadie said, hoping again that if she reminded Roz of this enough, it might sink in. "I was pretty sure you two would be able to work it out."

"That means you were a lot more sure of it than I was," Roz said. "But we'll take what we can get. And for now, that means a hundred yards of tulle."

"I can't wait to see it," Sadie said.

"You'll see it sooner than I wish," Roz said. "We've barely got any time to put this thing together now."

"It's going to be amazing," Sadie said. "I know it."

"How do you know that?" Roz asked.

"Because I know you," Sadie said.

"See?" Roz said. "I knew there was a reason I called you."

"I'm glad you did," Sadie said.

"See you," Roz said, and ended the call.

Sadie slipped the phone back into her purse, got out of the car, and went up to the house. But this time, after she let herself in, she didn't head upstairs to the office, where Josie had kept all of her private financial books and papers, or the attic, where the extra collection of personal effects had been stored. Instead, she turned into the room with the fireplace.

It was one of the few rooms in the house that hadn't yet been touched by the contractors who were already busy on renovations in other rooms, because it was Charlene's favorite room in the whole home, and she'd wanted to keep as much of the original furnishings as possible. So although they'd already made some decisions about the renovation before Sadie joined them as a consultant, they'd held this one until now, so that she could identify the provenance of everything from the small writing desk to the built-in bookshelves, the furniture, and even the ornate mantle over the fireplace.

Sadie had spent some time making an original appraisal of the room's contents, and taking notes that would allow her to find a more precise provenance for some of the pieces she recognized, or look up ones that were as yet totally unfamiliar to her. The built-in bookshelves were especially interesting to her, with beautiful carving on the narrow lips of the shelves that faced into the room, mostly floral patterns, but with a few details that seemed to give a nod to early Colorado history: a pair of horses grazing before a mountain in the distance, and what seemed to be the opening of a silver mine.

Sadie had never seen anything like it before, and she was very curious to find out if it had been carved in place or bought somewhere else, perhaps in a big city like Denver, and installed later. And she also wondered whether it was one of a kind, or if she'd discover a whole world full of carved bookcases when she began to investigate: perhaps a company that specialized in them, or maybe even a movement among individual craftsmen, all inspired by another craftsman's work, but adding their own touch to it when they imitated and expanded on the original idea.

This was one of Sadie's favorite things about working with antiques: No matter how much she knew, there was always something more to learn. And often something that seemed like a delightful oddity was actually a door to a whole realm of antiques she'd never been exposed to before. She'd pick up an interestingly carved nickel at an antique show, and discover that it was just one representative of a whole art form, practiced first by the American hobos during the bleakest years of the dust bowl and Great Depression. They spent the time they had on their hands carving new faces and images out of the profile of the Native American and the buffalo who graced either side of the buffalo nickel. In fact, the tradition persisted into the present day, kept alive by artists who carved all manner of things into the tiny coins: women's faces, flowers, memories of lost loved ones, even superheroes. She never knew when the act of picking up a new curiosity would introduce her to a whole new world.

But although Sadie had done a thorough inventory of the pieces in the conservatory, she hadn't been searching for any kind of secret in the pieces themselves. Now she began to execute a different kind of search. Instead of trying to identify when and where the writing table might have been built, and what kind of condition it was in, she opened each drawer, sifted through any stray papers that were still inside, peered into the cubbyholes designed to store mail, and even spent some time knocking on the various drawers and comparing the thickness of the wooden sides to the width of the space within a drawer, to see if they might have false bottoms.

But whoever had collected the family papers seemed to have thoroughly scoured this desk as well, already: She found nothing other than a small scrap of wrapping paper that had been wadded up in the back of one of the smaller drawers.

She then began a careful circuit of the room, checking anything else that might have provided a hiding place for whatever

Josie slipped into the room to find after receiving her mysterious phone calls. Sadie inspected each cushion of the chairs, checking for any splits or evidence of repairs in the material, and she even ran her hands over the wooden supports and backs, to see if anything of interest, no matter how small, had been fixed to any of them. Her heart skipped a beat when she discovered a piece of curling paper under the seat of a delicate rocker with handmade needle-point upholstery. But when she carefully turned it over to see what it was, she found only the manufacturer's name and address, along with a cheerful advertisement on the health benefits of rocking chairs. With a sigh, Sadie set it back down where it had been.

Since the furniture itself hadn't yielded any secrets, Sadie circled the room again, keeping her eyes on the molding, the flooring, any imperfections in the plaster walls. She even knocked across all four walls. A few places sounded more hollow than others, but that was to be expected with the studs and airspaces of an old house, and none of the hollow places presented any kind of access that she could make out.

Sadie's eyes finally came to rest again on the fireplace, which stood directly opposite her. It was the only place, she realized, that she hadn't thoroughly searched. Thankfully, it had been well-cleaned of ashes, so she wasn't in danger of winding up covered with soot, like a hapless Santa Claus. But although she didn't risk smudging her clothes as she searched it, it didn't give up any secrets either. The brickwork of the fireplace itself was solid, with the mortar still intact, though smoke-stained. The mantel was made of one imposing piece of red marble and fastened securely to the wall, with no room for papers, or anything else, to be slipped under a loose stone.

Even the grate itself, with the missing fleur-de-lis decoration that had provided one of the first clues of Ann's possible connection with the home, didn't have any other light to shed on the situation. Its grillwork was too open and delicate to hide anything. It had only been designed to set off the dancing light of the flames within, not to conceal secrets.

With a sigh, Sadie let her hand drop to the fireplace grate, her fingers trailing over the missing place where the fleur-de-lis that now graced Ann's necklace had originally broken off. To her surprise, the slight gesture caused the whole grate to move, far more than such a light touch should have moved it. And strangely, even though it had bumped out a full inch or two from the fireplace, it still seemed to be closely attached to the stone that surrounded the mouth of the fireplace.

Sadie knelt down to get a closer look. Had the metal frame somehow expanded, like the gates that protected the doors and windows of storefronts in some big cities? Had something actually come loose from the stone, which a minute ago had seemed so solid? Or was she just imagining things? Had she even really seen what she thought she'd seen?

Even with her face level to the grate, Sadie still had difficulty figuring out what had happened. She peered at the whorls and curlicues of the grate, and at the smooth stone of the fireplace, without any flash of insight—until she reached out to touch the place where the grate connected to the stone.

When she did this, she realized that an entire brick of the buff-colored rock that surrounded the fireplace had pulled loose from the others, still attached to the screen. Sadie reached for the broken piece of grating, and when she did, another inch or two of the rock pulled free from the wall.

Apparently it was a hidden mechanism of some kind, with the grating, especially at the point where the ornament had broken off, acting as the fulcrum of a lever that pried the stone free from those around it.

Sadie scrambled over to the stone. With a few more tugs, it came completely free from the wall, still attached to the grating, which tipped slightly under the weight of the brick. Sadie steadied it by leaning it up against the wall. Then she peered into the space the brick had left open when she pulled it free.

She could see nothing but darkness beyond the small patch of light that fell into the space from the ambient light in the room. She gave her eyes a minute to get used to the darkness, hoping that something in the space might emerge, but even after a long count, she saw nothing but a black hole.

She wasn't crazy about the idea of sticking her hand into a hole without first having any idea what was in it. But she also wasn't about to give up on finding out what was in it, if anything. So after steeling herself with the idea that the space was *probably* so well-sealed and dark that it *probably* couldn't host any creepy-crawly creatures, she put her hand inside.

At first she felt nothing, just the cool, smooth surface of the stone, very much like the face of the fireplace itself. But then, as she pushed her fingers gingerly back beyond the footprint of the removed brick, she realized there was an entire chamber beyond it, quite a bit bigger than the brick itself. In fact, she couldn't reach her hand to the back of the space. It seemed to be some kind of fissure in the rock itself.

But reaching to the back of the chamber, and even the presence of creepy-crawly creatures, quickly lost their place as her chief concerns. Because as she spread her hand out, trying to get the measure of the chamber, it brushed against something else: a sheaf of papers that, with another touch, she realized were contained in a card stock file folder, very much like the ones that held all the papers Josie had kept so perfectly organized in her upstairs office.

Sadie fumbled around in the darkness, realizing slowly, by touch, that the file she'd first discovered was not the only one, but rather the top of a small pile of folders. With some struggle, she managed to curl one up on itself and squeeze her own hand to a size that would allow her to draw a file out from the cramped hiding space.

She shook a thin film of dust off of it. The card stock folder was the color of a stormy blue sky, mottled and faded by age. The back was perfectly unmarked, but when she flipped it over, there was one of Josie's familiar adhesive labels, written in Josie's familiar handwriting.

It read, "Young Transportation."

17

A FEW MINUTES LATER, SADIE SAT DOWN AT JOSIE'S OLD OFFICE desk, with a pile of half a dozen identical blue folders in front of her.

They seemed, as she opened one after another, to contain similar pieces of information: hand-scrawled notes, names, addresses, dates, and numbers. None of the files contained more than a few pieces of paper. And none of the papers were any kind of official document, just Josie's own notes, taken in her own familiar handwriting.

But as Sadie sifted through them, she recognized that Josie's strong organizational instincts had been at work even here. Each file contained bits and scraps of information. But each also contained one identical page, which seemed to be a kind of record that Josie had invented herself, for her own purposes, even though it didn't bear the seal of any official business or institution.

Sadie pulled one of them free to study it more closely. Almost immediately, she realized she was looking at a file that somehow related to a child. A first name, Moses, was written at the top of the file. Below that were two fields labeled *M* and *F*. The *M* field was filled, but the *F* field was blank.

Despite the fact that they were labeled with initials only, it only took a minute for Sadie to recognize what they must be: spots to name the mother and father of a child. But besides the name at the top of the file, everything else was heavily coded. The letters next to the *M* were a scrambled mess that didn't resolve into any actual word that Sadie could read. Below the *M* and *F* fields were three lines that were clearly space for an address, but they were also filled with something that, at least at first glance, read as nonsense. Below that was a series of numbers, in a familiar grouping of three and four that obviously indicated a phone number, but instead of numbers, the spaces were filled with letters.

She was already starting to decipher even more of the handmade form itself. Strangely, it seemed to be duplicated, with a similar column on the right-hand side as the left, with another section for mother and father. *Is it a birth certificate?* Sadie wondered, her skin prickling. For all the guesses she'd made about Josie's connection with Ann, this was the first evidence of what might actually have happened all those years ago.

But why would any child's birth certificate need fields for two sets of parents?

Her heart beating faster, Sadie looked from one side of the sheet to the next, and back again. Josie hadn't been Ann's mother, she realized. Josie had been running some kind of underground adoption agency. That was why she had been so involved with the circumstances surrounding Ann's birth—although she had showed no signs of pregnancy herself.

And each of these files must relate to a different child.

So which of the files is Ann's? Sadie wondered.

Quickly, she flipped through each file, scanning the names for any clue. But it soon became clear that the names given to each child likely hadn't been ones they kept into adulthood. Along with Moses, there was a Blue, a Hopeful, a Lion, and a Jiminy Cricket. Even more frustratingly, in every file, those names were the only thing that Sadie could read at first glance. Everything else seemed to be in the same indecipherable code as the first file she had studied closely, nothing but an unreadable jumble of letters and numbers.

But then Sadie realized something else. The numbers, at least some of them, weren't all indecipherable. The phone numbers were, translated into garbled letters. But some numbers were arranged in three groups of two, set off by slashes, which seemed to be dates. And the dates on the forms seemed, at least at first glance, to be in the ballpark of the year of Ann's birth: the early 1950s.

Thank You, Sadie prayed, grateful for even the slightest break in what otherwise seemed like a totally impossible puzzle.

But when she went back through the files, searching for one that matched the dates of Ann's birth, she couldn't find anything that came close. She went through a second time, thinking perhaps she'd missed one in her excitement, but she only confirmed what she'd discovered the first time through: none of the dates were within even six months of Ann's birth.

Did I leave a file back in the fireplace? Sadie wondered. But she had carefully searched the space before bringing the files upstairs, pushing her hand, despite her fear of creepy-crawly things, all the way to a back wall, and brushing it over the horizontal surface as well, to make sure she hadn't missed anything. It was true that anything could have happened in the darkness, and she hadn't actually shone a light back there to be sure, but it would have been hard for a file the size of the ones she had before her to escape her notice. And the hiding space, built out of precisely fitted rock, didn't exactly seem to have a lot of nooks and crannies for a file to fall into and get lost.

More likely, Sadie reasoned, Ann's file was there on the table, and after all this work, she still couldn't recognize it. Perhaps, she realized, even the dates were in code: just one made out of numbers rather than letters. But she didn't have any more idea how to crack a numerical code than she did an alphabetical one.

Her eyes trailed down the page, looking for anything else she might possibly be able to make sense of, without any luck. It seemed to be just a dizzying collection of letters and numbers so chaotic that they didn't even seem to be in another language, but to be scrambled up out of no language at all.

But then she realized there was one other piece that she could recognize. At the bottom of each page was a set of numbers and dates, arranged in an accounting system grid that was probably second nature and virtually irresistible to Josie after all her years keeping the precise books she had been so proud of at the lumber company. They weren't full ledgers, but the simple order of dates, credits, and debits was still recognizable, even though each page only recorded a handful of transactions, if that was what they could be called.

Furthermore, Sadie realized with a jolt of excitement, the numbers were familiar. So familiar, she thought, that they might not even be in code. She couldn't tell with a single glance, but the numbers were very similar to the ones that she had pored over in Josie's original filing system, the checks that had been written from the lumber company to Young Transportation. And these files showed identical numbers leaving the Young Transportation accounting system as cash withdrawals, at almost the same intervals that Sadie remembered the deposits and debits appearing in Josie's personal accounts.

Could these amounts be the only pieces of information on these entire strange "birth certificates" that weren't impenetrably shrouded in Josie's personal code?

Sadie cast through the papers and files now spread across the desk, sifting through the new layer of Young Transportation files to find the ones she had been working on in previous days, which included the list Amanda had given her at the lumber company, of the unexplained debits to Young Transportation that she had discovered when she went over the books after Josie's death.

Just a few minutes later, she had Amanda's list laid out beside the stack of blue folders, comparing the dates and amounts of Amanda's list to the amounts on the first handmade birth certificate.

Almost instantly, she found the first match: a debit from Amanda's list that exactly matched the amount on one of the children's files. Quickly, she matched the rest of the files to every single one of the debits on Amanda's list. So Ann's file was likely among them. But how to find it?

Sadie scanned back and forth between Amanda's list and the dates on the children's "certificates." It was clear that the checks had been drawn down around the time of each child's adoption—probably to provide necessary funds to protect and provide for each young mother, Sadie guessed. Just as she'd suspected, there was no perfect match for the dates. She hadn't necessarily expected that: There was no reason that Josie would have made the deposit to her account the exact date that she drew the funds down from the lumber company—although if anybody would have been that precise with their bookkeeping, it would have been Josie, she reflected wryly.

Instead, she'd been looking for dates within a few days of the actual checks Josie had written from the lumber company accounts. Although Josie might not have deposited them that same day, surely she wouldn't have left them uncashed for weeks at a time, let alone an entire financial cycle. That wouldn't fit with her personal attention to detail. And even more important, since she was using the checks to embezzle from the lumber company, any irregularity with them would make her far more likely to be discovered, either by some curious clerk at the bank, or by someone else within the leadership of the lumber company.

But the dates on the ledgers in the certificates didn't seem to match the dates of the actual checks at all, although the amounts matched so perfectly.

Again, Sadie scanned from the ledger to the files, which she'd laid out side by side so she could get a look at all of them in a single glance. The first deposit she'd managed to match was dated July 9, 1951, but the date in the certificate ledger was more than a year later, on August 10, 1952.

Had Josie shifted the dates by a standard amount of time? Sadie wondered. *Perhaps she added a certain number of months to all of the dates?* But it wasn't an even number of months, she realized. The days had also changed.

She checked the next file. This time, the actual deposit was made on December 1, 1954, but the date in the certificate ledger was only a month later, on January 2, 1955. The next file she looked at referred to a deposit made April 18, 1956, but the matching certificate ledger listed it as May 19, 1957.

Suddenly, Sadie saw the pattern. Josie hadn't used any unbreakable cipher. She'd simply added 1 to all the numbers in the dates: 7/9/51 became 8/10/52; 3/18/56 became 4/19/57. She'd just been momentarily thrown by the fact that when Josie added 1 to 12, for the December date, she'd gone back to the beginning of the year, and chosen January, the first month, since there wasn't a thirteenth month. So 12/1/54 had become 1/2/55.

Suddenly, all the deposits and their dates made perfect sense. But Sadie's glance didn't rest on them with the satisfaction of her discovery. Instead, her gaze drifted up the page, to the date that she suspected indicated the birthday of each child. In some of the files, it was repeated on the scraps of paper that were also included, along with the handmade certificates. Or a date close to that date was included on the scraps, which suggested to Sadie that the scraps of paper might indicate due dates, while the certificates recorded the actual delivery date of each birth.

Had Josie used the system Sadie had just decoded on every date in the files? Sadie wondered. *And if so, would it reveal one of these dates to be Ann's birthday?*

Working quickly on a separate sheet of paper, so as not to deface the certificates, which might be the only records of the true parentage of the children they represented, Sadie scrawled down each possible birth date, subtracting one from each day, month, and year, just as she'd learned to do in cracking the ledger code.

As she did this, she began to recognize a pattern: The dates of the checks that Josie had drawn down from the lumber company and associated with each child were usually dated about six to eight months before the child's possible birth date—almost as if Josie began to collect funds around the time that she was first made aware of an impending birth.

Then, as she decoded the date on one of the last folders, her heart skipped a beat. It was only a day before Ann's birthday.

Sadie glanced at the name associated with the child: "Treasure." For some reason, tears sprang to her eyes. Ann might feel adrift in the world, and as if all the history she knew had been thrown into question by her discovery of the fact that the couple who had raised her were not her biological parents. But Josie, for whatever part she'd had in Ann's life, had named her a treasure from before the time she was even born. It reminded Sadie of one of her favorite psalms, which described God knitting together each person in each mother's womb, and marveled at the way all people were "wonderfully made."

Now almost certain that she was holding the file that held the key to the truths that Ann was so eager to learn, Sadie scanned the garbled letters and numbers that filled the other fields with intense curiosity, which turned quickly to frustration when it became clear that none of the rest of Josie's codes would yield up their secrets without a further fight. It was maddening to see the neatly arranged rows of text, especially in such familiar formats, but not be able to unlock the truths they contained. The fact that she could even guess now which of the lines contained which secrets: mother, father, birthday—made the frustration even more exasperating.

Unable to make the nonsense resolve into anything approaching sense, Sadie leaned back in her chair, staring down at the folder that lay open before her, to the boy named Moses, who according to the birth date she had decoded was the earliest file in the bunch. Her gaze drifted over the personal and financial papers of Josie's piled all around the blue folders she had just been working with.

Then she leaned forward with a jolt, a memory jarred from her mind by the sight of the folder labeled "Moses." A moment later, she was pawing quickly through the papers on Josie's desk again, this time setting aside Josie's well-organized piles of check registers, personal mail, and canceled checks, in search of a scrap she'd found wrinkled up in the back of a checkbook, as if Josie had stashed it there in a hurried moment, then forgotten about it for decades.

It hadn't seemed to mean much at the time, just a few names and numbers, another scrap of nonsense in what was starting to seem like an ever-growing pile of it. But combined with the pieces of seeming nonsense she'd just discovered, it might actually shed some kind of light. And one of the names on the piece of paper that had seemed like an oddity when she saw it at first now seemed like it might potentially offer an important clue: Moses.

I guess one of the things You're trying to teach me today is patience, Sadie prayed as she sifted through the contents of the desk for a third time that day, hoping that she wouldn't miss the scrap in her eagerness, and have to make a fourth search. But about halfway through the stack of papers on her left-hand side, she found it, still carefully pressed between the pair of check registers she'd placed on either side when she'd found it to flatten out the decades-old crumples and creases.

Moses, the scrap read. Below that was a time: *7:00 PM.* And a name, *A. Parrish.*

The discovery took Sadie's breath away. This scrap of paper was the only thing Sadie had ever found that connected Josie's secret life, described in the hidden files beside the fireplace, with the everyday details and financial records of her public life.

Sadie's mind raced. She pulled the file for the child "Moses" closer, to check the birth date, which was only a year before her own. And she turned the name *Parrish* over in her mind. She didn't know of an A. Parrish in town, but she certainly knew of a Parrish: Boyd Parrish, who had graduated from high school in Silver Peak only a year ahead of Sadie and Ann.

And Boyd Parrish, she knew, still lived in town. Or rather, outside of town, in a cabin that he'd built himself for the decade before he retired, a simple, rustic hunting cottage nestled among acres of pine that he and his wife had bought on the side of one of Silver Peak's sheltering mountains. They'd planned to use it as a weekend escape from their longtime home in Silver Peak proper, but after his wife's sudden death, Boyd had let go of that house and all its memories, and moved out to the hunting cabin alone, to make it his full-time habitation.

The place wasn't far from Sadie's, and was even closer to Milo's, where she boarded Scout. Because Scout loved to wander the pines, she actually saw Boyd relatively frequently, usually to give him a friendly wave and receive one back. She would try to nudge Scout to skirt Boyd's property, even though Scout's friendly instincts were always to trot up to and greet any nearby human being.

But maybe, she thought, standing to gather up her purse, *it was time to pay Boyd a bit longer neighborly visit.*

18

Sadie pulled up the long drive through the pines into the tiny circle of dirt track that served as both the grand entrance and the quick exit from Boyd's property. She gave a friendly *toot* on the horn as she parked, but to her surprise Boyd didn't emerge from the house as he often did even at the sound of Scout's cantering approach.

"Hello?" she called as she got out of the car.

The only answer she got was the ringing of steel against wood, which seemed to be coming from the back of the house. Bypassing the rough wooden stairs up to the front door, set in the cinnamon face of the great logs that composed the house, she circled around one side, and found Boyd with the arms of his red-and-black flannel shirt pushed high up his still-powerful arms, his black hair standing almost straight up, and his face red and shiny with sweat. He was surrounded by split logs and sawdust, and his face was brightly lit with unmistakable delight as he lifted a steel ax above his head and brought it down on the log placed on his chopping block, splitting it with a deeply satisfying crack into two pieces just the right size to be used as winter firewood.

Sadie wouldn't have thought that smile could get any brighter, but when she called her "Hello!" again, Boyd looked up and welcomed her with an even bigger grin.

"Sadie Speers!" he said. "Did you hear I needed some help bringing in this winter's firewood?"

"Not exactly," Sadie said with a smile.

"That's good," Boyd said. "Because it'd all be lies. I may need some help in the next few years, and by that time, I'll ask for it. But this year, this old man's still got enough in him to split his winter wood for himself."

He heaved another heavy log up on the chopping block and smote it into two with another impressive stroke. Then he scooped up one of the halves, replaced it on the block, split it neatly into quarters, then tossed the quarters into a nearby pile as if they weighed not much more than matchsticks.

"I can see that," Sadie said.

"Well, you just go back and report to anyone who's been spreading false rumors about me back in town that I've got it all under control. At least for this year," he said with a wink.

But with this, he did let the head of the ax fall to the ground, and then leaned on the sturdy handle to rest for a moment.

"Actually, I know why you're here," he said.

"You do?" Sadie said, playing along with mock surprise.

Boyd nodded. "It's this reunion, isn't it?" he said. "I spent so much time with your class you've forgotten I wasn't part of it. But I'm here to tell you, I paid my dues last year. I've already been to a reunion. You aren't going to get me back to another one."

"Well, if you spent so much time with us, maybe you *should* come to this one," Sadie teased.

Boyd held his hands up. "Nope," he said. "Not me. But I will tell you why I spent so much time with your class, since you seem curious."

"Very," Sadie said, although the question had never actually occurred to her until the present moment.

"Well, I'll tell you," Boyd said again. "Your class had the prettiest girls in the school. A man would have been a fool not to."

Sadie grinned. "I'm not sure I can argue with you on that point," she said.

"You'd be a fool to," Boyd told her. "It was plain as day. Everyone knew it. And of course, that's why I married a girl from your class."

With a pang, Sadie remembered that Boyd's wife, Madeline, had also graduated with her and the class that was about to celebrate their reunion. So perhaps that was why it had been on Boyd's mind, she thought. And perhaps why he'd felt the need to bring it up with a joke, to defend himself from the pain of Madeline's loss, which Sadie knew from experience could still feel fresh, even after several years had passed. Especially when an event like a reunion brought up again how very early a loved one had been taken.

"Actually, what I was hoping to ask you about doesn't have anything to do with the reunion," Sadie said. "At least not directly."

"Well, that's good," Boyd said. "Because as I said, I put in my time last year. You won't see me back for a good five, ten years after that." He laid the handle of the ax against his chopping block and came over to Sadie, wiping his face with a blue bandanna he pulled from his back pocket. "But what can I help you with? Nothing serious, I hope."

Sadie smiled, but hesitated, trying to think how to begin. Boyd had always been a jokester, so the two of them had had that in common. But the memory of Ann's reaction to discovering she was adopted was still fresh in Sadie's mind. She couldn't be sure that the few scraps of paper she'd found at Josie's home proved that Boyd was adopted. And if he was, she had no way of knowing whether that would be news to him or not, or if that news would be good, bad, or indifferent. But she knew it wasn't a joking matter, and was possibly an important revelation. So she wanted to tread carefully.

"Well," she said, easing into the topic, "I've been doing some historical research over at the Parker House."

Boyd's reddened face lit up. "Now, that's a great project," he said. "I have to say, I'm behind that one hundred percent. I've always liked that old place. And I guess like just about everyone, I was a little worried about what was going to happen to it once Josie passed. You never know what these out-of-town buyers are going to do. Turn it into a McDonald's. Or tear the whole thing down and put up a drugstore instead."

"Well, not the Jones family," Sadie said. "They're wonderful clients. I think they may actually care more about the preservation of the place than I do."

"Which is saying something, I'm sure," Boyd said with a laugh.

Sadie nodded and smiled back.

Boyd gave her an encouraging nod. "Well, I sure am glad to hear that," he said. "But I'm not real sure what it's got to do with me. But you can count me glad to help with anything," he said.

"It's about the Parker family history."

Suddenly, Boyd's face took on a strange look. It wasn't guarded, or worried, exactly. But it wasn't nearly as friendly and unself-conscious as it had been just moments before.

"The Parker family history, eh?" he repeated, almost warily.

Sadie wondered how much he already knew about his personal connection to the old house. It wasn't nothing, she guessed.

"That's right," she said. "And in particular, Josie's."

Boyd nodded, less as if he meant to show he understood or agreed, and more as if he was trying to think of something to do to buy himself time. "Josie, huh?" he said.

Sadie nodded.

Boyd's brow wrinkled. "I can't say I knew her very well," he said. "She was quite a bit older than us, as you know."

"She was well out of high school by the time we graduated," Sadie agreed.

Boyd nodded, as if glad to have found something to talk about. "And as you know, I was a bit more interested in the girls in the class behind me."

Sadie smiled.

"So I'm not sure how much I'd really have that might help you with any real historical research," Boyd said. "I mean, I knew her just about as much as anyone in town. I remember a sweet little sky-blue convertible she used to drive around when we were just about to graduate. It wasn't real expensive, but she did keep it nice. I have to say, it was about my favorite car in town. I know she worked at the lumber company. But I'm sure you already knew about that."

"I'm actually working through some of her papers," she said. "The family that owns the house now gave me access."

Boyd nodded, obviously trying to keep the conversation light. "Yep," he said. "Well, I guess they must have a lot of trust in you."

"I'm doing my best to live up to it," Sadie said. "But I've found some interesting things in the papers."

"Interesting?" Boyd said, so rattled now that he didn't seem to be able to do much more than repeat things that Sadie had already said.

Sadie nodded. She decided to go quiet and let Boyd be the one to take the next step in the conversation, just to see where he might go with it left to his own devices.

Boyd watched Sadie closely for a few moments, waiting for her to say something more. Then he glanced around at the woods, took a look at his house, kicked a bit at the pine needles and sawdust in the dirt of his backyard, and finally looked up again.

"So," he said, "how much access do you have to those papers?"

Sadie's eyebrows jumped. "Full access," she said quickly. Then, encouraged by Boyd's seeming willingness to talk more about Josie, she added another piece of information that might help her gauge how much he knew and didn't know. "And I've been finding some interesting connections in them, between Josie and some...local children," Sadie said. "Actually, not children anymore. People around our age now."

Suddenly, Boyd looked incredibly relieved. All the tension went out of his face, and his shoulders, which had been squared as if he was about to try to ward off a charging bear, relaxed into a more welcoming stance.

"So you know, don't you," he said.

Sadie was thrown for a minute by the completeness of his transformation. But it didn't take her long to recover herself. She didn't want to assume that she and Boyd were talking about the same thing. It was possible that he was talking about the adoptions. But it was also possible that he knew something about Josie, or something else about the Parker House entirely—things that she didn't know enough about even to ask. And she didn't want to keep him from sharing those things by diving in with what she thought she already knew. She wanted to give him a chance to share anything she might not know before she waded into the conversation with what she did.

Boyd raised his eyebrows, as if to say he knew she knew more than she was letting on. "You know, about the adoptions," he finally said, quietly.

Sadie felt a thrill of excitement. She had guessed from the papers she was looking at, and from all the strange connections between Ann and the Parker House, that Josie must have been somehow involved in a series of underground adoptions. But Boyd was the first other person who'd been able to corroborate that idea, with something more than stacks of old papers and the suspicions they raised in Sadie's mind.

She nodded.

Boyd heaved a sigh of relief. "I've got to say," he said. "That's kind of a relief to hear."

Sadie still wanted to tread carefully, not sure how much he knew, or how the knowledge of the fact that he was adopted, if he knew it, had affected him. "Why do you say that?" she asked.

Boyd settled down on a nearby log and gestured for her to take a seat beside him. "It's not fancy," he joked as she sat down. "But it's home."

When she was seated, she looked at him expectantly.

"Well, as I'm almost sure you already know, I'm adopted," he said.

Sadie nodded, not giving away whether she had really known this or not before, and prompted him to go on. "And Josie had something to do with it," she said.

Boyd nodded. "She arranged the whole thing," he said. "My birth mother was a teenager in a nearby town who got into some trouble, and wanted to keep it as quiet as possible. Josie was friendly with her parents, and she happened to know that my parents had been trying to have a baby, but weren't having much luck. So she connected the two of them. But times were different back then. My mother didn't want people in town thinking any differently of me because I was adopted. In that day and age, an unwed mother was a much bigger deal than it is now. And I guess women didn't all work right up to the time that they had their babies, like some of them do now, so it was a bit easier to raise a question in people's minds about whether I was really my adoptive mother's or not."

He shifted on the log beside Sadie. "And they also wanted to keep it quiet because my birth mother was so close, just a few towns away, and they didn't want to cause any trouble for her, in case people put two and two together. She was so young, and she just wanted to go on with her own life. She didn't need any rumors about the fact that she might have been out of town for a few months, on some mysterious business, right before a little baby was adopted by another nice family a few towns over."

"So it was a secret adoption," Sadie said.

Boyd nodded. "As secret as it could be," he said. "Secret even from me, until I was seventeen. Then, when I was going into the army, my parents knew I was going to wind up taking all kinds of tests and learning all kinds of things. My blood type doesn't even match the rest of the family's. I'm not sure I ever would have figured that out on my own, to be honest. But my adoptive mother was a nurse, and apparently it had been on her mind for years. Parents with their blood type could never have had a son with mine. She was terrified that I'd work it out and discover I was adopted before they had a chance to tell me themselves. So they sat me down before I went off into the army, and told me the whole story.

"But they swore me to secrecy then too," he said, "because I wasn't the only one."

Again, Sadie's skin tingled with anticipation. She had hoped that Boyd would be able to shed some light on his own adoption. It hadn't even occurred to her that he might be able to tell her something about the other files besides his.

"No?" she said.

Boyd looked at her. "Don't tell me you don't know about this," he said.

"About what?" Sadie asked.

"The other kids in town," Boyd said. "My adoption was from a nearby community. But because my mom knew Josie had handled it so well, when another high school girl in Silver Peak got into similar trouble a year later, she recommended that she go to Josie."

Sadie thought back on the files, her excitement building. If Boyd indeed was the "Moses" baby, as he very much seemed to be, the timing he was describing meant that the child he was talking about now was very likely Ann.

"Do you know anything about that woman?" Sadie asked, trying to keep her composure.

Boyd shook his head. "I would have been about one-year-old at the time," he said. "And probably much more interested in applesauce than in teenage girls. Although you know I was plenty interested in them by the time I was a teenage boy," he added with a wink.

"And your parents didn't tell you anything?" Sadie prodded, hoping to discover anything at all to take back to Ann.

Boyd shook his head even more emphatically. "Not only did they not tell me anything, they told me that I could never even tell anyone in town about my own adoption. They didn't want any of the girls whom Josie helped to have their secrets get out, just because we were careless with ours.

"So I guess in answer to your question," Boyd said, "Josie meant a lot to me. I figured, without her, who could tell where I might have wound up? I love my mom and dad. I'm so glad they're the ones who raised me. And if all I needed to do to give something back was not to tell anyone in town, so we could protect some other girls who might have been very much like my own birth mom, I figured I could do that. I never even told Maddy about it," he said. "But I guess it's all right now. We're pretty much all grown up. And Josie's been gone for some time now."

"You talk as though you knew that Josie had helped several girls in town," Sadie said. "Not just that first one."

Boyd thought for a moment. "That's true," he said. "I can't say I know who any of them were. But I guess word spread, according to what my mom said when they told me I was adopted. I think Josie even had worked out some system with a local doctor who was willing to help the girls out when they came to him in trouble. He provided birth certificates for children who had actually been born away from town, with the names of their adoptive parents in the place of their birth parents. That's how she could place so many children in new homes, with no one the wiser."

"I wonder if that might have cost her something," Sadie said, thinking back to the mysterious withdrawals from the lumber company accounts.

"Oh no," Boyd said. "At least not as I heard it. My mother was very emphatic about that. She didn't want me to think I had come from some kind of baby-buying service. She wanted me to understand it was very clear that no money changed hands. It was a private adoption, that's all. Just one that we needed to keep a secret, for the sake of the other mothers and kids."

Still, Sadie thought, it seemed Josie had needed large sums of money to pay for something having to do with the children she was helping to find a place in the world.

"How many other people know about this?" Boyd asked.

"Just me, right now," Sadie said.

"Do you plan to tell anyone else?" Boyd asked, concern flashing in his eyes. It had obviously been a relief to him to share the secret of his origins after all this time, but the sense that he had a duty to keep the secret was also still strong.

"Don't worry," Sadie said. "I'm not going to share it with the town paper. I respect what you and your family did all these years, to protect the lives of people you didn't even know. I don't plan to mention your name. But I do plan to share what I've learned with another friend."

"Has your friend been helping you with the research?" Boyd asked.

"In a way," Sadie said.

"But there's more to it than that," Boyd said, reading her face.

"I think, from what you've told me," Sadie told him, "that she may be another one of Josie's 'children.' Maybe even the one your mother first referred to Josie."

A smile spread across Boyd's face. "That's wonderful," he said. "And she grew up in Silver Peak here? With us?"

Sadie nodded.

"Well," Boyd said, "I'm not sure if she'd ever want to meet me, but as long as she didn't feel it would be violating her privacy, I'd be real happy to meet her one day. The way I see it, she'd be almost like a..." He hesitated, thinking to get exactly the right word. "Well," he said, "I guess kind of like a sister to me."

Sadie smiled. "That's a wonderful way to think about it," she said.

"I don't know about that," Boyd said. "But that is how I think about it."

"I wonder if you'd be willing to look at one more thing for me," Sadie said, leaning over to rifle through her bag, which she had settled in the grass beside the log they were seated on.

"I'd be glad to try," Boyd said.

Sadie pulled the Moses file out of her bag and placed it in his hands.

He read the label on the mottled blue tag. "Moses," he said. Then he looked up at Sadie inquiringly. "What's this?" he asked.

"It's your file," she said quietly.

"My file?" Boyd said.

"Josie kept files on each of the children whom she helped," she said. "I'm almost certain this is yours."

Boyd pointed at the old handwritten label. "But the name...?" he said.

"That was a kind of code," she said, "that she gave to you."

"Before I was even born?" Boyd asked, wonderingly.

"I think so," Sadie said.

Slowly, Boyd opened the file. He scanned back and forth over the scraps of paper, then settled on the coded certificate that Josie had made for each child. When he did, his expression changed to one of consternation. "But this is all...," he said, looking to Sadie for confirmation.

"...in some kind of code," she finished for him.

He gave a belly laugh. "I'm glad it's not just me," he said. He glanced back down at the page. "I have to tell you, sometimes the older I get, I open the newspaper, and at first it looks a lot like this to me."

Sadie grinned at him. "I get that feeling every now and then when my grandson sends me a text. Sometimes I think there are more acronyms in it than actual words. But when I tell him that, he just reminds me that Shakespeare made up words whenever he wanted to too. And he asks me why we should stop now."

"Kids," Boyd said with mock severity. "It's never a good idea to give them an education."

"That's what I always say," Sadie joked along.

But after a moment, both of them were both staring down at the page of coded letters and numbers again.

"What does it say?" Boyd asked after a long silence.

"I can read parts of it," Sadie said, "but not very much." She pointed out the birth dates and explained how she'd solved that code using Josie's checks, and then matched his code name with the scrap of paper she'd found among Josie's effects.

"I was actually hoping you might be able to help me with that," she said.

Boyd squinted at the page, turned his head back and forth, and then looked up, amiable but bewildered. "I'm afraid I've already given you all the help I can," he said. "The rest of this is Greek to me."

19

Ann smiled nervously as Sadie pulled the door of the Parker House wide to let her in.

"I came over as soon as you called," she said. "I think Roz thinks I'm not as committed to this reunion as I should be. But I'm not sure she's really very sorry about that."

As she had been all week, Sadie held her tongue about the simmering conflict between Roz and Ann. *Lord,* she prayed silently, *only You can untangle this. And I pray that You will.*

To her relief, Ann quickly seemed to forget about the conflict with Roz. "So," she asked eagerly, "you said you might have learned something?"

Sadie swung the door shut behind Ann and smiled at her. Ann smiled back nervously, looking for all the world like a teenage girl who'd just asked a friend to tell her how she looked in her first formal dress. That situation was very different from this one, Sadie realized, but at heart she also saw how they were the same: Both Ann and that hypothetical teenage girl were really wondering about the same thing: who they were in the world, and what other people could tell them to help them understand that.

"I think I've actually learned a few things," Sadie said, leading Ann into the room with the fireplace. There, she began to explain everything she'd discovered in the past few days, starting with a hands-on demonstration of the strange hidden chamber and the screen/stone mechanism that had allowed Sadie to finally find Josie's hidden files.

Then she led Ann upstairs, showed her the actual files, and explained how she'd cracked the dates that led her to Boyd and his confirmation that Josie had, in fact, been running a kind of underground adoption agency.

Sadie pulled the folder labeled "Treasure" from the stack and placed it in Ann's hands. "I'm not absolutely sure," she said, "but I think this is your file."

Ann looked down at it. When Boyd had looked down at the file Sadie had put in his hands only a few hours earlier, he'd been full of wonder. But Ann just looked worried, and perhaps even disappointed.

Ann flipped the folder open. She lifted the few scraps of paper that were in it, and then set them back in the folder and scanned down the handmade certificate Josie had prepared to keep track of the details of her adoption.

"I can't read any of this," Ann said.

"Well, we can read the birth dates," Sadie pointed out. "That's why I'm so certain this is likely yours. The birth date is just within a day of yours. And since Boyd suggested that Josie had an arrangement with a doctor who was willing to forge the birth certificates, I feel almost positive this must relate to your case."

Ann stared at her almost blankly.

"Did you see the name she gave you?" Sadie asked, tugging at the folder in Ann's hands. "Treasure. I just thought that was..."

At the look in Ann's eyes, Sadie trailed off. Now her blank look had changed to distress. Her eyes had suddenly filled with tears, which she tried to blink away, only to have them plunge down her cheeks.

"I'm sorry," Ann said, wiping them away with the flat of her hand. "I don't know what's wrong with me."

"It's a lot to take in," Sadie said comfortingly, squeezing her hand.

Ann squeezed her hand back, but at the same time, she gave her head a vigorous shake. "That's the problem," she said. "It's not a lot to take in. I know you've worked hard. I don't know if anyone else could have possibly found out as much as you have, especially in such a short time. But I feel like...I feel like we never really learn anything new with all of this. We just learn that the things we thought we knew *aren't* true. I thought my mom and dad were my parents, but it turns out they're not. I thought I knew what day I was born on, but it turns out I didn't even know my own birthday."

Her face crumpled even more as she said this. "I thought my name was Ann, but now it turns out I had another one, one I never even heard anyone call me before this."

"I'm so sorry," Sadie said. "I didn't mean to upset you by pointing that out. I just..."

"It's not your fault," Ann said firmly. "I'm not sure anyone did anything wrong here. It seems that Josie was really a wonderful woman, doing something very kind for all these people. But I just can't seem to get my feet under me, about what that means for me.

It just seems like everything's being taken away, and there's nothing to put in its place."

"Like what?" Sadie asked.

"Like knowing who my birth mother is," Ann said, giving the file a shake. "It's right here, isn't it? I mean, it must be. Where it says *M* for mother. But I can't read it. And neither can you."

"Well," Sadie said, taking the file from her, "I'm not sure I'd put it that way."

"You wouldn't?" Ann asked, wiping another tear from her eye.

"No," Sadie said. "I'd say we can't read it *yet*."

She set the file down on the table and opened it, looking again at the jumble of letters in familiar configurations but mixed-up order.

With a sniffle, Ann pulled her seat up next to Sadie and peered down at the unreadable page as well.

"How are we ever going to read that?" she asked.

Now that Sadie had confronted the garble again herself, she had no idea. In fact, a distinct sinking feeling was quickly replacing the optimism that she had just comforted Ann with. But Ann's insistence that she wished she could tell who her birth mother was did give Sadie a place to start.

She ran her finger under the two sets of letters that immediately followed the *M* line at the top of the page, and let her eyes slightly lose their focus, hoping that if she allowed her mind to wander, it might unscramble the letters with a single stroke of blinding insight.

But no such stroke of insight came.

"*Hmm*," she said.

"Do you see something?" Ann said, lurching forward eagerly. "What do you see?"

Sadie looked up to the heavens, wondering what she could possibly say to that. But as she returned her gaze to the desk, it fell on something else on the certificate: the duplicate set of parental names, and the fact that they were different from the original set, where just the mother was mentioned.

She laid her finger on the first set. "I think these two sets of parents are different," she said. "One set must be the birth parents, and one must be the adoptive parents. They're different, although they have the same labels. Do you see?"

Beside her, Ann nodded.

"And this must be your birth mother," Sadie said, tapping on the first set of names.

"Yes," Ann said quickly, "because Josie would have known who both my mother and my father were."

"That means…," Sadie said, dragging her finger over to the other side of the page, "that we know the answer to these two codes, for mother and father."

"My own parents' names?" Ann asked.

Sadie nodded. "Your mother's name was Diedre, if I remember correctly," she said.

Ann nodded. "And my father's name was Tim."

The two of them pored over the coded certificate. "Well," Sadie said, "it looks like the numbers of the letters match. Six for your mother. Three for your father."

"And look at the last names," Ann said. "They're exactly the same."

"You're right," Sadie said.

"But other than that, I can't tell what they have to do with each other. They're not one letter off, like you showed me with the dates," Ann observed, after quietly counting to herself. "And they aren't even the same letters my parents had in their names."

Sadie followed Ann's finger across the page as Ann reasoned through all this. But then, as Ann dropped her hands in her lap, Sadie jabbed her own finger at the page, pointing to the last letters in the matching last names in the spaces they believed held the identities of Ann's adoptive parents.

"Except for the last letter," Sadie said. In both of the identical scrambles of letters, the last letter was *C*—the same as the first letter of Ann's parents' surname: Cartwright. "See that?"

"Yes," Ann said, "but none of the other letters are in 'Cartwright.' What if it's just a coincidence?"

Now that she had identified the similarity in the last names, Sadie looked over at the first names again. "I don't think it's a coincidence," she said. "Because look at this."

She indicated the last letters of the codes in the spaces for the adoptive father and mother's first names. The last letter in the father's name was *T*—the first letter of *Tim*. And the last letter in the mother's name was *D*—the first letter of *Diedre*.

"They're my parents' initials," Ann breathed. Her own fingers trailed quickly over to the space where her biological mother's name was written, in code. Quickly, she read the last letters of the names. "*P*," she said, reading the final letter of the first name. "*G*," she said, reading the final letter of the last. "Do you think those could be my birth mother's initials?"

"I don't know," Sadie said. "It's so hard to tell if Josie used the same code throughout, or switched from section to section.

The code for the dates isn't the same as this one, whatever it is. But you know what…?"

Ann watched as Sadie pulled the file labeled "Moses" from the stack, and flipped it open to the handmade birth certificate inside. Then Sadie made a quick check of the last names of the adoptive parents. Sure enough, the last letter of both of them was *P*.

"For Parrish," Ann said.

"I think we can be pretty sure of that at this point," Sadie said.

Ann tapped her finger on the code for the birth mother's name in the Moses file. "But did she use the same code in this section of the file?" she mused.

"And how do we find out what those other letters translate to?" Sadie asked.

They stared down at the jumbled pages again together for a minute. Then Sadie drew in a sharp breath. As Ann gave her a questioning glance, Sadie pulled her phone from her purse, quickly looked up a number, and then dialed.

A moment later, Boyd Parrish answered at the other end of the line. "Sadie?" he asked.

"Hello," she said. "I'm sorry to bother you twice in one day."

"Oh, it's no bother," Boyd said. "What can I do for you?"

"Well," Sadie said, "I'm here with my friend."

"You mean my new sister?" Boyd said.

Sadie smiled. Ann didn't seem to be able to overhear what Boyd had said, but someday, Sadie hoped, whatever else happened, she'd be comforted by Boyd's perspective that every child whom Josie had helped find a home was in some way a brother or a sister.

"I guess you could say that," Sadie said.

"You tell her I can't wait to meet her," Boyd said.

At Sadie's hesitation, he added, "Whenever the time is right."

"I'll do that," Sadie said. "But in the meantime, I've got a question for you."

"Shoot," Boyd said.

"I'm wondering if you know anything about your birth mother at all," Sadie said.

On the other end of the line, Boyd went so silent that she wondered if the line had gone dead.

"Boyd?" she asked.

He cleared his throat. "I'm still here," he said.

Sadie winced at the serious tone of his voice. He had seemed so relieved to tell the story of his secret adoption at last that she'd been lulled into thinking that he wouldn't be too sensitive to this question. But asking about someone's birth mother, she realized now, was never a small thing. And it seemed like she might have just dived in this time without giving him enough warning.

"I'm not sure what to say about that," he said after a minute.

"I'm sorry," Sadie said. "I didn't think about what a big question that might be. I should have..."

"No, no," Boyd said, brushing her concerns away. "It's not that it bothers me to talk about it. It's just that I'm afraid it's not my secret to tell."

"Ah," Sadie said, understanding at last. Boyd hadn't just carried the secret of his own identity all those years. He'd carried the secret of his birth mother's name, as well. "So you did know her."

"Didn't know her," Boyd said quickly. "I...ah, I don't know why I never tracked her down. I guess I figured she knew pretty well how to get in touch with me if she ever wanted to. And she never did. So I just left it at that. And that was all right with me. She gave me the best set of parents a man could ever had. And I was satisfied with that."

"But you did know her name?" Sadie asked.

"Yes," Boyd said. "My mother told me when she said I had been adopted. She thought I might need to know it someday."

"Did she think you'd want to reach out to her?"

"I don't know what she thought," Boyd said. "But she said it was all up to me. I'd love to help you, like I said. But seeing as how I've never even reached out to make contact with her myself, I'm not sure it's fair for me to pass her name on to someone else. If she's even still with us."

"I understand that," Sadie said. "Whoever she is, she's lucky to have had a son like you. And I can see why you wouldn't want to share her name." Her finger came to rest pointing at the final letters of the jumble of code that indicated the birth mother's name on the Moses file.

"But I wonder if you might be willing to share her initials?" she asked.

"Her initials?" Boyd said in surprise. "Will that really help you?"

"I very much think it might," Sadie said.

"And you're not trying to find out who she is," Boyd said.

"No," Sadie assured him. "I just think this might help my friend find her own birth mother."

Ann looked at Sadie, obviously hoping for a clue to what was going on.

Sadie gave her an encouraging nod, and raised one finger to ask for patience.

"Well, if you think it will help," Boyd said. "Her initials were *A.M.*"

Sadie's finger moved quickly from the last letter in the first name, *A*, to the last letter in the surname, *M*. Her face broke into a grin.

"Thank you so much," she said, her voice rising in excitement.

"That help?" Boyd asked, his own voice rising in surprise.

"More than I can tell you," Sadie said.

"Well," Boyd said, sounding pleased. "I'm glad to hear that."

Sadie thanked Boyd and ended the call.

Then she turned to Ann.

"What's going on?" Ann asked.

"Boyd just confirmed that Josie used the same code on both sets of the parents' names," Sadie said. "At least in his file. So there's good reason to believe that she used the same code in your file, as well."

She pointed to the final letters of the codes for the birth mother's first and last names. "*P.G.*," she said. "I believe these are your mom's initials."

Ann's eyes widened eagerly. But then, just as with so many other discoveries they had made along the way, her face fell as she realized just how far they still had to go. "But it's just a pair of initials," she said. "They could belong to *anybody*."

"Not just anybody," Sadie said, "because when I spoke with Boyd yesterday, he told me that the next child adopted through Josie after him had a mother who was a high school student—in Silver Peak."

20

"Back with a friend?" Kimama said as Sadie and Ann came in the door of the Silver Peak Library.

At first, Sadie thought Kimama must be talking to her. But before she could open her mouth, Ann smiled back at Kimama. "I guess so," she said.

"More research for the reunion?" Kimama asked.

"Not exactly," Ann said. "I'm working on something more of a personal project."

"I'm surprised you've got time this close to the reunion," Kimama said. "Isn't it in just a few days?"

Ann herself looked surprised at this, as if she'd forgotten for the moment that the reunion was, in fact, only days away. Sadie looked at her with sympathy. She could believe that was actually what had happened, with everything else Ann had on her mind right now.

"She and Roz have it all in hand," Sadie said, jumping in quickly to cover for Ann.

"Well, I'm not sure that's exactly true...," Ann began.

"True enough for us to spend a little time on this project today, though, right?" Sadie asked her.

Ann nodded gratefully.

Sadie turned to Kimama. “We’d actually love to get a look at those old Silver Peak yearbooks you have,” she said.

Years ago, a group of Silver Peak High School alumni had made a display case to surround the library’s complete set of their school’s yearbooks. It contained a group of class pictures dating back to the previous century, a 1920s-era leather football helmet, and a 1950s-era varsity jacket, along with other curiosities, like programs from long-forgotten student dramatic productions.

“Are you sure this isn’t for the reunion after all?” Kimama said, coming out from behind the desk with a rattle of the keys for the cabinet. Sadie and Ann followed her across the library to the nook where the high school case was nestled, with the yearbooks on clear display.

Kimama gave them a wink as she opened the case. “Maybe it’s a secret project for the reunion?” she suggested. “A little surprise you’re keeping from Roz until a big reveal on the day itself?”

Sadie tried to give her head a cheerful shake, but the idea made her wince. That was just what they needed: a rumor going around town that Ann was making covert plans for the reunion, behind Roz’s back. In that case, Sadie’s optimistic comments about the reunion being almost planned wouldn’t just be optimistic. If Roz got the idea that Ann was trying to double-cross her in the planning, the reunion might not happen at all.

“Certainly not,” Sadie said, making a big production of pulling out the 1950s yearbooks, instead of the later ones that would have pictured her and Ann’s graduating class. “Actually, we’re just working on a bit of family history.”

Sadie didn't want to give away the fact that it was actually Ann's family they were working on. Ann didn't seem to be in any shape to answer questions about the situation, even if the person asking was as kind and interested as Kimama.

And with her unerring intuition, Kimama somehow seemed to recognize this. "Well," she said, gesturing to a nearby table, "I'll leave you to it."

"Thanks so much," Sadie called after her.

Then she bundled the short stack of early 1950s yearbooks in her arms and led Ann over to the table. When the two of them had settled at seats side by side, Sadie opened the first yearbook, the one for the year Ann was born. She'd picked out others for the previous and following years, but the best chance, she knew, was that the answer would be found in this one.

And finding it, she realized, shouldn't take long. It was a simple matter of flipping to the section of the class pictures that showed students whose last name began with *G*, in each class.

Sadie held her breath as she leafed through the relevant section of the freshman class. Any of the young, wide-eyed faces of the girls might potentially be Ann's birth mother, but it gave her heart a little pang to think of a girl that young struggling with decisions that would have been tough even for a grown woman to face. But none of the freshmen girls who had last names that began with *G* had a first name that started with *P*.

That, actually, was a relief as well, Sadie realized. She hadn't been sure how prevalent the initials would be in a town the size of Silver Peak. She could think of all kinds of names that might fit the description: Paulette Green. Priscilla Garner. Penny Groves. But how many of those possibilities would actually have attended

Silver Peak High School at the same time? The fact that she hadn't found any girls with the initials they were looking for in the freshmen class cut the odds down to the point that Sadie began to think, for the first time, that they might actually be close to finding the identity of Ann's birth mother.

She flipped to the sophomore class, scanning quickly past the *A*s, *C*s, and *F*s to the *G*s. About halfway through the block of students whose name started with *G*, her finger stopped and her eyes widened—but a moment later she recognized that, although the initials matched, the student was a boy, Peter Griffith, whose dark curly hair and bright brown eyes bore almost no resemblance to Ann's fair coloring.

"What if she's not even in here?" Ann asked. "What will we do then?"

"Well," Sadie said, trying to keep her voice chipper, "this is only the first yearbook we're looking through. We have that whole stack yet."

"But we haven't found even *one* girl who matches the initials," Ann persisted.

Instead of trying to come up with more words of encouragement for Ann, Sadie flipped to the section of class pictures for that year's junior class. A few pages later, she found the *G* section, which she began to scan through, trailing her finger from name to name.

Just a few names down, her finger stopped at "Gallagher, Pam." She stared down at it for a moment, verifying that she hadn't made a mistake: The name really did have the initials she and Ann had spent so much time searching for and discovering. And it really was the name of a young woman.

Then, slowly, she looked down the row of fresh young faces, searching for Pam's.

As she did, Ann let out an audible gasp.

A few seconds later, when Sadie's own eyes fastened on the picture labeled Pam Gallagher, she understood Ann's reaction instantly. The girl on the page looked amazingly like Ann. And since Sadie had gone to school with Ann when she was the same age as the girl on the page, Sadie knew that Ann had looked almost identical at that same age. The clothes and the hairstyles might have changed, but the family resemblance was unmistakable, with the delicate eyebrows, strong nose, and wide smile—and the same fair skin and almost platinum hair. Pam Gallagher and Ann looked so much alike that even someone on the street could easily have seen that Pam might have been Ann's mother.

Sadie had wondered what they would do if they found more than one girl in the yearbook with the same initials as the birth mother they were looking for. Now, just by looking at this picture, she knew they wouldn't have to make that decision. The resemblance was too clear.

"That's her," Ann said. "It's my mom."

Sadie put her hand on Ann's shoulder, while Ann drew the yearbook to herself, staring down into the picture as if she were trying to read an expression from a living face. Then tears began to run down Ann's face.

As they did, Sadie's mind continued to race. *They'd found Pam Gallagher in the yearbook. But where was she now?*

"Ann," she said quietly. But Ann put her hand up to indicate she wasn't ready yet to talk.

"I'll be right back," Sadie told her.

Ann gave her a grateful nod, and Sadie left her alone at the table to contemplate the first picture she'd ever seen of her birth mother.

While Ann searched for answers in the girl's face on the yearbook page, Sadie went over to the bank of gleaming computers that provided Internet access to the library's patrons. There was also a link to several more specialized databases, like one that allowed Silver Peak residents to search through the much larger collection of a Denver university, and another that gave them access to a virtual medical encyclopedia housed by one of the country's most prominent medical systems.

What Sadie was looking for, however, was more local. With a few clicks she'd learned from watching Kimama access it on previous occasions, Sadie brought up the database of the *Silver Peak Sentinel*, the daily local paper that had been publishing in town for over a hundred years. Every single issue had recently been compiled into a gigantic searchable database that brought up the actual facsimile pages of the old papers in response to any search.

Now Sadie typed two words into the blinking field that indicated the search parameters for the *Silver Peak Sentinel* archives: *Pam Gallagher.*

The first set of results were a jumble. It included all kinds of articles about women named Pam, with a flurry of surnames, from Anderson to Washington. One result even seemed to refer to an article that had run in the *Silver Peak Sentinel* at some point for the famous nonstick cooking spray. And mixed in with all of this was what seemed to be virtually the entire history of the Gallagher family in Silver Peak, although the chronology was wildly mixed up, as demonstrated by the seemingly random order in which the search engine had returned them.

The family had deep roots in the city. Just from a glance, Sadie was reminded that Pam was probably part of the family that had founded Gallagher Stables, which had built one of the largest buildings of all those that filled Silver Peak's downtown blocks. Of course, today it was no longer used as a stable. But the business had once been so big that the old stone building they had erected to house it was still large enough to house four different businesses with retail storefront space, and still have room for several spacious apartments upstairs. Most residents probably never bothered to look closely enough at the architecture to realize it was all one building, but if they did, the stonework still proudly proclaimed "Gallagher Stables," and a pair of sleepy-eyed mares looked down from opposite corners, carved into the Colorado stone.

Sadie sighed. Under normal circumstances, she would have enjoyed taking a walk down the rabbit trail of the Gallagher family history. But today she had a more pressing question on her mind. She reduced the search to return only answers that included the name "Pam Gallagher" in perfect order, and then ran the search again.

This time, the number of searches returned only amounted to a few pages. At the top was a notice of an award that the Silver Peak marching band had won in the 1950s, along with a list of all the members of the band at the time, including a mention of a Pam Gallagher in the trumpet section. Sadie smiled. Pam must have been an interesting girl to have chosen the trumpet over the flute or the clarinet, especially at that time in history.

The next article was a birth announcement, which gave Sadie a brief jolt of surprise, until she realized it was a birth announcement for Pam herself, announcing the arrival of a healthy baby daughter to her proud parents, and what looked to be two older siblings. A few years later there was another birth announcement, this time listing young Pam as one of the proud siblings welcoming another son to her parents' growing family.

So far, however, all the records were in the distant past. Sadie had seen nothing that even gave a hint as to where Pam might be now, or what she might be up to in the present—if she was still living. A moment later, Sadie realized why: It was very likely that Pam had gotten married. If she was still living, she was likely living under that married name. So a search for the girl she had been in high school was not likely to turn up her identity now.

Instead, Sadie typed in a new search: for *Pam Gallagher*, and *wedding or marriage*. Just two items came up: an engagement and a wedding announcement.

"What are you doing?" Ann asked.

Sadie got startled. She had been so absorbed in the search, and Ann had come up behind her so quietly, that she hadn't noticed her approach.

"I'm looking for Pam Gallagher," Sadie said. "Wherever she might be now."

"Did you find anything?" Ann asked, sinking down into the chair beside Sadie.

"I think I might have," Sadie said, clicking on the wedding announcement. It described a simple wedding, several years after Ann was born. Nothing too fancy: just lemonade and cake in the church basement, to celebrate the nuptials of the former Miss Pam Gallagher, and the lucky groom, Noah Payne.

"So her name wouldn't be Gallagher anymore," Ann reasoned. "It changed to Pam Payne."

Sadie nodded, already closing out the database of scanned *Silver Peak Sentinel* issues, to switch over to a more general search engine. "That's right," she said.

"But she could be anywhere," Ann said. "If she's even still alive," she added, more quietly.

"That's true," Sadie said, typing *Pam Payne* into a general Internet search. "But Silver Peak people have a tendency to stay local. Or at least return to Silver Peak. So I'm going to try a local search first." She typed *Silver Peak* after Pam's name in the search box.

"And I'm going to sort the returns for the most recent year," she said, adding the current year to her search parameters.

She turned to look at Ann and give her an encouraging smile. "Are you ready?" she asked.

Ann tried to manage a smile as she nodded. "I think so," she said.

But before Sadie could strike the Enter button, Ann put her hand over Sadie's. "I want to thank you," she said. "However this turns out, you've been such a good friend through all of this. I would never have gotten this far without you."

Sadie squeezed her hand. "I'm glad to do it," she said. "And you're right. I'm your friend no matter what happens. But if I've got anything to do with it, we're still going to find the answers to your questions."

She grinned. For what seemed like the first time in days, a true smile spread across Ann's face.

Then Sadie hit the Enter button.

The search engine worked for a few moments. Then a sea of returns flashed upon the page. A few of them were articles about Pam Paynes who were quite far afield, including one who seemed to be working in silver jewelry in the coastal mountains of California.

But then Sadie realized that, at the top of the searches, a local address and phone number had popped up.

Ann actually reached out toward the computer screen and tapped at it. "It's a Silver Peak address," she said. "Do you think it's her?"

"I don't know," Sadie said. "But it sounds familiar."

She selected the text of the address given for Pam Payne, and fed it back into the search engine. A moment later, she could see why the address had seemed familiar to her.

"The Silver Peak Rest Home?" Ann read from the screen, then turned to Sadie. "Do you think…?"

Sadie was already reaching for her purse as she finished Ann's sentence for her: "That's where she is."

21

Sadie took a deep breath as she piloted her car, with Ann beside her in the passenger seat, up the winding drive to the Silver Peak Rest Home. The residential facility was set in a stand of thin pines at the edge of town, and instead of being a single monolithic building, it was a collection of almost a dozen well-designed structures. They blended so beautifully with the forest setting that visitors to town sometimes asked residents about the lovely resort outside of town, with a tone of mild betrayal, as if the locals had been keeping the secret of the best vacation spot from them. They were always surprised when Silver Peak locals informed them, with a hint of mischief, that the beautiful "resort" they had been asking about was, in fact, the local rest home.

But there was some truth to the idea that the rest home had some of the feel of a resort. Sadie had always been glad that beloved friends of hers who were somewhat older had such a lovely community to retreat to in their later years. And whenever she came to visit, she did have the feeling that she was arriving at a kind of refuge, a place where things were peaceful and well-ordered.

Today, however, the feeling of peace she often felt as she approached the rest home was tinged with a frisson of expectation.

And, on Ann's behalf, a hint of anxiety. As Sadie had promised Ann, she'd be there no matter what. But she knew that not every story of finding an adoptive parent turned out to have a happy ending. Sometimes the traumas or issues that had led a young woman to give up a child were still present in the adult. Sometimes, even if she had overcome a great deal since the time she gave up her child, seeing her child wasn't just a pleasant reunion, but a reminder of everything she had struggled to leave behind.

And in this case, Sadie recognized, there was another factor in play as well. Not everyone in the Silver Peak nursing home still had all their wits about them. Pam Payne would be close to eighty years old now, if she was still alive. Even if she might have welcomed a visit from Ann in earlier years, would she still have all her faculties intact now? Would she remember the details of her younger days? Would she even remember who she herself was? Would she still have anything at all to share with Ann, to answer all the questions Ann had been struggling with over the past months? Or would this be just another one of what Ann had seen as so many disappointments along the journey that had brought them this far today?

When Sadie pulled up to the main building and parked, Ann looked up at the main doors nervously. "Do you think that's where she is?" she asked.

"I don't know," Sadie said. "But it's where someone will be able to tell us."

Together, the two of them walked through the lot and into the front doors. Just inside, a middle-aged woman with a short brown bob was seated at a greeter's desk, wearing a name tag that identified her as Dottie. "Welcome to Silver Peak Rest Home," she said.

Sadie smiled at her and went over, Ann trailing cautiously behind. "Thank you so much," she said. "I wonder if you can help us find the name of a resident we'd like to visit."

"Are you friends?" Dottie asked. "Or relatives?"

Sadie glanced at Ann. After a brief hesitation, Ann stepped forward. "Relatives," she said. As she did, her chin seemed to lift with just a hint of the courage she'd been trying to find during the last few days. "Her name is Pam Payne."

Dottie's face lit up. "Oh, Pam!" she said. "She's such a delight. You're lucky to call her family."

Ann's eyes widened. She seemed unable to say anything else.

"Um," Sadie said, stepping in, "can you help us with her room number?"

"Of course," Dottie said, with a few clicks at the computer that sat whirring on her desk. "But you won't have to go far. She's right here in the main building. It's one of the best ones, if you ask me," she went on, somewhat confidentially. "The apartments aren't lavish the way they are in some of the other buildings, but there's a wonderful community here. Since they don't have full kitchens, everyone comes down for dinner. And they always sound like they're having such a good time in there."

Sadie smiled.

Dottie gave a few more clicks on the keyboard. "And she is," she said, reading from the screen, "in three nineteen. That'll be on the third floor, just off the elevator." She gestured to the bank of elevators off the entryway, flanked on either side by large potted palms. "You see?"

Sadie nodded. "Thank you so much."

"Of course," the woman said. "And please tell her Dottie said hello. She brought me this homemade fudge she makes at Christmas every year since she moved in. So I try to do my best to stay in her good graces." She winked. "But actually, she's such a sweetheart that she doesn't need to bring anyone gifts. We all love her anyway."

"Will do," Sadie said with a smile as she steered Ann toward the elevators. Sadie was comforted by Dottie's description of Pam—it sounded like she still had all her faculties, and also that she was a special woman in her own right. But she also felt a pang of anxiety. For all this time, she and Ann had just been searching for an identity, or a name, sifting through files and codes and words on paper. But now they were about to come face-to-face with a living, breathing human being—one with friends, and thoughts, and her whole own life.

And if I'm feeling this way, Sadie prayed, *I can only imagine how Ann feels. I think You've led us here, Lord. Please go with us and help us now.*

For her part, Ann barely seemed to know where she was. She waited as if transfixed while Sadie summoned the elevator. When it arrived, Sadie ushered her on, hit the button for the third floor, then ushered her back off when they arrived.

Just as Dottie had promised, room 319 was clearly visible as soon as they stepped off the elevator, just kitty-corner across the hall. Its door was decorated with a beautifully arranged array of tissue paper flowers, which seemed, from the presence of other similar flowers up and down the hall, to be the evidence of some recent craft project. But the flowers on door 319 were both quite a bit more plentiful, and more artfully arranged, than many of the flowers that garnished other doors of the hall, as if the resident had thrown herself into the project with quite a bit more enthusiasm than some of her compatriots.

A simple lettered sign under the door number read *Pam Payne*. The door stood slightly ajar, as if to welcome in any visiting friends, or even passing strangers.

As the elevator doors swooshed shut behind them, Sadie took a step toward the room, gently nudging Ann along beside her. But, here, suddenly, Ann hung back, with surprising energy.

Startled, Sadie turned to look at her. Ann clung to Sadie's arm. "Wait," she said. "I'm not ready yet. I just need..." She took a deep breath and closed her eyes. Sadie couldn't be sure if she was thinking or praying, or doing something else. But she prayed herself. *Lord, please be with her. Please be with us all.*

Ann's grip on her arm eased. Then she let go of it completely. She squared her shoulders and started for her birth mother's room, with Sadie now trailing behind her.

When Ann reached the door, she raised her hand and gave a gentle knock.

"Oh, you don't need to knock," came a cheery voice from inside. "Just come on in!"

Ann's raised hand hung suspended in the air for a long moment at Pam's voice, as if it had frozen in time at the sound. But then she dropped it to the doorknob, pushed the door open, and stepped inside. Sadie waited behind, watching through the doorway, on the threshold.

An older woman sat in a comfortable, stuffed rocking recliner, wearing a neat navy collared housedress and a string of red beads at her neck that wouldn't have been out of place on one of the most stylish housewives of the 1950s. She looked up with a broad smile that was made eerie to Sadie only because the resemblance between her and Ann was still so strong, even all these years later. Except instead of remembering how Ann used to look, as Sadie had when she saw Pam's yearbook photo, now she felt that she was getting a strange preview of how Ann might look years from now.

Ann raised her hand, as if about to offer it to Pam, or perhaps as a gesture before speaking. But then she dropped it to her side again without saying anything, at a loss for words.

For a moment, a quizzical expression crossed Pam's face. But suddenly recognition began to dawn in them. Then tears sprang to her eyes. And suddenly, they were running down her face.

"Treasure?" she said. "You're Treasure, aren't you? I was afraid you'd never come back to me. My little girl."

She reached out her arms, and suddenly Ann had knelt in front of the rocking chair to embrace her, both of them laughing, then crying, then laughing and crying together.

After a moment that seemed both endless and impossibly short, Ann pulled back, slipping into a chair beside Pam's, while still holding her hand in both of Ann's own.

Quietly, Sadie took a seat on a nearby couch, not wanting to leave Ann on her own, but not wanting to insert herself into Ann and Pam's moment.

"How did you ever find me?" Pam asked, wiping away tears from her smiling eyes with an old-fashioned cloth hankie.

Ann simply wiped the tears in her own eyes away with the palm of her hand. "It's a long story," she said. "And I couldn't have done it without Sadie."

Quickly, Ann explained everything that had led them to Pam's door, from the original medical tests that first alerted her to the fact that she was adopted, to the clues to Josie's activities with Young Transportation that Sadie had unearthed during the course of her work on the Parker House.

"Well, you found your way here," Pam said, reaching up to touch a strand of Ann's hair. "And that's all that matters."

Ann smiled. But it was clear she still had more to say. "I'm so glad to meet you," she said. "And in some ways, it does answer so many of my questions, just to sit here in the room with you. But it was a shock to find out that I was adopted."

"I can only imagine," Pam said, her eyes wide and sympathetic.

"It made me feel like so much of the story I'd believed about my life wasn't true," Ann told her. "And that made me want more than anything to know what was."

"What was true?" Pam repeated.

Ann nodded.

"About me, you mean," Pam said, understanding. "And about how you were born."

Ann nodded again.

Pam took a deep breath. Then she gave a nervous smile. "I've held on to this secret for so long," she said. "My mother always thought that was the best thing for me, and I guess until now I just kept on believing her. But if anybody has the right to know the whole story, I guess it's you."

She looked down at her hands. "I never thought I was the kind of girl who'd be in the kind of trouble I got into," she said. Then she quickly looked up. "Not that you yourself were trouble," she said. "Of course not. You're a gift. I mean, look at you. Anyone in the world could see that." A smile lit her face again. But then it faded.

"But those were different times," she went on. "I fell in love, my junior year in high school. The boy was a wonderful guy. Kind, and sweet, and smart. It felt like nothing else in the world could matter more than the way we felt about each other. And then one day, I realized that we two weren't the only ones involved anymore. There was another one on the way." She looked up to meet Ann's eyes. "You."

Ann's eyes brightened with tears, but she looked steadily into Pam's face.

Again, Pam looked down at her hands, now clasped together with her long-lost daughter's. "I didn't tell anyone," she said. "Not for a few months. I kept hoping…" She paused. "I don't know," she said finally. "I don't know what I hoped. But finally I realized that I had to tell someone. So I told my mother."

She sighed, her face pinching at the memory of what had no doubt been one of the most difficult conversations of her life.

"A few days later, she introduced me to Josie. And we worked out a whole plan. I stayed in town for as long as I could, but just as the school year ended, I went away, because I was starting to show. I had you just before I started my senior year. You were so beautiful," she said, her voice breaking. "But I knew I couldn't take care of you. Not the way I would have wanted to. So I gave you to Josie, and she told me that you'd be well taken care of. And you were?" she asked, her voice rising almost plaintively. "It looks like someone took good care of you. And gave you a lot of love."

Ann nodded emphatically. "They did. My parents were the best ones you can imagine."

At this, Pam smiled. "And you grew up right here in Silver Peak," she mused. "I just never knew it. That's probably good," she said. "I would have had trouble keeping it a secret, if I had any idea you were anywhere near me. I wonder if we were ever in the same room together and just never knew?"

"It's possible," Ann said. "But I feel like, if we had, something might have told us that we meant something to each other."

"Or someone *else* might have told us," Pam said with a laugh. "Mercy sakes. I may flatter myself, but to me, you look just the way I did a few decades ago."

Ann took another deep breath. "There is one other thing," she said.

Pam looked at her expectantly, obviously willing to give any answer she could.

"My father," Ann said. "Who was he?"

"Oh," Pam said, her expression becoming cautious for the first time since they'd entered her room, "I never told him."

"You didn't?" Ann repeated, surprised.

Pam shook her head, her eyes full of compassion. "I couldn't bring myself to," she said. "It wasn't his fault. Or at least, it wasn't his fault any more than mine. I knew he couldn't take care of us. I knew he'd want to. I knew it would haunt him all his life if he couldn't. And he had so many dreams, so much to give. I wanted him to be able to go ahead and live his life, just like my mom was trying to arrange it so that I could go ahead and live my own. After I found out about you, I just never really... talked to him again." She looked off as she said this, her expression sad.

"So he never knew," Ann breathed.

"I still don't know if that was the right thing to do or not," Pam said simply. "But that was what I did."

"But you did have a good life," Ann said, as if she wanted to assure herself of that for Pam as much as Pam had wanted to assure herself that Ann had been placed with a good family.

Pam smiled. "The best. Much better than I deserved. I married a marvelous man, and we had a wonderful family and a full life. You've got two sisters," she told her. "Five nieces and nephews. And at last count, three grand-nephews."

Ann's eyes widened.

"That's going to take some getting used to," she said.

Pam nodded. "You can take as much time as you need," she said.

Ann sighed, then sat for a moment in companionable silence with Pam. Sadie watched her face, pleased to see that the anxiety that had marked it ever since Ann had come back to Silver Peak finally seemed to have fled for good.

But then another thought seemed to cross Ann's mind, drawing her eyebrows together questioningly. "And what happened to my father?" Ann said. "Do you have any idea? Is he still living?"

"Oh yes," Pam said, "he's still living. In this nursing home."

22

Unlike Pam's door, the door Ann and Sadie stood outside of now was almost unadorned, except for a color snapshot of a friendly-looking older man in a bright yellow Windbreaker, squinting a smile with a long ocean horizon stretching out behind him. The name of the man whom Pam had identified as Ann's father, Tim Riddle, was the only other information on the door.

After leaving Pam's apartment with many promises to return, and even a few more tears, they had found this room in a nearby building, just a few short minutes' walk from where Pam lived.

"This is different," Ann whispered to Sadie. "Pam has been waiting for me all her life. And even if she hadn't been waiting for me, at least she knew that I existed. He doesn't even know that she ever had his daughter. What do you think that will be like for him?"

Sadie, who had linked her arm through Ann's on the way over to remind her that she wasn't alone, gave her a comforting squeeze. "I can't even imagine," she said. "But I do know one thing."

"What's that?" Ann asked.

"I'll be with you when you go into that room," Sadie said. "And I'll be with you when you leave."

A smile spread across Ann's face. "Well," she said, "maybe that's all I really need to know."

She raised her hand to the door and knocked.

From within, they could hear a faint shuffling and rattling in the room. Then slow steps approached the door. A moment later, it opened. A tall, somewhat lanky man with a kind face opened the door with an expectant expression.

But when he looked from Sadie's face to Ann's, that expression quickly turned to one of shock. "Pam?" he said, his eyes wide.

When Ann didn't answer right away, Sadie glanced at her. Ann's eyes were full of tears, and it didn't seem like she'd be finding words to speak anytime soon.

Tim glanced back at Sadie, looking to her for explanation.

"I'm Sadie," Sadie said, sticking out her hand to shake his. "And this is Ann."

Immediately, Tim dropped his gaze to study his feet. "Oh, I'm so sorry," he said. "I've gotten confused."

Then he looked back up at Ann, as if he couldn't resist studying her face. "You just look so much like someone I used to know."

"Pam Payne?" Sadie asked.

Tim's eyes locked with hers. "Pam Gallagher," he said. "But…how did you know?"

"Because we just came from a visit with her," Sadie told him.

"Pam?" Tim said. "I didn't even know she still remembered my name. We haven't talked with each other since…" He trailed off and looked back at Sadie, again clearly seeking an explanation.

"Could we come in for a minute?" Sadie asked.

"Well, sure," Tim said, stepping back. He watched with bewildered curiosity as Sadie steered Ann into the room and helped her sit down on a plaid love seat. Slowly, Tim sank into a recliner surrounded by stacks of books and magazines that clearly indicated it as his seat of choice.

"Now," he said, with a clear eagerness in his eyes. "Tell me, how is Pam?"

Ann looked at Sadie for help, still unable to find a way to begin the conversation they had really come to have.

"She's good," Sadie said. "She's healthy. In good spirits."

Tim's gaze clung to Sadie's face, as if she hadn't said nearly enough to satisfy his curiosity. When she didn't add anything more, he began to search for something to say himself, still trying to understand what had brought them to his door.

"And are you two friends of hers?" he asked. He looked over at Ann again, still obviously unable to get over her strong resemblance to Pam. "Or . . . relatives?"

At this, Ann gave an audible sob. "Pam is my mother," she managed to blurt out, her voice breaking.

Tim's brow furrowed. "Well," he said, "I guess that would explain the resemblance. It's very striking, you know," he said. "You look just like her."

Tears began to run down Ann's face.

"I hope you'll take that as a compliment," Tim said, again looking to Sadie as if she might be able to shed some light on Ann's strong reaction.

To Tim, Sadie realized the announcement that Ann was Pam's daughter wouldn't mean nearly as much as it did to Ann, who had only just learned that fact herself earlier today. He had no idea that

Pam had had a baby as a result of her relationship with him. So to his mind, he was receiving a visit from the daughter of an old girlfriend. Even after all these years, Sadie could see that he still held feelings for Pam. But he was still completely in the dark about who Ann was—and her relationship to him.

In response to Tim's compliment, Ann just stared at him.

He looked back at her, still searching the lines of her face for something buried deep in his memory. "Well," he said after a moment, "I have to say, I'm very glad to meet you. But I'm not sure what brings you here today."

Ann looked down at her lap, overcome, then reached for Sadie's hand. It was clear that, for the time being at least, she'd said all she was able to.

Sadie took a deep breath. "Yes," she said, "I can see why you would be wondering about that. And you're right, Ann does resemble Pam quite a bit, as you can see. But what you need to understand is that Ann is adopted."

"Adopted?" Tim repeated. Then he shrugged and smiled. "Well, Pam always did love children. She always used to say that we…" He trailed off again, falling silent.

As he did, Sadie realized that the message she had meant to get across to him still hadn't gotten through. He'd understood that Ann was adopted. But he'd assumed, quite sensibly, that Pam must have been her adoptive mother.

"I'm sorry," Sadie said. "I don't think I was quite clear. Pam didn't adopt Ann. But Ann is adopted."

"Now how…?" Tim began, a puzzled look crossing his face.

"Pam is Ann's birth mother," Sadie told him. "She gave Ann up for adoption."

Now Tim's expression turned to one of pure surprise. And suddenly Ann found her voice again. "You're my father," she said. "My birth father."

"Me?" Tim said. There was wonder in his voice, but it was clear from the way he reacted that he knew it was a real possibility. "But she never… I never…"

He held his hands out in front of him, as if to steady himself, although he was already sitting down. At this, Ann reached out a hand and took his.

"You're such a beautiful girl," Tim said, reaching up to touch her face.

Ann smiled.

"But how is it possible?" Tim asked. "I never knew anything about it."

Quietly, Ann explained to him what Pam had just shared with her and Sadie: about how Pam's mother had arranged with Josie to have Pam go away for the duration of her pregnancy, and how Josie had arranged for a family in town to take Ann after Pam returned to Silver Peak.

When she finished, tears stood in Tim's eyes as well. "I loved your mother," he said, squeezing her hand. "I want to make sure you understand that. I loved her very much. I would have married her if I'd known anything about this. I would have tried to take care of you. I was probably too young to do it, and I don't know what kind of a job I would have done. But I would have tried. I hope you can believe that, one day."

"I believe it now," Ann said quietly.

Tim shook his head. "I never knew," he said. "I can't believe I never knew."

"She never told you," Ann said. "That's what she thought was best."

Tim took a long, shaky breath. "All I knew was that the love of my life had stopped speaking to me," he said.

It was interesting, Sadie thought, how he spoke about Pam, even after all these years. He didn't say "a girl I loved," or anything else that would make it sound as if the feelings he had for her were buried in the distant past. Instead, it sounded as if all his feelings for her were just as fresh as they had been back when the two of them were just teenagers, decades ago.

And the pain of the loss of Pam was still clear on his face as well. "I tried to get her to talk to me," he said. "I tried to get her to explain. One day, it was just the way it had always been. I remember, I had brought her flowers that day, ones that I picked by the barn while I was feeding the horses that morning. I used to do that a lot. She even had a little jar of water in her locker, so that the little bouquets I kept bringing her would last a bit longer.

"But she didn't want these," he said. "She didn't even want to talk to me. She wouldn't take the flowers. She wouldn't say a word. And that was just…how it was," he said, the pain and surprise from all those years ago still clear in his voice.

"I tried," he said, turning to Ann. "I mean, for weeks, I tried. I still went to her locker every day before school, just like I always did. Then she started coming in later, and later, so I started trying to find her after school, when classes were over. But she'd just walk on, without telling me anything, no matter what I said.

"For some reason or other, she just didn't want to have anything to do with me," he continued. "I could see I was upsetting her. The more I tried, the worse it got. So finally, I just…gave up.

"That was at the end of the school year," he said. "And that summer, she just...vanished. Nobody really knew where she went. And when she came back, it was as if I didn't exist. As if nothing that happened between us had really ever even...happened," he said.

He took a deep breath, his hands upturned in his lap. "I never could believe she'd be interested in a guy like me," he said. "I never knew what she saw in me, or why she'd stay as long as she even did. It hurt like the dickens. But I guess I finally decided she had just come to her senses. Realized I wasn't good enough for her. Decided to get on with some kind of a better life."

He looked at Ann again. "But I never stopped loving her," he said. "I had a good life. I did. And I had a good wife. But Pam..." He stopped. "She always meant something special to me. You say she's doing well now?"

"Very well," Ann said, squeezing his hand. "She's right over in the main building, in one of the small community apartments."

"Oh, I know that," Tim assured her. "I know exactly where she is. I just thought she still wouldn't want to see me. If she even remembered who I was."

"That wasn't the impression she gave us," Sadie said gently.

Tim gave a hopeful smile. "And I guess we have at least one thing to talk about now," he said, turning that smile on Ann, who smiled back.

"I think you might be right about that," Sadie said.

23

"Well, what do you think?" Roz asked, gesturing around at the lights and chatter of the reunion.

"Very nice," Edwin said, diplomatic as always. "Now, if you'll just excuse me." He slipped away into the sea of familiar faces.

"Now where is he going?" Roz asked. "Didn't the two of you just get here?"

Sadie nodded with a smile. "Yes," she said, "but we did have a bit of time together before we got here. We were able to walk here, thanks to your getting the venue moved from the ranch into town."

"A victory," Roz said, looking around. "Although I did have to concede serving actual champagne. And let's not forget the hundred yards of tulle."

Despite the slight stinging tone of Roz's words, Sadie could hear the happiness and pride in her voice. The fact was that the reunion looked wonderful. At Roz's insistence, they had taken over the town square, where so many important events in the lives of so many Silver Peak residents had already taken place. Now that the reunion was in full swing there, Sadie couldn't really imagine it having taken place anywhere else.

But Ann had made her mark on the planning, as well. The reunion was hardly the roughing-it version that Roz had admired, with weary travelers searching for one last piece of pizza, eaten straight from the box.

Instead, the square had been transformed by a canopy of lights and, yes, tulle, which hung overhead, seeming to create a bridge between the crowd below and the bright stars above. Guests were nibbling happily on a delicious, healthy buffet prepared by Andi Taylor, the best local caterer in town. Local high school students, including Theo, circulated in the crowd, offering to collect empty cups and plates. It wasn't as fancy as Ann had imagined, or as simple as Roz had wanted to insist.

Instead, it was perfect.

Sadie linked her arm through her friend's. "How are you feeling tonight?" she asked.

"Tired," Roz said emphatically. But then she laughed. "And happy."

"To have it over with?" Sadie joked.

Roz shook her head. "Not just that," she said. "I have to admit, it's wonderful, getting all these folks in the same place again. And with all the work we put into it, I'd be happy if it went on all night. But with this crowd, I think we may have more than a few who make early exits."

"Well," Sadie said, "at least they were here."

"That's exactly right," Roz said. She squeezed Sadie's waist. "It's not quite fair," she said. "Because I already get to see my favorite friend from high school all the time."

"Oh, really?" Sadie asked. "And who's that? Edwin?"

Roz gave her a warning nudge. "We've been each other's best friends since we were kids," she said. "Don't try to renegotiate the terms with me now." She looked out at the crowd.

"But I have to say," Roz went on. "It's really lovely to see all these faces we haven't had a chance to see in so long. Not even the ones we were close to. In fact, maybe especially the ones we weren't close to. Because they all shared a part of life with us too. It brings back so many memories to see them all again."

Sadie smiled. "It does," she said.

"Like Gerry Saunders," Roz said. "Do you remember the time he got his head caught in the bleachers before the big basketball game? What was he even doing sticking his head in there?"

"I don't know," Sadie replied. "I think I remember someone threw his shoes under the bleachers. And Gerry thought he'd just reach through and get them, instead of walking all the way around to the back."

"And then he was stuck!" Roz crowed. "For an hour!" Her shoulders bounced with laughter. "I hadn't thought about that in years," she said. "But when I did, I laughed so hard that I probably added even more years to my life."

"Well, the good thing is, he turned out all right," Sadie said. "He's a lawyer now. Edwin says he remembers him arguing a case before his court."

"I don't know how Edwin kept a straight face through that," Roz said. "With the memory of Gerry waving his hands around, trying to get free of those bleachers."

"Well, maybe that's the lesson of these kinds of reunions," Sadie said. "I used to think everyone else was so grown-up. And the people who were older than us, I used to think they had it all figured out. But the older I get, the more I realize—we're all still just kids. We might learn a thing or two along the way, but at heart, we're just the same. We've got all this sympathy and warmth for the kids we grew up with. But if we knew the stories of everyone else we met, we'd probably feel the same way about them too. I just wish I could keep remembering this feeling. I think it would help me to be a better person."

"I don't know," Edwin said, emerging from the crowd as she said this. "I think you're pretty great, just the way you are."

"Grandma!" Theo said, coming over with a plate of canapés. "You look great. What did you say this was, again? Your tenth reunion?"

Sadie gave him a playful tweak on the cheek, then popped a canapé in her mouth before he darted off into the crowd, laughing.

"Enjoying yourself?" Roz asked Edwin with a smile.

"Absolutely," Edwin said. "It's just that…do you hear this song?" he asked.

Sadie hadn't been paying any attention to the band that was playing, but now that Edwin drew her attention to it, she could hear the first strains of the song that had been "theirs" all those years ago, when they had first dated in high school.

"Edwin," she said, a smile breaking out on her face. "Did you request this?"

"Request what?" Edwin said, taking her hand to lead her to the dance floor.

As he did, the band leader spoke over the introductory vamp. "And this song tonight has a very special dedication. It's going out to Sadie, from Edwin."

A little swoon swept through the crowd.

Sadie blushed as Edwin led her onto the floor and took her in his arms to dance. Soon the smiling faces turned away from them, and Sadie was lost in the moment with Edwin and the song. They didn't have to say anything special to each other; they just looked into each other's eyes as the music played. All the years they'd known each other, and all the things they still felt now, did the talking for them.

"Thank you for the dance," Edwin said huskily when the music ended.

A more peppy number started up as soon as their song ended, and the two of them began to shuffle off the dance floor as the rest of the crowd broke into all kinds of antics around them.

As they reached the edge of the dance floor, Ann gave them a small wave.

"Just give me a minute," Sadie said, squeezing Edwin's hand. He touched the small of her back as she slipped away from him to catch up with Ann.

"How's it going?" Sadie asked, after Ann greeted her with a hug.

"It's good," Ann said, releasing Sadie. "Thanks to you."

"You're happy with the party?" Sadie said, gesturing at the swags of tulle and lights overhead. "It looks beautiful. And I have to say, the food is delicious."

"Oh," Ann said, waving her hand impatiently, "I'm glad you're having a good time. But that wasn't what I was talking about. I'm good because I've finally got the answers I came to town looking for. And I could never have found them if not for you. I don't know if I'll ever be able to thank you."

"That's what friends are for," Sadie said.

"I know," Ann said. "But not everyone who says they're your friend is a true friend."

Sadie smiled at her.

"I've been over to the rest home a few times since we went together," Ann said. "It's been so good just to spend time with Tim and Pam. I'm learning so much about them. And about me. I think Jasper may actually make a trip over there with me before I leave town again."

"That would be wonderful," Sadie said. "Maybe he'll feel like he has more family than he thought he had, instead of fearing that his sister is being taken from him."

"I hope so," Ann said. "Because that's how I feel now."

"And I should thank you too," Sadie said. "If it hadn't been for your curiosity about your parents, I might never have done the research I did on Josie. But Charlene and Jason are delighted with the 'secret history' of the house. They especially love the fact that we were able to find the secret compartment in the fireplace."

"I guess I might be pretty delighted if someone found something like that for me in a house I'd just bought," Ann agreed.

"And Amanda at the lumber company was so relieved to understand what Josie had been doing with the money. Josie was a kind of mother to her, I think," Sadie said. "And kind of like you finding out a truth you didn't expect about your family, she hadn't known what to think about the embezzlement. Did it mean that none of the love Josie had shown her for all those years was real? So in a way, she got back a piece of her family when you got back a piece of yours, as well."

Ann smiled. “And she’s not the only one,” she said.

“Oh, really?” Sadie asked. “What do you mean?”

“Well, I told you I’d been back to the rest home several times to see Pam and Tim,” she said. “But that isn’t really the whole story.”

“No?” Sadie asked.

“No,” Ann said. “Because the last time I went, I didn’t talk to them.”

“Why not?” Sadie asked, her voice rising in alarm.

Ann smiled. “Well, all the times I’d gone before then, I’d gone to see Pam, and then gone over to visit Tim,” she said. “But this time, when I went looking for Pam, they told me that she’d just gone over to the garden.”

Sadie nodded.

“And when I got to the garden,” Ann said. “There she was. With Tim.”

“They hadn’t talked in decades,” Sadie said. “But they’d shared so much when they were young. I wonder what that was like.”

“I think it must have gone well,” Ann said. “Because when I got there, she was sitting beside him with her head on his shoulder. As far as I could tell, they weren’t saying anything at all, just sitting side by side. They couldn’t see me, because I’d come up from behind.”

“And you didn’t say anything,” Sadie guessed.

Ann shook her head. “Not that time,” she said. “After all those years, I wanted them to have their moment. And so I just slipped away.”

She squeezed Sadie’s hand. “Thank you,” she said. “I know I’ve said it before, but I’ll never be able to say it enough.”

Sadie gathered her into a hug. It felt wonderful to have her old friend near enough to be so affectionate once again. But after a minute, Sadie released Ann, patting her on the shoulders.

"I don't know what I'm doing," she said, "stealing you from your own party. You need to get back there and enjoy it, after all your planning."

"You know what?" Ann said. "All week long, I was sure there was no way I was going to enjoy this reunion. I couldn't be happier to be wrong."

She took a few steps back toward the party, then turned around. "You coming?" she asked.

Sadie shook her head. "I'll just be a minute," she said.

As Ann drifted back into the party, Sadie looked out at the lights and the crowd, scanning the faces of her old friends. Some of them were so different that she might not recognize them at first glance. But now, gathered in clusters of old friends, laughing and sometimes even moving the way they did all those years ago, everyone seemed familiar, and even well-known. It wasn't that nobody had changed a bit, as Theo had teased, Sadie thought. It was that, when such old friends gathered, they could still see each other for exactly who all of them had always been.

With a happy sigh, Sadie headed back to the party, to join all of her friends.

About the Author

Carole Jefferson is the pen name for a team of writers who have come together to create the series Mysteries of Silver Peak. *Reunion Dance* was written by Vera Dodge. Vera grew up in small towns in the Midwest. She lives and works in Brooklyn.

Read on for a sneak peek of another exciting book in Mysteries of Silver Peak!

The Counterfeit Caper

"Sadie, you've hardly touched a bite. Are you all right?"

Sadie looked up from her plate to see Cecile Daly staring at her from across the table. Cecile's bright blue eyes, pixie blonde hair, and petite figure toned by a daily jog, made her appear much younger than her sixty years.

"Oh, I'm fine," Sadie replied with a smile, realizing she'd been pushing the creamed peas around on her plate without actually eating them. And they were delicious creamed peas too. Everything on the menu at the Drover Dell Diner was delicious, and all made from scratch.

"I think she's nervous about the auction this afternoon," Roz confided, giving both Cecile and Alfred Daly a smile. "She couldn't talk about anything else during the drive from Silver Peak."

"Are you hoping to buy something in particular?" Cecile asked Sadie.

"Well, there are several things listed on the auction bill that caught my attention," Sadie said, "but I need to see them before I know if they're worth bidding on." She didn't mention the item that had her stomach tied up in knots, afraid she might jinx herself if she spoke of it.

Sadie pushed up the sleeves of her coral-hued crew-neck sweater, feeling a little warm on this cool September day. "I've been to hundreds of auctions in my life, but I'll admit this one has given me a small case of the jitters. It's silly, I know."

"Nothing silly about it," Alfred said, reaching up to straighten his blue bow tie. He wore a dark gray suit that provided a sharp contrast to his thick, wavy white hair. "The Ferris family estate auction has had people talking for months. I've heard there are antique dealers coming in from all over the state."

"That's true." Sadie plucked the white linen napkin from her lap and placed it next to her plate, giving up on the creamed peas, meat loaf, and mashed potatoes she'd ordered for lunch. "The auction sheet was over ten pages long, and that's not including the smaller items for sale."

Cecile s peared a small golden beet from the roasted beet salad in front of her. "And they can sell that much in one afternoon?"

"No," Sadie replied, "most of the larger items from the estate and carriage house were slated to go up for sale this morning, like the old horse-drawn sleigh and carriages, the vintage gazebos, the cars, and all of the other outside items the Ferris family owned." She glanced down at her watch, just to be certain their lunch didn't go too long. "This afternoon, they'll be selling the antiques and collectibles from the inside of the Ferris mansion."

Roz eagerly rubbed her hands together, her bangle bracelets jangling on her wrists. "I just can't wait to see it all! Sadie tells me some of the items were made all the way back in the seventeenth century."

Alfred nodded. "That's right. And most of them will go for a pretty penny, I'm sure."

"And that's why I'm nervous," Sadie confided with a small chuckle. "And probably not very good company today, either."

"Nonsense," Alfred countered, peering at her through his wire-rimmed glasses. Amusement gleamed in his gentle gray eyes. "You and Roz are both wonderful company. Cecile and I were thrilled when you called and asked us to join you for lunch."

"We certainly were," Cecile chimed. "In fact, we need to do this more often."

"I agree," Sadie said as the waitress stopped by to refill their water glasses.

The Drover Dell was a small diner located in the heart of downtown Breckenridge and had been in business for over forty years. The diner's daily specials, listed on a large chalkboard in the front window, always included their popular bison burgers and home-cut, sweet potato fries. Alfred and Cecile had introduced the diner to Sadie and her late husband, T.R., over two decades ago, and the four of them had enjoyed many a lively meal there.

Today was no different, as Cecile talked about her plans to start taking French lessons in anticipation of a trip to Paris that she hoped to take with Alfred. "If he ever retires," Cecile said, giving her husband a playful wink.

"Retire?" Alfred said, feigning horror at the word. "I'm much too young for that. I've got another fifteen or twenty years left in me before that happens."

"Then I may have to go to Paris without you," Cecile teased, before their conversation turned to their families and mutual acquaintances.

Sadie told them about her grandson, Theo, and his upcoming college tour. "It's still preliminary, since Theo is only a junior, but he wants to get a jump on things. And to Alice, it's a great excuse to spend a big chunk of one-on-one time with Theo before he's out of the house. Which means I get to enjoy Sara spending the next two weeks with me."

"How fun!" Cecile exclaimed. "How old is she now? Fourteen?"

"That's right," Sadie replied with a wistful sigh. "She and Theo have grown up so fast." Despite her wish that her grandchildren were still young enough to rock to sleep at night, Sadie thanked God for them every day, and for her daughter, Alice. All three of them were such a blessing in her life.

Roz and the Dalys were a blessing too, she realized, as she listened to Roz tell Cecile and Alfred about her two sons.

After a few minutes, Alfred turned to Sadie. "So, have you planned your strategy for today's auction?"

Sadie chuckled. "The only strategy I have is to bid higher than the next guy, if possible." She tilted her head to one side. "Are you sure you don't have time to drop in at the estate auction?" She knew that, as a professor of American history at Colorado Mining College, Alfred enjoyed antiques and artifacts from the past as much as she did. "Even for a few minutes?"

"I wish I could," he said wistfully. "But I have a meeting at two that I just can't miss."

Cecile said, "The chair of the history department is looking for someone to fill the assistant chair position that just opened up." A proud smile curved her mouth. "I think he's got his eye on Alfred."

Roz's green eyes widened. "My, how exciting for you, Alfred."

He chuckled. "It may sound that way, but as the assistant chair I'll just get most of the work and none of the glory." He turned to his wife. "Along with some late-night meetings, dear."

Cecile reached over to pat his arm, her skin still a lovely, golden tan from the long hours she'd spent in her garden over the summer. "I won't mind. You deserve a promotion after all the time you've given the college."

Roz picked up her coffee cup. "With the recent spate of burglaries in Breckenridge that I've been reading about in the paper, I'm not sure I'd feel safe staying home alone."

"I've heard about them too," Sadie said, turning to Alfred and Cecile. "Have there been any break-ins in your neighborhood?"

Cecile shook her head. "Fortunately for us, the burglar, or burglars, seem to be targeting the high-end houses located on the outskirts of town. The most recent break-in happened at the King of Fake's house."

Roz blinked. "The king of what?"

"Fakes," Alfred said with a smile. "It's a moniker the man coined himself." He turned to Sadie. "You know who we mean, I'm sure."

Sadie nodded. "Brent Fielder." She smiled at Roz. "He's one of the country's biggest collectors of famous fakes, frauds, and forgeries."

Roz laughed. "I think the three of you are pulling my leg!"

"No, it's true," Cecile said.

"Every word of it." Alfred, a former Eagle Scout, held up his hand in the two-finger Boy Scout salute. "Although, to be fair, Fielder collects many authentic antiques and artifacts too."

Roz didn't look convinced. "But why would someone want to collect fakes?"

"I think the novelty of it is part of the appeal," Sadie mused.

"And it actually can be lucrative too," Alfred added. "There are several stories of fake antiquities fooling experts in the field, and of bringing a huge amount of money from collectors who are none the wiser. But those high-quality fakes are rare, which makes them appealing to a certain segment of collectors. It's usually the folklore behind the fakes that gives them the most value."

"Like the Great Brewster Chair acquired by the Henry Ford Museum back in the seventies," Sadie said in agreement. "The museum paid nine thousand dollars for a chair that was once believed to have belonged to William Brewster, one of the men who established the Massachusetts Bay Colony way back in 1620."

"And it was a fake?" Roz asked.

Sadie nodded. "Turns out it was built in 1969 and designed to fool the experts. The museum still displays it as an example of how authentic a fake antique can appear."

"And they paid nine thousand for that example," Alfred said with a smile. "The Great Brewster Chair is the kind of item that the King of Fakes would love to have for his collection."

Roz looked bemused. "So did the thief steal some of Brent Fielder's fakes or his real collectibles?"

"The police aren't releasing that information," Alfred said with a shrug.

"And it might not matter," Sadie ventured. "Since most of Fielder's fakes have fooled the experts at one time or another in the past, he could pass them off as the real thing."

Alfred leaned back in his chair and steepled his fingers together. "The recent Pederson burglary is the one that's got everyone talking at the university. Oliver Pederson lost an original Monet painting valued in the six figures, along with several pieces of his wife's diamond and emerald jewelry."

"I heard the mayor's house was robbed too," Cecile said.

"Oh my," Sadie said, shaking her head. "Do the police have any leads?"

"Maybe." Cecile placed her napkin on her plate. "My cousin works at the police department, and she hinted that they may be closing in on the thief."

"Let's hope it's true," Alfred said, then turned to Sadie. "And speaking of mayors, how is Edwin?"

"He's good," she said with a smile. "He seems to thrive in his duties as Silver Peak's mayor. I'm so proud of him."

"You should be," Roz told her. "He's doing a great job."

When the waitress approached their table to gather some of the empty plates, Sadie glanced at her watch again. "Oh, Roz, we need to scoot if we don't want the afternoon session to start without us."

Roz rose from the table. "Well, it looks like we're going to eat and run." Then she looked at Sadie's plate. "Do you want a doggie bag to take with you?"

Sadie considered it for a moment, given the large amount of food still left on her plate, then she shook her head. "No, I don't want the food sitting in my car all afternoon."

"I'll take it," Alfred said with a smile. "There's nothing better than a cold meat-loaf sandwich for a midnight snack."

"Oh, Alfred," Cecile said, trying to stifle her laughter.

Sadie laughed too. "Yes, please, do take it, Alfred. That way it won't go to waste."

Alfred asked the waitress for a doggie bag while Sadie and Roz headed to the cash register to settle up their bill.

A few minutes later, the four of them stood on the brick sidewalk outside the diner. "Good luck at the auction," Cecile told Sadie, reaching out to give her a hug. "Let us know how it goes."

"I will," Sadie promised, bidding farewell to Alfred as Roz hugged Cecile.

Then they were on their way.

Three hours later, Sadie and Roz sat among the crowd of bidders and onlookers at the Ferris estate auction.

"Are you still nervous?" Roz asked, wearing the pair of emerald-green cat-eye glasses she'd fished out of her purse on the way over.

"No, but I am starving," Sadie said wryly, wishing she'd eaten more of her lunch. "Who knew the auction would take this long?"

Roz grinned. "The food truck is selling soft pretzels with cheese. That might hit the spot."

"Don't tempt me," Sadie replied. She'd been trying to ignore that food truck, with all of its sweet and savory temptations, since they'd arrived at the estate auction three hours ago.

They'd already been here much longer than she'd expected. She'd hoped to spend part of the afternoon getting ready for Sara's visit tomorrow, but at this rate, she'd be lucky to be home by dusk.

Undeterred, Sadie sat up and squared her shoulders, not planning to leave the auction until the item that had brought her to Breckenridge came up for sale. She looked around the large auditorium, her bidding card clasped in her right hand.

To her dismay, the Ferris estate auction had caught the attention of several antique buyers in the area, along with some of the long-distance buyers that Alfred had mentioned.

The Ferris family had settled in Breckenridge in the late 1800s and been well known around the state for their philanthropy. Sadie and her late husband, T.R., had attended a large charity gala at the Ferris mansion several years ago, and Sadie had marveled at the huge array of antiques and collectibles that had filled the home.

When ninety-eight-year-old Eulalie Ferris passed away a few months ago, Sadie had been surprised to learn that her heirs planned to sell off all the household contents, including the antiques. As with many auctions, there were some additional consignment items added from private owners, to draw even more interest in the sale.

But of all the lavish antiques and collectibles on the auction bill, Sadie had her heart set on only one of them. It was the antique phonograph that she'd seen at the Ferris gala all those years ago. A Victor Orthophonic Credenza model—the rare one with a tooled Moroccan leather front, it was an exact match for the phonograph once owned by her grandparents. The Orthophonic models were a huge technological leap over the old Victrolas, with fuller, richer sound that was capable of reproducing the new electric recordings that came with the talking picture era. Grandpa had taught her to dance to the 78 rpm records played on that phonograph. She'd sung hymns with her grandmother with music from the phonograph. She'd even enjoyed her first dance with Edwin to the 1960 hit song "This Magic Moment" played on that phonograph.

She'd never seen another one like it since the Ferris gala and had even offered to buy it from Eulalie at the time. Eulalie had politely declined, but now Sadie had her chance. She couldn't ever remember being this nervous and excited at an auction before, and she took a deep breath to calm herself.

"Take another breath," Roz said with a smile, reaching out to gently pat her arm. "You've got this."

"I hope so, but you never know. There are a lot of dealers here today. I just wish it wasn't taking so long."

"I know what you mean." Roz leaned back in her chair. "We've been here long enough that I've actually decided to bid on something."

Sadie appreciated the fact that Roz enjoyed attending antique auctions with her, although she rarely bid on anything. "What is it?"

"One of the mystery boxes," Roz said with a smile. "You know how much I love surprises, and I should find at least one thing I like inside one of those large boxes." She tucked a strand of gray hair behind her ear, the motion causing a melodic tinkle of the gold bangle bracelets adorning her right forearm. More than one antique buyer had approached Roz today to comment on her vintage butter-yellow peasant blouse and pinstriped blue-and-yellow maxiskirt. Roz had soaked up the compliments and couldn't wait to go home and tell Roscoe, since he'd given her the outfit for her birthday.

Sadie chuckled. "You know you're taking a risk, right? They put stuff in those mystery boxes that they believe no one will bid on."

"Oh, I know that," Roz said breezily. "But those mystery boxes don't usually cost too much, do they? I've already decided I won't pay more than twenty dollars."

"That sounds about right for what they're worth." Sadie's gaze moved to the auctioneer at the front of the auditorium. Marvin Burton was one half of the partnership of Burton & Best Auction Services. Marv Burton and Leo Best had been in business together for over twenty years and were both excellent auctioneers. Marv's wife, Starla, assisted at every auction, along with their adult daughter Lisa, who had joined the business a few years ago.

"Item number one hundred fourteen is a Swiss clock, circa 1910, with gold overlay and hand-carved mahogany details," Marv announced to the crowd. "Let's start the bidding at two hundred dollars."

The Victor Orthophonic Credenza model phonograph, the top of the Victor line and built in the late 1920s, was item number 116 in the program, and Sadie could see it lined up on the platform behind the auctioneer. She'd had a chance to examine it before the auction began and was thrilled to see the Moroccan-leather-front cabinet and spring motor were still in excellent condition. Starla had even cranked the machine to play a 78 rpm record.

Smooth, rich music had emerged from the open doors of the large cabinet, filling the auditorium with Beethoven's "Ode to Joy."

While Sadie appreciated the demonstration, she feared it may have drawn even more interest from potential buyers.

As she watched the bidding for item number 114, her heart began to beat a little faster. Despite her impatience, there was something about the sound of an auctioneer's rhythmic patter and the enthusiasm of the bidders around her that lent a wonderful excitement to the air. She'd learned a long time ago that it was easy to get too caught up in that excitement and overbid for an item. That's why she already had a top bid of two thousand dollars in mind for the phonograph and had made a promise to herself to go no higher.

"Sold!" Marv shouted with a sharp rap of his gavel against the wood podium. "The Swiss clock goes to bidder number five hundred seventy-one, with a winning bid of six hundred and thirty dollars."

A spatter of polite applause echoed in the auditorium as Marv's assistant, Lisa, picked up a plain cardboard box about the size of an electric roaster oven and carried it to the empty display table next to Marv.

Marv grinned as he laid one beefy palm on top of the box lid. The mystery boxes had each been sealed shut with tape to keep the curious from taking a peek inside. "And here's item number one hundred fifteen. This is our first mystery box of the day, ladies and gentlemen. The first of four."

Roz sat up straight in her chair. "Ooh, this could be it."

Sadie smiled. "What are you hoping to find in there?"

"Oh, I don't know," Roz said, one hand clasping her bidding card. "Some vintage jewelry would be nice. Or books or some milk glass dishes or vases. I could find anything in there. That's what makes it so fun!"

Sadie laughed. "Let's just hope it's not some old burlap feed sacks. That happened to me once with a mystery box, remember?"

"I sure do," Roz said, laughing with her. "But you managed to make some cute place mats out of them. As I recall, you sold enough of those place mats to recoup the money you spent on the box."

"Plus a little extra," Sadie said with a nod. "That's called making lemonade out of lemons. Or bucks out of burlap, as the case may be."

Sadie heard Roz chuckle as they both turned their attention toward the auctioneer.

"Time for a little mystery, ladies and gentlemen," Marv announced. "This is our first mystery box of the day, and I've heard that it contains some delightful items." He grinned, revealing a silver crown around one front tooth. "Let's start with ten dollars, folks."

Sadie saw a man in the front row raise his hand in the air. "Ten!"

Marv nodded in the man's direction to acknowledge the bid and then continued his fast-paced chant. "Ten-dollar bid by the gentleman up front. Now eleven, now eleven, will ya give me eleven?"

Roz's hand shot up. "Eleven!"

"Eleven is bid by the pretty lady," the auctioneer said. "Now fifteen, now fifteen, will ya give me fifteen?"

"Twenty!" a man shouted from the back.

"Oh, I hate that," Roz whispered to her. "Why do they have to jump so high?"

"Probably hoping to scare off other bidders," Sadie said.

"I've got twenty," the auctioneer said, "now twenty-one, now twenty-one, for this fine mystery box. Will ya give me twenty-one!"

"Twenty-one," called out the man from the front row.

The auctioneer pointed at him. "We've got twenty-one." His gaze moved to Roz. "Twenty-two? Will ya give me twenty-two?"

"Twenty-two," Roz shouted, half-standing up from her chair. Then she turned to smile at Sadie. "Two can play at that game."

"Pretty lady bids twenty-two," Marv said. "Now twenty-three, now twenty-three..."

"Twenty was your high bid," Sadie reminded her, getting caught up in the excitement herself. "And there are three more mystery boxes."

"I know." Roz flashed another smile. "But I really want this one. I just have a good feeling about it."

The man in the front row raised his arm in the air. "Twenty-three."

"Oh no," Roz breathed, then bit her bottom lip.

"I've got twenty-three. Now give me twenty-four, now twenty-four." Marv paused for a moment, his keen-eyed gaze scanning the room. "Last chance for twenty-four."

Sadie stood up and cried, "Twenty-four!"

Roz turned to gape at her. "What are you doing?"

"Shhh," she said with a smile. "I have to pay attention."

"Twenty-four," Marv announced, looking once more around the room. After a long pause, he said, "Going once...going twice. Sold!"

Marv's gavel struck the podium.

"You won!" Sadie reached over to give Roz a hug. "We don't know what you won, but you won!"

"You mean *you* won," Roz said with a grin.

"No, you won," Sadie insisted. "Remember the four dollars I borrowed from you the other day when we had breakfast at Flap Jack's? Well, consider yourself repaid."

Roz laughed. "Well, then I guess I did win." She raised both arms in the air, her gold bracelets jangling at the movement. "Woo-hoo! I can't wait to see what's inside my box."

"We'll find out soon." Sadie shifted in her chair. "The phonograph is up next. We can leave after it sells."

A wave of excited murmurs swept through the crowd as two men carefully hoisted the Victor Orthophonic Credenza model and carried it to the table near the podium. As the gorgeous Moroccan leather trim shone under the bright auditorium lights, the tune of "This Magic Moment" began to play in Sadie's head. She shook it off, needing her full concentration for the bidding ahead. She knew from experience that one of the most important parts of the bidding process was assessing your competition.

Sadie took a slow, deep breath, telling herself not to get her hopes up too high. But she could already picture the phonograph for sale in her shop and even had a spot picked out for it. Her grandparents' phonograph had been willed away long ago, but Sadie still had all of their old 78 rpm records.

"Are you ready?" Roz whispered to her.

"I think so," Sadie said, waiting for the bidding to begin.

Marv gave the phonograph a long, appreciative look before turning his attention to the audience. "Ladies and gentlemen, item number one hundred sixteen is truly special. I've been in this business a long time, and I can honestly say that this is one of the finest Victor Orthophonic phonographs I've ever come across. This was the top o' the line, folks. The crème de la crème."

"It is lovely," Roz murmured.

"It was purchased by the Ferris family around 1928," Marv continued, "and remained in the family through all these years. It's been well-maintained, and as many of you heard earlier, the sound quality is amazing."

"Oh, Sadie," Roz said, holding out her hand to show her fingers trembling, "now I'm nervous too!"

"All right, everybody," Marv called out to the crowd, "let's start the bidding!"

A Note from the Editors

WE HOPE YOU ENJOY MYSTERIES OF SILVER PEAK, CREATED BY the Books and Inspirational Media Division of Guideposts, a nonprofit organization that touches millions of lives every day through products and services that inspire, encourage, help you grow in your faith, and celebrate God's love in every aspect of your daily life.

Thank you for making a difference with your purchase of this book, which helps fund our many outreach programs to military personnel, prisons, hospitals, nursing homes, and educational institutions. To learn more, visit GuidepostsFoundation.org.

We also maintain many useful and uplifting online resources. Visit Guideposts.org to read true stories of hope and inspiration, access OurPrayer network, sign up for free newsletters, download free e-books, join our Facebook community, and follow our stimulating blogs.

To learn about other Guideposts publications, including the best-selling devotional *Daily Guideposts*, go to ShopGuideposts.org, call (800) 932-2145, or write to Guideposts, PO Box 5815, Harlan, Iowa 51593.